BRAC

D1276411

APR   2023

DOWNFALL

ALSO BY MARK RUBINSTEIN

FICTION

The Mad Dog Trilogy

Mad Dog House

Mad Dog Justice

Mad Dog Vengeance

STANDALONES

Love Gone Mad

The Foot Soldier: A Novella of War

Return to Sandara:
A Novella of Love and Destruction

The Lovers' Tango

Assassin's Lullaby

NONFICTION

The Storytellers:
Straight Talk from the Planet's Most
Acclaimed Suspense and Thriller Authors

Beyond Bedlam's Door:
True Tales from the Couch and Courtroom

Bedlam's Door: True Tales of Madness & Hope

DOWNFALL

A NOVEL

MARK RUBINSTEIN

OCEANVIEW PUBLISHING
SARASOTA, FLORIDA

ISBN 978-1-60809-546-9

Published in the United States of America by Oceanview Publishing

Sarasota, Florida

www.oceanviewpub.com

10 9 8 7 6 5 4 3 2 1

PRINTED IN THE UNITED STATES OF AMERICA

For Linda

"For a deadly blow let him pay with a deadly blow; he who has done a deed must suffer."

—Aeschylus

"We tell ourselves stories in order to live."

—Joan Didion

DOWNFALL

NOVEMBER 1982

PROLOGUE

CARRYING A MEDICAL bag, the doctor approaches the apartment building.

It's close to eleven o'clock at night and Brooklyn's East Nineteenth Street is dark and deserted. The branches of bare sycamore trees sway in a frigid November wind.

Opening the outer door, he enters the building's vestibule. Before pressing the button on the directory, he wonders if at sixty-four he's too old to be making house calls. His colleagues insist that medicine isn't practiced this way, not anymore.

Giving up the house calls would have made Claire happy. She's always hated how the telephone would ring in the middle of the night when a patient called in distress. But he's always felt an obligation to his patients.

Maybe they could have avoided the separation if he'd paid more attention to Claire and less to the practice. But here he is, entering a building late at night, a place where a few older people are still patients in his ever-dwindling practice.

Okay, he regrets having never foreseen what would happen when he reached his mid-sixties, when new patients never materialized and he started to become irrelevant as a physician.

Oh how he hates having regrets. But there are no regrets about refusing to make the payoffs to those bastards. He'll never concede a thing to those crooks. Not now, not ever.

In the building's vestibule, he's about to reach for the directory call button—apartment 3-B—Donovan. Feeling a draft of icy air on his neck, he realizes the outer door hasn't closed properly.

About to turn back and shut the door, he catches a glimpse of a figure standing in the open doorway. Before he can register who it is, his back explodes. The impact is so massive he's thrust forward, and there's no feeling from his chest down. He knows his spine has been shattered, and he realizes his heart has burst—and he's bleeding out.

So this is what dying feels like, he thinks as he starts falling, and there's another blow so powerful it thrusts him farther forward, and then another as the world fades, then goes dark.

But none of this has happened yet.

CHAPTER ONE

Sitting at a table on the glass-enclosed porch of the Skyline Diner, Rick Shepherd smiles as he does each time he sees the sign on the wall behind the counter:

Life is Uncertain
Eat Dessert First

It's good to appreciate humor, no matter how upset you feel about what's going on at the office with Kurt Messner.

Upset? It's anger.

Anger? It's more than that; it's rage. And it's smoldering inside him. It's erosive and could lead to very bad things. Bad things?

Sure, it sometimes feels like he could kill that son of a bitch.

Murder? Really?

Don't be a drama queen. Leave that to your ex-wife.

It's just a figure of speech.

He wonders how it came to the point where, as a thirty-four-year-old physician, he feels he's living the wrong life.

The wrong *life*? That too is absurd. Okay, so it's not the wrong life, but it feels like he's living in the middle of a mistake.

A huge mistake—like having joined East Side Medical Associates a few years ago.

Kurt Messner, an orthopedic surgeon and the group's managing partner, is driving everyone berserk. He cares only about having wall-to-wall patients, nonstop from 9:00 a.m. until 5:00 p.m. so he can maximize the bottom line. It's all about the money. A medical office isn't a carousel, and yet, the pace of the practice is dizzying.

Rick knows he's little more than a cog in a well-oiled medical machine. It sometimes feels like they're spitting out patients on a conveyor belt. Yes, it's the wrong practice. For him. He never imagined being a doctor would involve the compromises he's been forced to accept.

Okay, so he's not happy with the practice.

But living the wrong *life*? That's no way to feel about things. There are good things in his world and it's important to appreciate them. There's Jackie and Dad and Mom and Katie, but there's gotta be a way to change the direction of his professional life.

He still tastes last night's wine, now fermented on his tongue. His queasy stomach isn't helped by the diner's lingering aromas of eggs, home fries, and bacon. Having awakened early this morning from a clammy sleep, he's steeped in an alcohol-induced fog. While he never uses drugs—doesn't even smoke a joint—he feels narcotized. He takes another sip of a third cup of coffee generously refilled by Mary, the fifty-something waitress. It's bland Silex crap, but it's hot and black, and by now, he feels caffeinated enough to return to the office whirlwind.

His watch says it's 12:20; gotta get back—patients are stacked and waiting.

His half-empty coffee cup makes a good paperweight for a five-dollar bill—a decent tip for Mary, who's gotta earn a living. He's occupied one of her tables for almost a half hour at lunchtime, ordering nothing more than the coffee.

* * *

Amid the blare of Lexington Avenue, a cold November wind knifes at his face. A pedestrian swarm clogs the street amid honking horns, wailing sirens, and the whooshing air brakes of trucks and busses. The Number 6 subway roars beneath the sidewalk, sending vibrations and the smell of ozone up through the metal grating.

It's Manhattan's symphony of madness.

Turning from Lexington onto East Seventy-Ninth, Rick contemplates the patients he'll see—people beset by diabetes, heart failure, afflictions of the bowels and bones. Hopefully, he'll avoid Kurt Messner, with whom he has a mutual abomination society.

He's suddenly jolted by sirens shrieking and the ear-bleeding blast of a fire truck's air horn. An EMT van and a string of police cruisers streak toward a crowd gathered outside the entrance to East Side Medical Associates. *Did someone have a heart attack in our doorway?*

Patrol cars and emergency vehicles approach with their light bars flashing and sirens burping.

Threading through the crush of people, Rick manages to get close enough for a look at what's going on.

Yellow and black police tape stretch across the sidewalk.

Two EMTs off-load a collapsible gurney from an ambulance.

A Channel 7 Eyewitness News van pulls up. Two guys get out of the vehicle: one with a shoulder camera, the other holding a portable microphone.

"What's going on?" Rick asks a young man at the periphery of the crowd.

"Some guy got shot right here on the street."

Shot in broad daylight? On the Upper East Side? In front of our office door? The city's going down the crapper.

A siren whines to a halt, police radios squawk, people babble, flash-bulbs explode in sudden bursts of light. Crime scene techs wearing Tyvek suits, booties, and gloves are going about their job. Threading through the throng, Rick gets closer and peers at a tarp-covered body lying on the sidewalk. A glistening delta of blood—the edges dried in the cold air—has oozed from beneath the canvas. Brown shoes protrude from one end of the covering, toes pointing skyward.

"Excuse me, Officer," Rick says to a cop standing behind the tape. "That's my office and I've gotta—"

"Nobody crosses the line," the cop says.

"I'm a physician. I need to—"

"Sorry, Doc. We're processing a crime scene."

Nearly reeling with disbelief, Rick turns, weaves back through the crowd.

*   *   *

At Lenox Hill's emergency room, he grabs a phone. "East Side Medical Associates," says the receptionist.

"Hi, Carla, it's Rick. I can't get back from lunch. The cops've blocked the entrance."

"I know. Can you believe this? Someone was killed right outside our door."

"Do you know who it was?"

"I don't think he was a patient. We're closing up and we'll have to reschedule the afternoon appointments."

Jesus, only five minutes ago he was amused by that sign, LIFE IS UNCERTAIN, but now, those words bring a chill to his bones.

CHAPTER TWO

AT SIX IN the evening, Rick is back at the apartment sipping a glass of wine.

He waits for the alcohol to flood his brain circuits. When it does, he'll float in that nimbus of indifference he craves.

It's earlier than usual for Rick's fiancée, Jackie, to be home from her law office.

He tells her about the shooting.

"Was he a patient?"

"I don't think so. I've been watching the news, but there's no word on the guy's identity."

The TV is still on, but the volume is muted. Rick snatches the remote, turns up the volume.

Chuck Scarborough begins the 6:00 p.m. broadcast.

"A thirty-three-year-old man, now identified as Robert Harper, an elementary school teacher, was shot to death just after twelve noon today on East Seventy-Ninth Street in Manhattan."

There's an outside camera shot: East Seventy-Ninth Street between Lexington and Third: police cars with light bars flashing—an ambulance, a firetruck, and EMT personnel. The Medical Examiner's van is on the scene.

There's a close-up of the private entrance to East Side Medical Associates.

Scarborough goes on. *"Harper, who taught at the Iverson School located on East Seventy-Eighth Street, was returning from his lunch break, when he was shot by an unknown assailant."*

"How awful," Jackie says. "And right in front of your office door."

The camera switches to an on-site reporter. Huddling against the wind, she says, *"Witnesses reported seeing a man fire three shots from a pistol into the victim's back. The attacker was described as wearing a dark overcoat, a Navy watch cap, and a scarf covering most of his face."*

"This is unbelievable," Jackie says. "In broad daylight. Sounds like a mob thing."

"A witness saw the assailant walk quickly to Third Avenue, where he hailed a taxi at the corner of Third Avenue and Seventy-Ninth Street. Police are asking anyone with information to call the crime hotline."

A chyron crawls across the bottom of the screen, displaying the call-in number as the reporter says Harper was the father of two young children and lived with his wife in Queens.

As she talks, a photo of Robert Harper appears. A head shot.

An electric jolt pierces Rick at the sight of the man's face. Then comes a sense of disbelief.

"Oh, my *God*," Jackie gasps. "Rick, he could have been your *twin brother*."

It's uncanny. Robert Harper looked just like Rick. He was about the same age—mid-thirties—had a full head of short, blondish hair, a square jaw and blue eyes.

The guy was a dead ringer, a doppelganger.

Of course there are subtle differences, but Jackie's right: there's a brotherly resemblance, if not something more. A quick glance on a busy street and anyone could mistake the poor guy for Rick Shepherd.

Dread washes over Rick. *I'm looking at a picture of myself.*

"Rick, that man could be your *double*."

"My double's dead."

"And he was killed at the entrance to your office."

The pores on Rick's face open. Sweat varnishes his cheeks.

Who wants me dead?

As the reporter's voice drones on, Rick's thoughts swirl through a roster of possibilities. There've been no serious arguments with anyone—not a single soul—certainly, nothing that could lead to murder. Has there been friction in his life? Of course. Shit happens in any life, everyday things, minor irritations, petty disagreements, things barely worth remembering. But never anything serious. The last actual fight he'd had was during the eighth grade.

The highlight reel of his life streams through Rick's mind—elementary school, high school, a brief stint in the Boy Scouts, friends, acquaintances, the medical society, the hospital. His thoughts circle like a centrifuge but certainly no one would want to shoot him down in cold blood.

The newscast continues. There are interviews with Harper's fellow teachers and staff members, his students—eighth-grade kids—freaking out, hugging each other, sobbing.

Mayor Koch is being interviewed on camera. *"This is unacceptable. Our streets must be kept safe from predators . . ."*

As Koch continues speaking, Jackie turns to Rick with widened eyes. "Rick, a man who could've been your *twin* was killed in *front of your office*." She reaches for him with shaking hands. During the two years they've been living together, he's never seen her this distressed. Wrapping his arms around her, he feels her trembling.

Am I in someone's crosshairs? If I am, why? What's going on?

His heartbeat throbs in his wrists.

This is so unreal.

Maybe he *is* living the wrong life.

The booze-buzz is gone. Cold clarity takes hold.

In a warbling voice Jackie says, "Rick, we have to go to the police."

CHAPTER THREE

THE NYPD'S 19TH Precinct is housed in an Italian Renaissance-looking building on East Sixty-Seventh Street between Lexington and Park.

Typewriter clatter resounds through the squad room. A squall of background voices can be heard. People moving in all directions lend a chaotic feel to the place.

Rick and Jackie sit facing Detective John Howell at his desk.

Howell's a paunchy, fifty-something guy with thinning hair. He wears a tweed sports jacket, a white shirt that's pulling at the buttons over his belly, and a blue cloth tie hanging loosely from his neck. A small mustard stain is apparent on the tie. Looking slightly bored but apparently trying not to show it, he scribbles a few cursory notes as Rick talks. Occasionally glancing at Robert Harper's photo, Howell squints and the skin around his eyes tightens; he then peers at Rick as though he's making a comparison. Despite trying to appear receptive, the guy looks skeptical.

Howell draws a deep breath, leans back in his chair, and shrugs. "Okay, Doc . . . I'll grant you there's a resemblance, but the vic was fleshier than you; he coulda lost a few pounds, sorta like me." He pats his belly bulge, then lets out a chortle.

Does this guy think this is funny?

"And you look like an athlete. Am I right?"

"I once played baseball," Rick says. "A long time ago. But, Detective—"

"I can tell," Howell interjects. "You're in good shape. And Harper?" he says, looking at the photo. "It's obvious the guy never played ball in his life. Granted, with a passing glance, he sorta resembled you."

"Detective . . ." Jackie interrupts in a warbling voice. "You just said it: 'A passing glance.' When you're walking on the street, you could've easily mistaken that man for Rick. We saw the resemblance the second the picture came up on the TV. And the shooting happened in front of Rick's *office*. The conclusion is obvious."

"Okay, okay," Howell says, leaning his elbows on the desk and sighing heavily. "I get it. I do."

Fucking guy's bored, just wants to get home and grab a beer.

"It happened in front of your office and there *is* a resemblance." Picking up the photo of Robert Harper, he again scrutinizes it, peers at Rick.

Is this guy patronizing us?

"You can't dismiss this as *coincidence*, Detective," Jackie says in a voice now tinged with irritation. Though it happens rarely, her lawyerly composure is about to shred.

Jackie's law school friends said she ripped opponents to pieces in moot court.

"Okay, I said *I get it*," Howell nearly snarls. He turns to Rick. "So . . . let's check off all the boxes."

"Meaning?"

"I'm gonna ask you some questions and I want you to answer them as honestly as possible."

"Sure."

"Is there anyone in your life you'd consider an enemy?"

"How do you define an enemy?"

"Someone who'd pass you on the street, turn around, come up from behind, and pump three bullets into your back, *that's* how."

"Harper was shot three times?" Rick asks. The words feel like they're being torn from his throat.

"Yup. He took three slugs in the back. You got *that* kinda enemy, Doc?"

"Not a chance."

"Anyone who might hold a grudge?"

"No one I can think of. Actually, there's absolutely no one *ever* in my life who would want me dead."

Rick has no enemies. *Not even Kurt Messner. Yeah, Kurt's an overbearing jackass—a real Prussian kommandant, and we've occasionally had words—but would Kurt have me killed? No way.*

"Okay, Doc, you have a specialty?"

"Internal medicine."

"Any patient with a really bad result?"

"There's never been anything terrible."

"Whaddaya mean *terrible*?"

"Some patients die, some you see once and they never come back . . . you don't know why. Maybe there wasn't the right chemistry. Or their insurance coverage changed and they're out of your network. It could be anything."

"No patients who're unhappy with their results?"

"Not that I know about."

Any criticisms?"

"No."

"Any malpractice suits in the works?"

"None that I know of."

"Any complaints to the county medical society?"

"None."

"Trouble at the hospital?"

"No."

"Any friction with nurses, other doctors, staff . . . you know, the usual workplace bullshit?"

"None."

"Any friction with *anyone*?"

"None I can think of."

"Any run-ins lately . . . a road rage kinda thing, an argument with a neighbor?"

"No."

"You live where?"

"Not far from here. In Manhattan, Eighty-Fourth and Third."

"An apartment building, right?"

"Yes."

"Any kooks in the building?"

"A few."

"There always are." Howell's lips curl into a semi-smile. "Any arguments? A noisy neighbor who leaves garbage in the hallway, someone's dog crappin' in the elevator?"

"One noisy neighbor, but there've been no arguments. Nothing like that."

"You never complained to the super?"

"We brought it up with him, but the tenant doesn't know we reported it. Nothing's going on there."

"Any strange occurrences?"

"Like what?"

"Anyone hassling you? An argument over a parking spot. Any minor issue that could escalate into something serious?"

"Nothing like that."

"Have you noticed anyone loitering near your building when you leave for work in the morning?"

"No."

"Anyone at the office or hospital who doesn't look like he belongs there."

"No, nothing like that."

"How 'bout crank calls or hang-ups?"

"A few over the last couple of weeks."

"How often?"

"Once a week, maybe less."

"Does the caller say anything?"

"No, just hangs up."

"Happens to everyone in the city. How 'bout weird voicemail messages at home, the office, the hospital?"

"None."

Howell nods, pauses for a moment. "You said you're divorced, right?"

Jackie lets out a loud sigh. Rick knows it's meant for his ears. "Yeah, but that's not an issue."

"Hey, Doc, it can always be an issue. How long you been divorced?"

"Four years."

"Where's the ex?"

"Fort Myers, Florida."

"When was your last contact with her?"

"There's been none since the divorce."

Jesus, this is agonizing. Any more talk about Allison and Jackie'll get pissed.

"Any kids?"

"No."

"Does the ex work?"

"She's an architect."

"Was the divorce amicable?"

"Yes."

"Any money issues?"

"What we had was split down the middle."

"Has she remarried?"

"Yes."

"How do you know?"

"You hear things."

"What's her name?"

"Allison . . . I'm not sure of her last name now."

"Her maiden name?"

"Becker."

Howell writes it down, sneaks a peek at Jackie.

"Why the divorce?"

"C'mon, Detective. Do we hafta get into that?"

"Yeah, Doc, we do. Why the divorce?"

Jackie hates when Allison's name comes up as it sometimes does with friends. Especially since Jackie's been pushing for them to get married and he's been stalling.

"We had very little in common. It was just physical attraction . . . a mistake."

"About you two . . ." Howell eyes Rick, then nods at Jackie. "It's exclusive?"

"Yes."

"You're sure of that?" Howell's eyes shift to Jackie. A smile in his voice threatens to reach his lips.

Shit. It's a cringeworthy moment, just excruciating. Rick's thighs tighten.

"It's exclusive," Jackie says.

Jackie's voice is a giveaway. Rick knows she's seething inwardly.

Howell nods, regards Rick, waits.

"We're sure," Rick says with a nod.

"Any ex-boyfriend who might have it in for the Doc," Howell asks, eyeballing Jackie.

"Not at all," she says. Her voice sounds tight, strained. Rick knows she's holding back from shooting darts at the guy.

He turns back to Rick. "Any trouble at the office?"

"Not really."

"Not really?" Howell arches an eyebrow. "Whaddaya mean *not really?*"

"The managing partner's a pain in the ass, but it's nothing serious."

"Managing partner? What kinda practice?"

"A group practice. A bunch of specialties . . . internal medicine, OB-GYN, urology, orthopedics, dermatology, you name it."

"How many partners?"

"Nine."

"*Nine?* That leaves lotsa room for disagreements, wouldn't you say?" Howell tilts his head.

Rick realizes Howell must think he's hit pay dirt.

"Any disputes? Money issues? The pecking order?"

"Just some disagreements."

"About what?"

"The managing partner wants bigger profits. But it wouldn't lead to this . . ."

"Lead to *what?*"

"To murder."

"What's this managing partner's name?"

"Look, Detective . . . it's not necessary to—"

"Just for the record, Doc."

"Messner. Kurt Messner. C'mon, Detective, no *way* does this involve him."

Shit, this could lead to even more complications at the office. As though things aren't bad enough.

"Look, Doc, you're worried someone might wanna kill you, so just lemme do my job." Howell scribbles away. "Whatever you say stays here . . . for the time being. Got it?"

"Yeah."

"How 'bout the family? Any problems there?"

"Nothing important."

"C'mon, Doc, gimme somethin' to work with."

"My parents are separated. My father lives in Brooklyn. My mother's in Manhattan."

"How long they been apart?"

"Two years."

"Amicable?"

"I'd say so."

"How old're they?"

"He's sixty-four; she's sixty-one."

"Anyone new in the picture? Either one of them . . . a boyfriend, girlfriend, or should I say *companion*?"

"No, nothing."

Howell's face crimps into a mask of disbelief.

"They're in their sixties, what can I say?" Rick shrugs.

"So? Whaddaya think, Doc, it all goes south when you hit fifty?"

Howell's lips twist into a semi-smile.

"There's nothing going on there."

Howell notches that same eyebrow, looks skeptical.

He's gotta be a cynic. How can you be a detective and not think the world's full of shit?

"Any brothers, sisters?"

"A sister."

"Where's she?"

"East Eighty-First Street."

"Married? Separated? Divorced?"

"She's single. Lives alone. Never been married."

"Any problems there?"

"No."

I'm not getting Katie involved in this shit.

"Do you gamble . . . play the horses, bet on ball games?"

"No, never."

"Do you owe anyone money?"

"No."

More back-and-forth—question after question popping like a string of firecrackers—about the family, the practice, friends, acquaintances, neighbors, drug use, absolutely everything. Rick's thoughts roil as he answers them, and he's certain nothing good will come of this interview.

This guy knows how to get under your skin. Must have learned this shit in detective school or whatever these guys go through. Or maybe it's just his personality.

How does Rick make sense of this?

Murder. At his office door.

A guy who could be mistaken for him.

Who did it? A patient? A former patient? Not a chance.

Kurt Messner? Sure, there are frictions and sometimes the office feels like a war zone. But it's a *cold* war. A *civil* war. Kurt? Murder? No fucking way.

"So far, Doc, I don't see this homicide as having a *thing* to do with you. Absolutely *nada*. Just seems like an unfortunate coincidence to me."

Maybe Howell's right. It could be a random thing. Some poor bastard who just happens to look like me was in the wrong place at the wrong time. And now he's a corpse in the morgue.

"Who knows?" Howell says. "It could have been somethin' goin' on with Mr. Harper."

The detective could be right. What does Dad always say? *Don't jump to concussions.*

"Look, Doc, I understand your concern, but just go on with your life. If somethin' comes up—like if those hang-ups get more frequent or someone makes a threat—give us a shout."

Though Howell makes sense, something gnaws at Rick—a not-so-vague sense of wrongness. It's there, burrowing beneath his skin.

Howell adds, "Don't lose sleep over this, Doc. This case'll get a lot of attention. The brass is worried because this happened in a good neighborhood in broad daylight and Hizzoner's gonna get involved."

Howell tosses his pen onto the desk. "Like I said . . . this probably had somethin' to do with Harper's life, and nothin' to do with yours."

CHAPTER FOUR

TWO NIGHTS LATER, the telephone jangles.

The sound is so penetrating, Rick feels like he's being gored.

Is it a school bell? Shit no, it's that burglar alarm from the dry cleaning store a few doors down on Third Avenue.

It's another break-in. The city really *is* going down the drain.

"Rick. Get the phone."

Is it a dream? No, it's Jackie's voice.

"Rick. Wake up. Get the *phone.*"

Jesus, another hang-up? In the middle of the night? This is getting serious.

In the darkness, he makes out the night table. Yes, it's the phone with its burbling trill. He virtually jumps up, sits at the edge of the bed, shakes his head, tries to clear the cobwebs. His body trembles as his hand slaps at the receiver, knocks it off the cradle. His brain hasn't kicked into gear yet.

Groping in the dark, he sees the illuminated numbers on the night table clock.

Jesus, it's 1:10 in the morning.

His heart feels like its somersaulting in his chest.

It's gotta be the hospital. There's a patient in distress.

The bed bounces as Jackie sits up.

The bedside lamp on Jackie's side clicks; light fills the bedroom. The phone is in his hand, now at his ear. His heart is beating an erratic tattoo in his chest.

He hears a sob followed by the rattle of ragged breathing.

"Mom . . . ?" he croaks.

"Rick . . ." Then there's a cough followed by a choking sound.

Another swallowed sob.

"Mom, what's wrong?"

The fog of sleep evaporates.

"It's . . . it's your father." A quivering voice says, "Oh, Rick . . ." A hiccup.

"*Dad?* What happened? What's wrong?"

"He's dead."

A blast of disbelief. *Dad's been in good health . . . dead at sixty-four? No way.*

Yet, his insides plunge. It feels like a mallet slams into his chest. And the reverberation sends what feels like an icicle through his spine.

"Mom? What happened?"

Her voice is strained, phlegm-filled. "I told him to stop . . ."

"Stop what?"

That cold feeling spreads. An icy current runs through his chest down to his arms. Now he's shivering.

"I warned him about those house calls . . . especially at night."

Muffled sobs.

House calls? Was he in an accident?

"Mom, what happened?"

"Your father was making a house call and he . . . he was shot . . . murdered."

CHAPTER FIVE

STARING OUT THE window, Rick gazes up at a slush-colored sky.

From his mother's apartment on the tenth floor, traffic on Third Avenue looks like a sluggish caravan moving uptown through the morning gloom. The sounds of horns blaring and sirens shrieking penetrate the double pane windows and form an eerie backdrop to the darkness of it all. The sky, the street, even the façade of buildings along the avenue match Rick's mood—bleak, somber, foreboding.

When Mom's call came last night, it was a shock wave of unreality.

But disbelief is giving way to reality—to loss and emptiness. It's seeping in: his father is dead.

Will the world ever seem normal after this? Will I ever feel whole again?

It feels like a sinkhole has opened inside of him and it widens with each passing moment.

The brutality of it all feels like a punch in the face. The barbaric act of one human being against another—a life obliterated so suddenly—has blown its way into Rick's life.

And into the life of his family.

Dad's dead. Murdered in cold blood. How unbelievable.

This is no Robert Harper shooting. This is the death of a loved one, his father. This one is up close and personal.

How can Rick feel so paralytic, so numb, yet feel this raw? As though he's been gutted.

As a physician, he swims in an ocean of medical misery. He's seen enough death to fill a morgue many times over. Medicine strips everything down to the essentials: life or death. Being or not-being. Yet, he's never viewed the body of a loved one.

Dad's gone? Shot in the middle of the night. While making a house call. It's unbelievable.

How do you accept the violent death of someone you love?

Then there are the morbid rituals: Would he be asked to identify the body? Go to the morgue and see whatever's left of him? And then there's a wake, a funeral, prayers, mourners, condolence calls, bullshit of every kind.

Of course he'll have to ID the body.

He can't let Mom or Kate do it. Mom's too broken up and Kate's too fragile. Uncle Harry can't do it. Poor guy, with all the misery in his life, he could never handle looking at the body of his twin brother.

Death has hijacked Rick's life. And the lives of those he loves.

Jesus, how flimsy the protective walls we build around ourselves are—they're eggshell thin—ready to crack open in an instant. That's all it takes, a moment in time and everything changes.

He thinks of that sign in the diner: *Life is uncertain. Eat dessert first.*

There's more to that little adage than meets the eye.

Your day-to-day existence seems so routine, so predictable, so mundane. Until that single moment in time. A second is all it takes.

Murder.

It just doesn't happen to someone you know or love.

Until it does.

And there was the Harper shooting . . . my look-alike. Jesus, what's going on? It's a good thing Mom didn't see the evening news after it happened. If she had, she'd be a nervous wreck.

And now Dad. When was the last time I saw him?

A few weeks ago when he and Jackie took him to that Brooklyn trattoria he loved. His father talked about how he enjoys the give-and-take with his patients, and teaching the med students is a special pleasure. Or *was* one. And he mentioned the house calls, the last sad remnant of his shrinking practice. Medicine sustained him, especially since the separation. What were the last two years of his life like? Miserable, for sure.

His birthday was coming soon, would've been his sixty-fifth. Though he reminded himself again and again, Rick kept forgetting to get him something. Anything, a small token of appreciation would have been meaningful. But he failed. He'd been too tied up with his own petty world between the discord at the office and the everyday chores of living life.

He shudders, recalling that telephone conversation with his father, the one that happened only yesterday. Those last words he said to him—how lacking in empathy he'd been—were the words of a fool, a selfish one. If only he could redo that talk, take back what he said, replace it with something compassionate; but death precludes that—it means no do-overs. Sadness washes over him in a tide of regret.

It feels like the world's lost its mind. It's broken in some way he can't quite define. Or has it tilted more on its axis and everything's pointing in the wrong direction? It all seems so goddamned insane. And suddenly Rick feels untethered in the world, rootless, as though part of what kept him stable in this life is now gone.

It suddenly hits him and he shudders with the realization.

Dad was shot down. Robert Harper was blown away in front of the office. Were those bullets meant for me? First the son and then the father. What the fuck is going on?

He feels his insides tremble. He could drop a Xanax and wait for that little white pill to short-circuit the dread threading through him.

The drug company rep leaves boxed samples of them off at the office every month. But he can't depend on a pill to get him through this shitstorm. He's gotta keep it together, if not for himself, for Mom and Katie, both wrecked by what's happened, especially for Katie. And for Jackie, too. Everyone close to him is upended.

His mother and Kate sit on the sofa, holding hands while Jackie prepares tea. Mom's eyes are red, the lids swollen. Clutching a handkerchief, she dabs at her nose. She looks destroyed. She must feel guilty about having left Dad. Even more remorseful than Rick feels. Guilt has a way of sneaking up on you, of grabbing you by the neck when you least expect it. And then, *Bam*, you're immersed in a world of hurt.

Kate's gamine face is curdled into a mask of distress. Dark semicircles are slung beneath her bloodshot eyes. Grief has seized her, and Rick knows she could be tempted to sink back into using. And now there's no father to facilitate getting her into another rehab program.

Rick turns from the window. "Is Uncle Harry coming?"

"He's driving in from Connecticut," Mom says.

As if Dad's brother hasn't had enough misery in his life.

"I can't believe it," Kate says. "Dad's *dead*?"

Getting to her feet, she begins pacing.

Rick looks for the telltale drug signs in Kate: pinpoint pupils, slightly slurred speech, if not slurred, then slowed, and a becalmed voice. Is she downing Xanax? Uppers? Downers? Opiates—codeine, Vicodin, or Percocet? At one time or another, she's been on every one of them along with her loser of a boyfriend, Mike Brock. And the detox treatments have only given her a temporary reprieve. Within a month or two, she's back on whatever she can get her hands on.

Yes, there's a shock-blasted look in her eyes.

But it's not from drugs. It's from grief, the thief of joy.

Embracing her, he rubs her back. Sobbing, with her shoulders heaving, she leans against him. He says nothing. This is no time for brotherly nostrums.

Is now the time for *anything*—for patients, office politics, people in the street, hordes rushing to get nowhere, people going about their work-a-day lives as though nothing of consequence has happened? All of them indifferent to this family's pain, to their suffering. That's just the way it is. Will he find himself just going through the motions of living life while the world moves on?

Violent death does that. It rips at life's seams, leaves a hole in everything.

But he can't dwell on this shit. There's too much to do—there are the chores of death.

Contact a funeral home. Close up Dad's practice, take care of the house in Brooklyn, call the telephone company, the bank, a lawyer, the electric and gas companies, the accountant, the attorney, Social Security, all the minutiae of a life suddenly ended. And there's Mom, alone now, gotta help her.

"I left word at the office," Jackie says. "I won't be going in today."

Rick's reassured by her nearness, by knowing she's here for him, for his mother, and for Kate. Jackie has an analytical mind while Rick operates more on instinct. But they work well together—sugar and spice. Their only real clashes have orbited around his delaying their getting married.

"When's the detective getting here?" asks Kate, pacing the floor again.

"It's rush hour. The trip from Brooklyn must be awful," Jackie says.

When the intercom buzzes, Rick's heart falters. *A detective. Some hard-bitten guy who sees this kind of thing every day.* He's reminded of Howell two nights ago.

Howell: reassuring them there's no reason to worry. What bullshit.

Two shootings close together, his unlucky look-alike and his father.

Hard, cold logic tells him it can't be coincidence. There's more to this than the random spinning of the universe. Something's going on and it's dangerous.

No, it's more than dangerous. It's lethal.

And this morning there were two more hang-ups.

Two shootings, one in Manhattan, the other in Brooklyn, two days apart. What connection can there be? An attempt on the son and then the father is shot.

The intercom buzzes. Jackie picks up the receiver. "Yes . . . ?"

Alfredo, the daytime doorman, says, "Please tell Mrs. Shepherd a detective's here."

That feeling of disbelief washes over him again. An NYPD detective is downstairs in the lobby, *here*, coming to Mom's home.

It's unreal.

CHAPTER SIX

RICK OPENS THE door to a guy who appears to be in his late thirties.

He looks like he was once a jock: solidly built, slope-shouldered, closely cropped hair, pale blue eyes, good looking in a rugged sort of way. Looks like he's been around plenty of blocks, knows the world.

"I'm Detective Art Nager, NYPD," he says flashing his badge.

"Yes, Detective. I'm Rick Shepherd. Please come in."

Nager walks with an easy athleticism, has a world-weary look. Yet Rick senses something empathic, even kindly, in his eyes. You don't expect that from a guy who works homicide cases for a living, a guy like Howell. Rick's gut tells him Nager's not hard bitten, hasn't been worn down by the job, hasn't lost his capacity for compassion.

Mom, Kate, and Jackie rise to greet him.

Rick makes the introductions.

"I'm sorry for your loss," Nager says as his eyes swerve to each of them. "This must be a shock to you all." His words sound genuine; not shopworn platitudes.

Mom's chin quivers. Tears trickle down her cheeks. Kate looks no better than Mom.

Turning to Rick, Nager says, "I understand from Mrs. Shepherd that you're a physician, too . . ."

"Yes. Maybe we should talk in the den," Rick says, hoping to spare Mom and Kate any details about the shooting.

Nager nods. He reads the signals.

Kate and Mom head back to the living room as Rick, Jackie, and Nager go into the den.

Rick closes the door, gestures toward a chair. "What can you tell us, Detective?"

Setting his overcoat on a chair and sitting down, Nager says, "I was at the crime scene last night. What we know so far is that Dr. Shepherd was making a house call at an apartment house in the Flatbush section of Brooklyn. He was shot three times in the back while he was in the building's vestibule."

Shot three times in the back? Jesus, that's what happened to Robert Harper.

"His body was discovered by a tenant who went out to walk his dog at about eleven fifteen, so the coroner estimates the time of death somewhere between ten forty-five and a little after eleven. We found his wallet next to the body. A card in the wallet said to call Mrs. Shepherd in case of an emergency."

"Was it a mugging?" Rick says, trying to process what he's hearing.

"The cash was taken, but his credit cards were still in the wallet. And the doctor's bag and wristwatch were untouched. If it was a mugging, the perpetrator may've been spooked and took off before he could grab them."

Rick can hardly believe they're talking about his father's death.

"Forensics will be working on every angle and we'll probably have more details within a day or so. I know this is difficult for you right now, but I'd like to ask you some questions . . ." He pulls a small notebook from his breast pocket.

Rick nods and casts a glance at Jackie. Her face is milk white. He knows exactly what she's thinking—three shots to the back, the same way Robert Harper was gunned down.

"Mrs. Shepherd and the doctor have different addresses. I assume they were living apart."

"Yes, they've been separated for about two years," Rick says, even as his throat constricts.

"Can you tell me why?"

"My mother felt Dad's priorities were wrong," Rick says. "At some point, she thought he was seeing someone . . ."

"An affair?"

Rick feels like he's choking. "Yes, that was about two years ago," he says. "That's when she left him and moved here." Surprisingly, his voice is steady; there's no tremor and his thoughts flow clearly. Is he detaching himself from the horror of it all? Is this how you deal with murder?

"Was it an amicable separation?"

"Yes."

"No conflicts like, say . . . over money?"

"None that I know of. In fact, he sent her money every month."

"You mentioned your father's priorities. Tell me about that."

"Yes. He was, how can I put it? He was committed to his patients. It sometimes seemed like they were his first concern. The home phone rang constantly with patients calling. He probably rode the elevators of half the apartment buildings in Brooklyn making house calls. My mother felt the house calls were dangerous, especially at night, that he could be mugged or worse. He was so involved with his practice that my mother felt left out of his life. And when the affair happened, she'd had enough so she moved out."

"Was he seeing anyone at the time of his death? A woman . . . some kind of relationship?"

"I don't think so. Why's that important?"

"Lemme give you the basics. When a woman's murdered, we first look at the husband or a boyfriend. When a man's murdered, we look at his business associates, an ex—if there is one—and his love life. Many victims of murder are killed by people they knew. It's just a jumping-off point so I have to ask these kinds of questions and I realize they can be . . . difficult."

"I get it," Rick says as his stomach begins doing a slow roll. "But I don't think there's anyone else in his life; certainly no one who would do *this*. If there is someone, he's never said anything about her." Rick suddenly realizes he's talking about his father in the present tense and feels a shudder ripple through his chest.

"A dumb question, Rick. Did your father have any enemies?"

"Not that I know of," Rick answers, recalling Howell's questions.

Enemies . . . a rage-filled patient . . . a former patient, someone who'd had a lousy result . . .

"Any malpractice suits?"

"No. His patients idolized him." Rick clears his throat. "Actually, they think he's a god. He's one of the few doctors who still makes house calls."

Jesus, I'm still talking about him in the present tense.

Rick's thoughts swerve to his father's patients: he was adored by them. It had been that way for years. On major holidays, homemade treats poured into the house: honey struffoli, sour cream coffee cakes, soda bread—every ethnic variation of a holiday gift for the Medicine Man of Brooklyn.

Nager follows up with a plethora of questions: about arguments, friction with neighbors, friends, acquaintances, any recent incidents, strange telephone calls, if there had been any problems with anyone in his father's life.

The same questions Howell asked.

"No, none of the above," Rick says. "And if there were problems, I think he'd have mentioned them to me."

"Was there any change in his behavior over the last few weeks or months? Anything at all?"

"No change, but he was unhappy that his practice was drying up. That had been going on for more than a year. Actually, it began about two years ago. He realized people don't want to go to an older physician. He was a solo practitioner whose practice was shrinking every month. The reality is clear: it was dying."

Rick's chest tightens at the thought of his father's waning practice. And of his death.

Nager nods as Rick speaks. The guy seems to understand the professional abyss Dad faced.

After a brief silence, Rick says, "I'm guessing you're thinking this wasn't a random attack."

"I can't really say right now. We'll have a better idea when forensics goes through everything and we have more information. And to be thorough, we'll need to get his phone records and personal papers . . . bank statements, office records, things like that."

"This happened in the Flatbush section?" Rick says.

"Yes, at fifteen thirty East Nineteenth Street in Brooklyn."

A shock wave batters Rick. "Jesus, that's where we lived when I was a kid, before we moved to Brooklyn Heights, where my father's been living alone for the last two years. I know he still had a few patients in the building where we'd lived."

"Do you know anything about a woman named Catherine Donovan?"

"No. Who's she?"

"The patient your father was going to see when it happened."

"How do you know he was going to see her?"

"Her next-door neighbor told us he visited her quite often. She has a heart condition."

Rick shakes his head. "I never heard of her."

"We'll be talking with her very soon." Nager explains that detectives on the crime scene team have been going door-to-door in the building and are speaking with people who live in the private houses on the block. "It's a thorough canvas for possible witnesses," Nager says. "We'll know pretty soon if anything turns up . . ."

"Meaning what?"

"We want to know if anyone saw or heard anything. If they saw a car pull up and if anyone got out of it and followed your father."

Nager slips the notebook into his jacket pocket. "Rick, is there anyone you can think of who might've held a grudge against your father?"

It suddenly hits Rick. "Wait a minute, there *is* someone who hated my father . . . Mike Brock, my sister Katie's ex-boyfriend."

"Tell me about it."

Rick glances toward the den door, makes certain it's closed so Kate won't overhear him. "The guy's a drug addict. Kate met him at a rehab facility. Dad ragged on her all the time to stop seeing him," Rick says, picturing Mike Brock riding a Big Twin Harley and wearing a black leather jacket—his whole wannabe Hells Angels act, and the outlaw motorcycle crowd he hangs out with.

"What else can you tell me about him?"

"When Kate was living at home, our father tried to get a restraining order against Brock, but she moved out of the house with him and bounced around the East Village living with him and his friends—a few nights in one place, a couple in another. It was a bone in my father's throat."

Jesus, if I could get my hands on that bastard I'd break his fucking neck.

Nager nods and pulls out a small notebook, jots something in it.

"She's clean now. She has her own place—thanks to money our parents have been laying out for her. Now, she works as a dog walker here in Manhattan."

"Rick," Jackie interjects, "tell the detective what happened with you and Mike Brock."

"Once when I visited Kate," Rick says, "she had bruises on her face. It turned out Mike had hit her. A few minutes later, I heard his motorcycle pull up in front of the house. When he got to her apartment, I threw him against a wall, told him I'd kill him if he ever touched her again."

"So there was bad blood between you and him, and between Brock and your father?"

Rick nods, aware his chin is trembling.

"We'll check him out. You know where he lives?"

"As far as I know, he doesn't have a fixed address."

"Before I leave, I'll talk with your sister."

"Detective," Jackie says, "are you familiar with what happened the other day . . . a man named Robert Harper was killed in broad daylight on East Seventy-Ninth Street here in Manhattan?"

"Sure, it's still in the news."

Jackie's eyelashes are tipped with tears; they look like dewdrops. She tells Nager about Harper's resemblance to Rick and about the meeting with Howell.

"That *is* a strange coincidence," Nager says.

Regarding Rick, he says, "A man who looked like you got shot in front of your office; and then your father was shot the same way." Nager's lips tighten. "Is there any connection between this man Robert Harper and your father?"

"None that I know of."

"The Harper matter isn't a Brooklyn case, but I'll contact Manhattan North and we'll look into it." He jots something else in his notebook. "You're sure no one else might have it in for your family?"

"I can't even *imagine* it," Rick says. "But there's something else . . . we've been getting hang-ups lately."

"How often?"

"Three, maybe four in the last few weeks . . . but they're getting more frequent."

After asking for details, Nager says, "It's best for you to stay in touch with Detective Howell about those hang-ups."

Rick nods, recalling Howell's dismissive attitude.

Nager hands Rick a business card.

The room is silent. Through the closed door, Rick hears Mom sobbing in the living room.

Jesus, how do we get beyond this?

"A few necessary details . . ." Nager says, getting to his feet and reaching for his overcoat. "I need someone to identify the body. Will it be you?" he asks, peering at Rick.

"It's me," Rick says, standing on legs that feel like they're liquefying.

"The body's at the Medical Examiner's Office . . . Kings County Hospital on Clarkson Avenue in Brooklyn. You know where that is?"

Nodding, Rick is aware of that choking feeling returning. "I'll go as soon as rush hour is over."

"A few other things . . ." Nager says. "We'll need access to your father's office. We'll take his records and go through them for any possibles. Can someone let us in?"

"You know where it is?"

"Yes, his cards were in his wallet."

"I'll let the superintendent know you're coming. It's a private entrance at the corner of a yellow brick building."

"Fine. And we'll need to go through the house in Brooklyn Heights. It's twenty-one Cranberry Street, right?"

Rick nods as he pictures the old clapboard house on a quiet street only two blocks from the harbor.

"We'll have to look through his checkbook, bills, bank records, credit card statements, anything that might give us a lead to who might've done this. Can someone let us in?"

"I have a key," Rick says, visualizing the living room, dining room, the den, the overstuffed chair where Dad sat in the evenings reading medical journals.

"I can let you in," Jackie says. "I'm taking some time off."

"Is noon today okay?"

"I'll be there."

*   *   *

Rick hears Kate's sobs coming from the den. Can she hold it together long enough to give Nager any information about Mike Brock?

Suddenly, the door opens. Kate's face is bone-white as she heads for the hallway bathroom, enters it . . . and slams the door. Rick hears her retching into the toilet bowl.

"She's in no shape to talk right now," Nager says. "We'll touch base tomorrow morning. As soon as Kate can tell me anything, we'll come by."

Rick walks the detective to the door, steps with him into the hallway.

"We'll do everything we can to find out who did this," Nager says. "And again, Rick, I'm sorry for your loss."

As a physician, Rick's witnessed the condolence calls of friends and relatives when patients died. He's always wondered how people can express heartfelt sympathy without coming across as trite, formulaic, or even insincere. But Nager's words seem genuine. He feels a connection to the guy.

As the elevator door opens, Rick realizes he's so weary, his bones ache. If this is part of grief, it's exhausting.

You know you'll outlive your parents—it's a given—but until it happens, death is just an abstraction. Death propels certain truths to the fore: sure, you know you'll die.

But what happened to his father—getting shot down for no apparent reason—is fucking insane.

And then it happens. A cold wave of fear invades Rick, seeping through his chest, then down his arms into his hands and fingers, which are now ice cold. Someone tried to kill him by sinking three bullets into his back—mistaking Harper for him—and it's possible that the same person put three slugs into Dad.

Obviously, there was a plan: first the son, then the father.

And for the first time in his thirty-four years, Rick Shepherd wonders how death will take him.

CHAPTER SEVEN

As HE CLIMBS the steps of Brooklyn Borough Command, Art Nager feels a hot, sour surge billow up from his stomach and splash the back of his throat. It tastes like battery acid.

Goddamned reflux. A fancy way to describe heartburn. Tums in the morning, Maalox at night. And too much coffee. Of course, he had to stop at the coffee shop on the corner of DeKalb for another cup of coffee. Goddamned heartburn's kicking up already and it's only ten thirty in the morning. And he knows he'll down more of that bitter bilge from the squad room's Mr. Coffee machine. Then he'll feel that backwash of stomach acid crawl up his gullet. Christ, how he hates that feeling, like the inside of his chest is on fire. *That's why they call it heartburn, dummy.*

He's been drinking black coffee for twenty-five out of his thirty-eight years. Despite Mom's warnings, it never stunted his growth. He's six-two, two hundred eighteen pounds and was once an All-City high school football player. But now, he worries about what stomach acid will do to the lining of his esophagus, but not enough to give up drinking the shit.

The trip back from Manhattan wasn't too bad; traffic was relatively light. Waiting for the elevator, Nager thinks about Rick Shepherd.

Guy looks like an athlete—they're about the same height, and from the drape of his sports jacket, it's obvious he has thick shoulders and arms—looks like he played ball before he got to be a doc. Nager really felt for that family. When someone you love is murdered, you carry that load for the rest of your life.

The Shepherd case might be tricky; if it was a random shooting or mugging, it'll likely fall into the dust bin and be a long shot with the evidence they have so far. That was one of Pop's favorite expressions: *It'll be a long shot.* Pop was a gambler. Always played the odds, whether at the track or a ball game—the Dodgers, the Yankees—it hardly mattered which team was playing. There were bets to be made, spreads to bet on.

At least the Shepherd case will keep Nager from thinking about Ellen and what happened to their marriage. A flash of their ten-year-old son, Bobby, sends a warm flush through him. He'll have the boy this weekend. The kid's dying to see *E.T.* Then, it'll be dinner followed by a banana split at Juniors, the boy's favorite place, even more than Jahn's ice cream parlor.

Arriving at the squad room, Nager spots his junior partner, Liz Callaghan, sitting at her desk. Six months earlier, Assistant Chief Pildes asked him to mentor her through Homicide, virtually begged him to be her rabbi.

"Why me?" he'd asked Pildes, aware he didn't relish the chore of breaking in a newbie.

"Because she's a looker," the Chief said. "And these fuckin' guys are Neanderthals. With this crew, I'll have a harassment claim on my hands in a heartbeat. Besides, she's connected. And I *know* you're a gentleman."

Yes, she's connected. Liz Callaghan's father, now retired, was once Assistant Chief of the Brooklyn Command.

What if she doesn't measure up? Her father still has sway with the higher-ups, guys who can make or break a career. Being her rabbi could turn into political suicide. But she's been a quick study and has a mind like a steel trap. In fact, Nager's impression of her is, among other things, that she has a mischievous intelligence.

Liz Callaghan: thirty-one years old and single. He wonders why a woman with her looks has never been married. He knows that fact from peeking at her personnel file. The Chief was right on the money: she's definitely a *looker*—or what back in the day in the Sheepshead Bay area they called a *traffic-stopper*. She's got the fairest skin Nager's ever seen and huge blue eyes you can sink right in to. Wears her strawberry-blond hair pulled back in a bun. Nager's always liked women with buns and ponytails.

Her record say she graduated *Summa* from Brooklyn College. After a solid stint as a beat cop, she took the exam and made Detective Third Grade.

There's something different with Liz as his partner. When he became a detective third grade—Jesus, it feels like a hundred years ago—his mentor was Don McCreary, now retired and living with his wife on City Island in the Bronx. Before long, you knew the other guy's life—his wife, his kids, his biases, his background, his peccadillos and maybe some of the not-so-minor vices, too. You stayed close, even if he were a guy you wouldn't ordinarily have as a friend off the job.

But with a woman, it's different. There are no personal questions. And no jokes with even a tinge of sex to them. Not even an innuendo. They're taboo. Even a look or an innocent hand on the shoulder—or, God forbid, a pat on the ass—might lead to trouble. Even though Liz doesn't seem like the overly sensitive type, you never know. The most benign comment could trigger a complaint . . . followed by a hearing and then a shitstorm.

"Hi, Art," Liz says as he enters the squad room. She tosses aside a copy of the *Post* and shoots him that high-wattage smile that can make him fantasize there's a possibility of something beyond a professional relationship.

"How're you this morning?" she asks.

"I'm good, Liz," he says, sitting at his gunmetal gray steel desk.

"How was the trip to Manhattan?"

"Good . . . good," he says reaching into the top drawer of his desk for a roll of Tums. He rips out two tablets and chews the chalky stuff. Instant cooling of the heartburn. Now he's tempted to head over to Zelnick's desk and grab one of those belly bombs from the Dunkin' Donut box. But if he does, his stomach will start spewing like Vesuvius.

"You guys finish up the canvas?" he asks.

"Yeah—and the results are disappointing. No one claims to have heard or seen a thing."

"No one passing through the lobby just after it went down?"

"Just that dog walker," she says.

"That's too bad."

"The community council's gonna go crazy over this," Liz says, swiveling her chair to face him. "The doc was a beloved fixture in the neighborhood."

"Yeah, the captain's gonna worry Hizzoner might get involved."

"How's the vic's family?"

"They look like death warmed over. Especially the daughter. She's a basket case."

"I can only imagine."

He reaches for another Tums. A little insurance won't hurt.

"Do the on-site photos show anything that wasn't evident last night?" he asks, aware he's always uncomfortable at crime scenes.

"Nah, they show exactly what we saw. The doctor was shot three times in the back. Like Doc Gilroy said, three bullets penetrated the spine and blew through his heart. Really tore him apart. The ME said from the angle of entry and exit wounds, the doctor had probably begun to turn around just before the shots were fired, but basically, he never knew what hit him. He died quickly. The slugs are being examined by Ballistics as we speak."

"Too bad there was no CCTV in the vestibule or outside the building."

"Nope, not in that neighborhood."

"Anything else about this Mrs. Donovan?" he asks.

"While you were talking with the ME, I spoke with the neighbor who discovered the body. He said Dr. Shepherd made plenty of house calls to the Donovan woman. He thinks the woman has a heart condition. I confirmed he was going to see her."

"Poor guy, never got to see her, that's for sure."

"But *I* did," Liz says. "While you were directing the canvas team, I spoke to her. She's a wreck."

"Well, the doctor was killed on his way to see *her*. That would rattle anyone's cage."

"I think something else was going on."

"What?"

"She was home alone when it happened," Liz says. "Her husband was working at his bar; he's usually there 'til two or three in the morning."

"Anything else?"

"She phoned the doctor at about eight thirty, said she had heart palpitations. The doctor said he'd be there in about an hour. But of course, he didn't show, and at some point, her alleged palpitations stopped."

"*Alleged?*"

"Yeah."

"Why *alleged?*"

"Here's why. She falls asleep in her living room chair; tells me she woke up when she heard sirens on the street and noise in the hallway. The doctor still hadn't showed. And he never called. While she's talking to me, she's stammering and fidgeting."

"So you're suspicious?"

"Yes. Because while we're talking, I notice an open bottle of wine on a buffet table in the foyer. I'd estimate maybe a glass of vino was gone. And there's a wineglass on the coffee table. A little wine residue is on the bottom and there's a lipstick impression on the rim. She'd obviously had some wine before nodding off."

"But the kicker is there was *another* wineglass on the coffee table. A clean one. My guess is she was waiting for someone, and I'm betting it wasn't the husband. I'm thinking maybe she was waiting for the doctor for something other than her heart."

"Interesting little factoid."

"You always say these little observations can be more important than what a suspect says."

He nods. "But she's not a suspect, is she?"

"Not yet."

Nager nods. "Anything else?"

"Bottom line, Art, I'm guessing something was going on between Mrs. Donovan and the doctor. And since you're the ladies' man, you oughta question her."

He laughs. *Yeah, sure. Divorced, living alone in a shitty apartment, paying child support on a detective's salary; no woman in my life, some ladies' man.*

"I'll do it, but right now, let's go over what we know about the crime scene."

"The cash was gone but the prescription pad wasn't taken, so I doubt the perp was a junkie."

"Let's not jump to conclusions either way, Liz."

Nager recalls how as a novice detective he'd sometimes seize on a small fact and make premature deductions based on that observation. His rabbi, McCreary, would say *that's barroom logic, Art; don't be a conclusionist.* And he was usually right. Finding a drug addict lying dead in an alleyway or a dead man at the bottom of a stairway might look like an accident. But forensic testing and squeezing a witness could reveal something else—they were well-planned executions.

He sure misses McCreary. It sometimes feels strange—like it's an inversion of how things oughta be—that he's the senior detective on these cases. He never envisioned himself mentoring a junior detective, especially one like Liz Callaghan.

The fax machine sends out three short rings. "It'll be the preliminary forensics report," Liz says, waiting for the first sheet of paper to be churned out. It slides slowly onto the tray.

She snatches it. "Yes. Ballistics ID'd the bullets as nine-millimeter slugs. The diameter, rifling, and grooves say they came from a Wilson Combat model, the Tactical Supergrade Professional, semiautomatic."

"A Wilson Professional? That's the Rolls-Royce of handguns," Nager says. Though he's never held one, he knows it's sleek, solid, and manufactured to precision standards. "A Wilson Pro." He lets out a soft whistle.

"It's pricey, right?" she says.

"Yes, a few thousand, depending on the model. That alone puts this situation in a different light."

"You think we're dealing with a hit man?"

"The perp wasn't carrying the usual street-piece like a Raven or a Taurus. I don't wanna jump to conclusions, Liz, but it *might've* been a professional hit."

"The three bullets were grouped closely in the vic's back," Liz says. You think it was an execution?"

"A gangland execution usually involves a small-caliber bullet to the back of the head, but not always. This is unusual, especially the Wilson Pro."

Liz's eyes shift to the fax tray. She pulls out two more sheets of paper, scans them. "No GSR on the doc's coat where the bullets entered his back."

"Gunshot residue can travel up to five feet from the muzzle," Nager says.

"Meaning the shooter was at a distance."

"So, Liz, what's your thinking?" He always lets her speculate, tries not to be overly didactic. And besides, he enjoys listening to how she uses logic and thinks about things.

"A close grouping from a distance probably means the shooter has experience," she says. "I'm guessing the perp's put in some serious range time."

"Right you are."

Liz flips to the next page. "Only the vic's fingerprints were on the wallet. No other prints. Like I said, the cash was gone, but the credit cards were left."

"Did the perp wear gloves?"

"Here it is, next paragraph. Cornstarch granules were on the wallet. Cornstarch is used to powder surgical gloves, right? And there was residue from nitrile surgical gloves. The same residue was found on the three shell casings lying on the floor."

"Okay, so the shooter has a high-end weapon. He wears powdered nitrile gloves when he loads the pistol and when he fires it, so he leaves no prints on the casings. He does the vic with closely grouped shots from enough distance so there's no GSR on the body.

He doesn't bother to pick up the spent shell casings, so he's not worried about the gun being ID'd. I'm thinking he's an expert marksman."

"Why do you keep saying 'he'?"

"It might sound sexist, Liz, but a fully loaded Wilson Pro weighs in at a good three pounds. And it's got a hefty kick. You've gotta be pretty strong to get that kind of grouping from a distance of more than five feet. It's most likely the perp was a guy."

"So maybe we rule out a drug-related homicide," Liz says.

"It goes way down on the list."

"He took steps to avoid leaving his prints on the shell casings," she says. "That might mean there's a chance his prints are on file somewhere, that he might have a rap sheet. Or he's been in the service: Army, Navy, Special Forces."

"That's a huge group of possibles," he says.

"Hundreds of thousands of men."

"For sure, this was a planned hit," Nager says. "I'm guessing the perp was lying in wait. Or followed the doc from his house to where it went down. So, how did he know where the doc lived?"

"If that's what happened, he had book on the doctor."

"Absolutely. It sounds like a well-planned execution. Another question is did the shooter take off by car or by foot? And the canvass tells us no neighbor saw or heard a thing," he says. "We canvassed the building and every house across the street. So, if it wasn't a drug-related homicide, why'd the perp take the cash?"

"Maybe to make it look like it was a mugging," she says.

"Okay," he says, "right now, we have a few people of interest—Mrs. Donovan and possibly her husband. You said he was supposedly at his bar when it happened, right?"

"Yup."

"We'll talk with her and get to him before he has time to construct an alibi."

"I really think the doctor and Mrs. Donovan had something going on," Liz says.

"Could be."

"I guess you never really know what's happening between a man and a woman," Liz muses.

What does she mean by that? Am I reading things into inconsequential words?

"Yeah . . . jealously can be a powerful motive." Leaning back in his chair, Nager says, "A few other things. First of all, the doctor's family mentioned that Harper homicide in Manhattan."

"You're talking about that shooting on Seventy-Ninth Street the other day?"

"Yeah. It turns out the son's also a doctor. His name is Rick Shepherd. And this guy Harper who was gunned down apparently looked a lot like the young doctor Shepherd. And Harper was shot three times in the back. So it's a similar type of homicide. On top of that, it happened in front of the son's office."

"In front of his *office*?"

"Yup. So, there could be a connection between our doctor in Brooklyn and the Harper case in Manhattan. It could be someone out to get the whole family. Or at least to take down the son and the father. The son thinks someone might be gunning for him, but has no idea who it might be. So, let's get in touch with Manhattan North and see what they've turned up.

"Another thing . . ." Nager adds. "When I talked with the son, he told me that Dr. Shepherd had a bad relationship with his daughter's boyfriend, or now, her *ex*-boyfriend. According to the son, he's an abusive guy by the name of Mike Brock, a biker type, who hangs out in the East Village."

"So we have a few possibles," Liz says. "Mrs. Donovan and her husband and this Brock character."

"Yup. And the son, Dr. *Rick* Shepherd, told me he had a physical run-in with this Brock character, a few years ago. So, let's try to locate this guy and see what's going on."

CHAPTER EIGHT

RICK HATES LATE autumn and winter.

It begins getting dark at four thirty in the afternoon and everything seems bleak, ominous; it sometimes feels like the world's coming to an end. Or is it just his mood? It's two thirty and he's sitting alone in the apartment. Jackie's at her office clearing up some things before she takes the next few days off.

After today's visit to Kings County Hospital's morgue, he wonders how long the view of his father's body will haunt him. Rick knows that some images, once seen, can never be forgotten. The pathology building with its morgue in the basement—replete with its banks of refrigerated cabinets and the air redolent of the sickly odor of rotting corpses mixed with antiseptic solution—even felt ghoulish when he was a medical student doing a pathology rotation.

When the attendant opened a stainless-steel cabinet and the body was trolleyed out on a sliding track for identification, Rick's knees went weak and he felt close to vomiting. When the sheet covering the corpse was lowered to the chest, the utter disbelief, the horror of looking at the lifeless, sunken face of his father, left Rick gasping for breath.

Trying to banish thoughts of the morgue, Rick thinks about Jackie and how good it is to have her in his life. There's so much she gives him: her intelligence is steeped in warmth and empathy.

They'd met two years ago. He'd been sitting at the bar in a bistro on Second Avenue when he became aware of two women entering the place and taking seats at the bar. He couldn't help but fixate on the blonde—Jacqueline or Jackie—with her green eyes, high cheekbones, and honey-colored hair highlighted by the peach-tinged lighting of the restaurant. She and her friend—Penny—were debating whether to have dinner there or go elsewhere.

He'd always been reluctant to start conversations with women he didn't know. They seemed to dwell in some mysterious estrogen bubble he never felt comfortable trying to penetrate. Yet, that night he turned to them and said, "You should try this place. The food's very good."

So they began talking. He loved Jackie's laugh, was riveted by her smile—it seemed innocent, yet somehow seductive. As they spoke, there seemed to be a series of barely detectible intimacies between them, as though they shared an unspoken connection.

For days, he replayed their conversation, recalled the inflections of her voice, her gestures. And with the memory of each moment— especially the luminous look in her eyes as he walked her home and they kissed goodnight—a wash of warmth and lightness flowed through his chest.

Jesus, that was nearly two years ago, a different world than the one he now inhabits.

And here he is, immersed in darkness. He knows he's stumbling over the trip wire of guilt and feelings of regret. Every minute he's not absorbed in the pain of grieving, he feels he's betraying his father. If only that last conversation with him had ended differently.

Street noises bleed through the living room window: a siren's wail, the rumble of an eighteen-wheeler heading uptown on Third, the laughter of young men spilling out of the sports bar down the avenue. The cacophony of Manhattan.

And here he is, drinking wine in the middle of the afternoon, while sitting in the apartment instead of being at the hospital seeing patients. Doing the opposite of what Rick knows his father would be doing if their roles were reversed.

Right now all he wants to do is insulate himself from the world and ensconce himself in this apartment that feels like a sanctuary.

God, this wine tastes like Listerine. Nothing seems right.

He can't even *think* about watching TV—especially the news—can't listen to music, or laugh at a joke, or even *imagine* being with friends right now. He hasn't picked up the phone since it happened, just lets the answering machine record the cascade of condolence calls coming in. They seem canned, inauthentic, but what can anyone possibly say without sounding mawkish?

A blast of sound from Third Avenue sends a spike of alarm through him. It's a tractor trailer barreling over a loose manhole cover. He's now aware of every noise: water running through pipes in a wall, the neighbor slamming her apartment door or playing her stereo too loudly.

Rick is vigilant, tense. He's certain Robert Harper's death wasn't a random thing. He knows for whom those bullets were intended.

And Dad's murder?

Who would want both of us dead, and why?

It'd be a waste of time to see Howell again. He'd brush him off, saying "give us a shout" if anything happens. Like if bullets smash into Rick's back.

The highlight reel of improbable possibilities streams through his mind for the hundredth time: Were there any enemies or negative experiences—however inconsequential or remote—with anyone, past or present, that could account for his father being killed and Harper taking the hit that was meant for Rick?

Am I in some maniac's crosshairs?

He scours through a roster of his not-so-great medical outcomes. Some patients were terminal even before he saw them—they never had a chance to last more than a few weeks. Others took unexpected downturns soon after treatment began. Their families understood; no one blamed him. In fact, they were thankful for his compassion during their loved one's demise. And the patients he now sees? He has good relationships with them. And he spends time explaining things to their families.

Of course, in any medical practice there are always mixed results. It's a reality. But why would any patient or a family member feel the urge to go after him? And why would that same patient track down and murder his father? They had separate practices. The connection to his father can't have a thing to do with medicine.

Guzzling the rest of the wine, he senses danger lurking at the edge of his life, thinks about dropping a Xanax. That shit's addictive, even at a low dose.

No way do I want to take that road. I can't dull myself with alcohol or a drug. I gotta stay focused.

The killer is out there—doing the ordinary things people do— maybe riding the subway or hailing a taxi, going about the most mundane routines as though the murders were just another day at the office.

The telephone rings.

Everyone at work knows he's taking the week off, so it's not the office. Dave Copen and Phil Lauria are covering for him. The answering machine will pick up. But by the third ring, he's seized by a strange urgency, so he gets up and grabs the telephone receiver.

"Hello?"

There's a background hiss along with small, distant voices on the line.

Holding his breath, he listens.

Someone's there. There's the sound of shallow breathing.

A click.

Are the hang-ups coming more often? Definitely.

Holding the telephone receiver, Rick's skin prickles as the pores on his face open. He drops the receiver back onto the cradle.

In the bathroom, he opens the medicine cabinet and downs a Xanax.

But there aren't enough pills in the world to ease his fears for his own safety or to lessen the pain and regrets of his father's death.

He chokes back tears, recalling the last words he spoke to his father.

Only the evening before he died.

Just two nights ago.

Words that'll stay with him for the rest of his life.

Words he'll always regret.

And there's no way to take them back.

CHAPTER NINE

IT'S MIDAFTERNOON AS Nager and Callaghan head down the steps of Brooklyn Command.

"If Mrs. Donovan has a job, she won't be home at this hour," Nager says.

"She worked at Macy's but quit a few weeks ago for reasons I don't know," says Liz. "It's nearly three, so there's a good chance she'll be home now."

Standing on the sidewalk, Nager realizes, not for the first time, that he and Liz are almost eye-to-eye. She's gotta be a good five-ten in bare feet. And her boots add another few inches.

"We'll see if she has anything else to say," Nager says, gazing across DeKalb Avenue.

"I decided not to press her but I'm sure something was going on between her and the doctor," Liz says.

"What makes you so sure?"

"A woman's intuition," she says with a subtle hint of a smile. "My antennae shot sky high the moment we started talking."

"People are just so full of shit," Nager says, shaking his head.

"Art, have I ever told you you're a cynical man?"

"Cynical? I'm skeptical."

"A distinction without a difference."

He shrugs. "Cynicism, skepticism, who cares? Just remember, Liz, people lie all the time. I've sweated a million suspects and witnesses, too—every kind, every race, every ethnic origin, every age—and they all lie like rugs. Bottom line? Trust no one."

"Not even doctors?"

"Doctors? A lousy way to live—imagine dealing with sickness and death every day of your working life. I don't know how they do it."

"How about homicide detectives?"

He shakes his head. "I don't know how we do it, either."

"You tired of the job, Art?"

"Right now, it's what I have."

"Trouble with the ex?"

Nager knows Liz has overheard him on the phone arguing with Ellen, but he won't unload his baggage on Liz. If she were a guy, he'd long ago have told her the ball-busting his ex has put him through. But he knows better than to open up that can of worms with a woman partner.

Approaching the sedan, he knows he feels too wiped out to drive. Not enough sleep last night; just tossing and turning. So he says, "You wanna drive?"

"Oh, so now you trust *me* behind the wheel?"

"Of course."

"Then how come *you* always drive?"

"Because I'm a male chauvinist."

She laughs. "Haven't you noticed it's always the *guy* who drives?"

"Yeah, yeah. I get it. So from now on, *you* drive."

He tosses her the keys.

She snags them in midair, opens the door, and slips behind the wheel.

Turning the ignition key, she says, "Let's take Nostrand down to her place."

"You got it."

Liz cranes her neck, looks in both directions, makes a U-turn crossing the double yellow line on DeKalb. As she does, a blizzard of pigeons swooshes up from the asphalt.

Nager likes the way Liz drives—self-assured, no hesitation the way it could be with so many of the other women he's been with. *Am I a male chauvinist? And she's right: it's always the man who drives. Jesus, I'm a fucking Neanderthal.*

His thoughts swerve to his ex, Ellen, and how when he drove, she was such a pain-in-the-ass-back-seat driver: *Watch out! Slow down. You're too close to the guy in front of us.* But this is different; he's the passenger and he's being driven by a woman who's brimming with confidence. And competence.

* * *

Liz drives to Nostrand Avenue and turns left, maintaining a steady speed—twenty-five miles an hour—to stay with the wave of green traffic lights. She knows the quickest way to get to the southern part of Brooklyn is to drive at that pace. Any faster and she'll end up catching red lights all the way down to Sheepshead Bay. She laughs at the wise-asses who peel rubber at every light only to come to a screeching halt a few red lights down the avenue.

Driving along Nostrand, Liz realizes how little Brooklyn's changed over the years. The borough still has its ethnic enclaves: neighborhood ghettos like Russian-Jewish Brighton Beach, Irish Sheepshead Bay, Italian Bensonhurst, or Black Bed-Stuy.

She realizes how the stores along Nostrand Avenue reflect the borough's different nationalities: Afro-American outlets sell Haitian and Jamaican meat patties; they give way to Italian butcher shops hawking sweet sausages and braciole. Passing an Irish bar with a shamrock sign in the window, she recalls the nights when she was a teenager and her mother sent her to Paddy's to coax Dad out of the place and help him walk the three blocks home.

Farther south in the Flatbush section, stately maple and sycamore trees line the roadway, their bare branches forming a dappled arcade in the November sun. Well-kept private homes line both sides of the avenue. Liz would love to live in one of them . . . someday. But right now, it's just a fantasy.

At Avenue P, she turns right, drives to East Nineteenth Street, turns right again, and parks in front of 1530.

Getting out of the car, she and Art stand in front of a six-story, red brick building on a quiet, tree-lined, residential street.

"Maybe we should've called to make sure she'd be home," Nager says.

"Why let her prepare herself?" Liz says. "I'll bet she'll be as nervous as she was when I talked to her last night."

"Good point," he says. "A prepped witness is a lousy witness."

In the building's vestibule there's no sign of last night's homicide.

The only remnants are gouged-out areas in the wall where the crime scene team extracted three bullets that lodged in the wall after passing through the doctor.

* * *

Nager recalls the doctor crumpled on the floor, exit wounds on the front of his body the size of grapefruits. And blood had oozed everywhere, some dried and crusted, some still moist and shimmering, looking like currant jelly. Gouts of flesh and blood, a lake of it beneath the body. There was blood-splatter on the walls too. As with most of the bodies he's seen, there was the smell of excrement as the vic's body loses control of its functions at death, and the bowels empty.

The whole Homicide team was there: the technical people wearing booties, Tyvek coveralls, and gloves; the on-call ADA; the photographer, flashing one photo after another; even a couple of uniforms. The whole grisly enchilada. And, of course, the coroner's van was parked in front of the building while Doc Gilroy—a thin, older guy looking as cadaverous as the corpses he dissects—assessed the body's lividity and temperature and estimated the time of death.

For Nager, there's a sense of darkness to what happened in the vestibule. The coppery smell of blood can often make him feel like he'll toss his cookies, and for a brief moment he thought he'd lose his dinner. He never likes joining the on-site team after a homicide goes down. Processing a crime scene is almost as tough as talking with the vic's family. Too much of his own baggage is tied up in it.

So here he is, in the entranceway before you come to the bank of mailboxes. The directory panel is on the vestibule wall to his right. It has printed names of the building's occupants alongside vertical rows of buttons. A round, two-way speaker sits in the middle of the bronze plate. Eight apartments to a floor, six stories, forty-eight separate dwellings. A typical setup for a residential building in the boroughs.

"It's Three-B, Donovan, right?" he asks.

"Yup," Liz says, nodding.

Poor Doc apparently didn't get beyond reaching for the buzzer.

Nager presses the button for apartment 3-B.

A short wait.

"Yes?" A voice comes through the speaker.

The voice surprises him. It's sweet-sounding, but not syrupy. Definitely not what he had expected. Nager was sure Catherine Donovan's voice would sound like it'd been marinating in booze and cigarettes for decades. Shit, why does he think this way? But he knows *exactly* why he expected the voice to sound like a whiskeyed version of Brooklynese—he grew up on East Seventeenth Street, only a few blocks from here. He knew the people living in this area, mostly middle- and lower-middle-class residents, hard-core earthy Irishmen and women.

The neighborhood reminds him of high school, and he can virtually picture the girls back then: gum-snapping teens wearing black jackets with club names stitched on them—*Earth Angels* or *Party Dolls*, logos lifted from the doo-wop songs of the fifties. He was certain Catherine Donovan would be an adult version of them, would remind him of his ex, Ellen—Brooklyn-bred and tough as masonry nails.

But Mrs. Donovan's voice suggests otherwise. It's soft, even sweet, implies vulnerability. He feels a surge of empathy for her after what she endured last night.

But like McCreary always said, *Don't jump to conclusions. The word "prejudice" really means "pre-judging" someone. Don't let your prejudices become self-fulfilling prophecies.*

"Mrs. Donovan, it's Detective Art Nager, NYPD. My partner, Detective Callaghan, spoke with you last night. We'd like a few minutes of your time just to ask you a few more questions."

There's a pause, a longer one than Nager expected.

He glances at Liz.

She shrugs, shakes her head, and her eyes widen.

A buzz, then a clicking sound comes from the inner door's magnetic lock mechanism.

CHAPTER TEN

WHEN APARTMENT 3-B's door opens, Nager smells a fragrance reminiscent of lilac.

And cigarette smoke.

With the safety chain still in place, Catherine Donovan peers through the narrow space; she's backlit by pearly light flooding through the living room window.

Nager holds his badge to the opening. She inspects it, nods, unlatches the chain, and fully opens the door.

Catherine Donovan is a forty-something woman with dark hair tied back in a bun. She has refined natural features, but not the kind etched by a surgeon's knife. And she looks just like she sounded—gentle, soft-spoken, and someone who'll cave under intense questioning. Nager's not quite certain how he knows this, but he does. Despite McCreary's warning about jumping to conclusions, Nager knows first impressions count for something. And he senses something about Catherine Donovan: she's not some hard-ass Brooklyn type who's been around the block a million times.

She's not like Ellen, someone who lives to burrow under his skin every chance she gets.

Mrs. Donovan's hazel eyes dart from Nager to Liz, then back to Nager. Her brow furrows. "Yes? What is it, Detectives?"

Nager thinks there's something sad—even soulful—in her eyes. He's certain she's had her share of misery.

Yup, don't be a conclusionist. Remember old McCreary's words.

"Mrs. Donovan, we need to talk with you about the homicide in the building," Nager says. "May we come in?"

He uses the word *homicide* to see if it makes her defensive. Liz suspects the woman is covering something up, and his junior partner's first impressions are usually spot-on. That's one of the things he likes about Liz: she has an intuitive and anticipatory kind of intelligence. Even though she's a newbie, Liz has one of the best bullshit meters he's encountered in a long time.

Catherine Donovan stands aside, beckons them to enter the apartment. She's wearing dark slacks and a cream-colored blouse. Very little makeup, no jewelry. Her appearance suggests refinement, even gentility. And Nager's always preferred women who don't smear on the warpaint.

The living room is furnished with a sofa, a club chair, an old-fashioned divan, and a glass-topped coffee table. The place is so retro, it reminds Nager of Mom's furniture, right outta the forties.

"I already told the detective everything I know," Mrs. Donovan says in a warbling voice as her chin tilts toward Liz.

"Understood, but we have a few more questions for you," Nager says. "May we sit down?"

"Sure. Make yourselves comfortable." Her tone is casual, even nonchalant. Nager's sure she's feigning indifference. He long ago learned a flippant or glib manner can be the refuge of an uncooperative witness—or of a suspect hiding something. But what's Mrs. Donovan trying to conceal? Liz thinks she knows what this woman's secret could be. *We'll soon find out.*

Nager and Liz sit on the sofa while Mrs. Donovan settles herself into the club chair, slings one leg over the other—does her best to look detached as though this is just another ordinary day in her life. But that crossed leg swings back and forth—like a pendulum. Yes, she's nervous. Nager knows the worst part of nerves is the anticipation of what's going to happen next, so he waits a few beats before speaking. After a prolonged pause, he begins questioning her.

"When did you call the doctor?"

Mrs. Donovan's lips lighten. "Like I told the detective," she says, again nodding toward Liz, "I think it was close to nine."

"What made you call him?"

Her eyebrows rise and her eyes widen; it's clear the question surprises her. "I already told you," she says, again glancing at Liz. "I get these palpitations." She stares at Nager, wide-eyed, cants her head, like she's impatient, can't wait to get them out of her place. Her lower lip begins quivering. And she's leaning forward, ever so slightly, as though she's trying to anticipate his next question.

So he waits another beat, just to heighten the tension. He long ago learned to respect the power of silence. Most people—especially suspects, though Mrs. Donovan isn't a suspect, yet—can't tolerate a sudden vacuum of silence; they feel a need to fill a conversational void and end up divulging things they hadn't meant to disclose.

Mrs. Donovan fidgets as her eyes dart back and forth between Nager and Liz, then settle on a pack of Parliaments on the side table. She's about to reach for a cigarette, then thinks better of it and stops.

"So you called the doctor," Nager says. "And what happened? He just didn't show?"

Her eyes narrow, then she shakes her head. "No, he didn't."

"Were you worried about him?"

"Not really," she says in a slightly tremulous voice. "He's one of the few . . . he *was* one of the few doctors who still made house calls. I thought maybe he got delayed by, you know . . . another patient, or maybe something was going on at the hospital."

"When did you realize he wasn't coming?"

Her eyelashes flutter. "I'm not sure. When I get these things—these palpitations—it feels like my heart's jumping around in my chest and it frightens me. But then they stopped and I . . . I just fell asleep, here in this chair."

"Then what?"

She clears her throat. "I woke up when I heard the commotion in the street. You know . . . sirens, and there were people talking and yelling in the hallway. It was like the whole building was in an uproar. So I realized something was wrong. But . . . but why are you asking me all these questions?"

Nager can virtually *feel* her wariness. Liz is right, something was going on between Mrs. Donovan and the doctor. It was more than worry about some so-called palpitations.

"I told your partner all of this," she says in a strained voice. Her eyes settle on Liz. It's clear to Nager that she'd feel more comfortable talking with a woman. He notices how Liz shifts her gaze toward him, a hint for the witness to focus on the person asking the questions.

Mrs. Donovan uncrosses her left leg, then slings the right one over the left. "I don't know what else to tell you. When my doorbell rang, it was the detective." Her chin again tilts toward Liz.

"Mrs. Donovan, let's go over a few things you *didn't* tell Detective Callaghan."

Her lower lip really begins quivering; so does the skin over her chin, and her body looks like it's tightening. Nager is sure she's getting more nervous.

"How long had you known Dr. Shepherd?"

"Oh, I think it's been a couple of years . . . maybe less." She shifts her position in the chair.

Nager hopes Liz will follow up on that question. But for the moment, he lets it go—no frown, no widened eyes, nothing to convey skepticism about the bucket of bullshit she's handing him. He'll let her stew in uncertainty about where this line of questioning is headed. A witness's expectation is the worst part of being interrogated by a detective. It propels the witness's thoughts to begin speculating, to wonder if there are hidden meanings or implications in what's being asked. And that can lead to unexpected revelations.

Mrs. Donovan grabs that pack of Parliaments from the side table, taps the bottom of the pack, extracts one, reaches for a table lighter. With her hand shaking, she snaps it a few times.

Nager waits for her to complete the delaying tactic. Finally, she lights up, inhales deeply, then contrails of bluish smoke flow out of her nostrils.

"How'd you meet the doctor?"

"He was recommended by a neighbor. You see . . . years ago, Dr. Shepherd and his family lived in this building and . . . and he treated some of the other tenants. Still does, or did, until . . . you know." She takes a drag on the cigarette, exhales more smoke, suppresses a cough, then clears her throat. "Like I said . . . he's one of the few doctors around who still makes house calls." The cigarette wags between her lips as she speaks. "He's very kind, really compassionate." She sets the cigarette in a large glass ashtray sitting on the side table.

"So you began seeing him about two years ago?"

"Yes, for my heart condition."

She's elaborating and justifying. Needlessly. She's being defensive.

Nager gives her his best *You've gotta be shitting me* look—even as he senses Liz is itching to begin her questioning. Liz can be relentless, in a gentle but effective way. Nager squints, tosses Mrs. Donovan a slight nod, purposely assumes a skeptical look as his eyebrows meet midline, then he turns to Liz and says, "Any questions for Mrs. Donovan?"

*   *   *

Liz leans forward, rests her elbows on her thighs; she knows it's time to up the ante, so she begins. "What medication do you take, Mrs. Donovan?"

There's an intake of breath by the witness. She didn't anticipate that question. "Oh . . . I, uh . . . I don't take any."

"Of course, you've been to the doctor's office?"

"Yes, sure." Mrs. Donovan's eyes narrow. Liz knows the witness senses what's coming.

"Where is it?" Liz says, pretending she's genuinely curious.

Donovan's eyes narrow. "What are you trying to imply, Detective?"

"I'm not implying anything, Mrs. Donovan," Liz says, knowing she's got to push the witness if they're going to get anywhere.

One of the first things Liz learned was the art of innuendo-laced interrogation.

Mrs. Donovan's composure is faltering in the face of the insinuation that something was going on between her and the doctor. Soon her poise will shred and she'll open up. Liz hears the increased warbling in her voice and the skin over the woman's chin is trembling big-time, which tells Liz that Mrs. Donovan is afraid the true nature of the relationship will be revealed. So, it's time to bear down, but not too harshly. She shoots Mrs. Donovan a skeptical look—brow furrowed, head tilted. Enough to let her know she thinks she's hearing anything but the truth.

The tip of Mrs. Donovan's tongue slides across her lower lip. She picks up the cigarette and takes another drag.

"Mrs. Donovan, you told me last night that you'd been working for Macy's as a buyer, right?"

"Yes."

"But not now. Why is that?"

"Too much stress. I just couldn't take it anymore."

"And you're married, right?" Liz says, knowing what's not said can be more powerful than an accusation.

Mrs. Donovan nods. The color drains from her face; it's a sudden paling, a surefire tell. She grabs the cigarette and takes another deep drag.

"Where was your husband when this happened?"

"I told you . . . he was working at the bar."

"When does he get home?"

"Oh, by about two a.m., sometimes later . . . but that's about to change. He's selling the place; he has a lawyer working on it."

"What do you usually do 'til he gets home?"

"I don't see where that's any of your business, Detective." With a shaky hand, Mrs. Donovan sets her cigarette back in the ashtray.

She's lost her cool. Now's the time to get aggressive.

"Anything that happened here last night *is* our business, Mrs. Donovan," Liz says in a voice more basso than before. *Sometimes you have to come on like gangbusters*, Liz thinks. "And that includes an open bottle of wine along with two glasses sitting on your coffee table." There's a brief pause. "Let me remind you . . ." Liz says, "this is a *homicide* investigation, and the district attorney won't look kindly on any attempt at obstruction."

Donovan's body jerks like she's been jolted by a cattle prod. Her face tightens. She begins blinking like a broken traffic light. "I'm not doing anything illegal. I've already told—"

"You're withholding information, Mrs. Donovan. That's obstruction." Liz narrows her eyes; it's a way of telling a witness her story lacks credibility.

"Do I need a lawyer?"

"At the moment, you're a witness in a homicide investigation, not a suspect. You can call a lawyer if you'd prefer, but it isn't necessary. You see, Mrs. Donovan, it so happens we know about your relationship with Dr. Shepherd . . ." Liz falls silent, lets the accusation fill the air in the room.

A glottal sound erupts from Mrs. Donovan's throat. She grabs that cigarette, slips it between her lips, sucks on it, lets out a smoky sigh.

"You have neighbors, Mrs. Donovan. They talk. Just use what you know about life. C'mon, this isn't rocket science."

Liz knows Catherine Donovan's suffering the sting of embarrassment, not only about her trysts with the doctor, but from being confronted as a liar. And there can be pay dirt in tossing out a suspicion stated as though it's hard-core fact.

"Please . . ." Donovan whispers, nearly choking as her face flushes. "You've got to understand . . ."

"Understand what, Mrs. Donovan?"

"My husband and I are on the verge of divorce—and if he finds out—things could get really ugly."

"Just tell us the truth," Liz says, again leaning forward with her forearms on her thighs, establishing physical closeness, a semblance of intimacy. "We're all on the same side here."

"Okay, okay," Donovan says. Her chest rises and falls with a deep inhalation, the precursor of an admission. Her eyes jump from Liz to Nager. "Just promise me that what I say stays here."

"That depends on what you tell us, Mrs. Donovan," Liz says.

"And you don't have to say 'Mrs. Donovan' every time you ask me something."

"I understand, Mrs. Donovan."

Though she's coming on strong, Liz feels sorry for this woman; her life is no piece of cake. But she's been an uncooperative witness up to this point and business comes first. "Just tell us the truth," Liz says in a voice now more gentle than before.

The witness bites her lower lip, then says, "I met Dr. Shepherd nearly two years ago. He was making a house call and we fell into conversation and . . . we began seeing each other. He was separated when we met."

"Did you always meet here, in the apartment?"

"Yes. He'd bring his doctor's bag so it'd look like . . . well, you know. It was always late in the evening. Lots of older people live here; they go to bed early. But he made it look like he was making a house call."

"Let's get back to last night . . . start from the beginning."

"I telephoned him and asked if he'd like to come over."

"Why last night?"

"My husband and I had an argument and I was feeling down." Tears well in her eyes. "Listen, Detective, he's a . . . Dr. Shepherd was a good man. He didn't deserve what happened to him."

"Do you know if he was seeing *other* women while you and he were together?"

"No . . ."

"*No*, he wasn't, or *no*, you don't know?"

"I don't know." Tears shiver at the edges of her eyelids. "We were just two lonely people."

Liz asks lots more about Mrs. Donovan's liaison with the doctor— one question after another—and a few more bits of information emerge, but nothing that'll lead anywhere productive.

"I know this much," Mrs. Donovan says, "he's . . . he was lonely . . . living in a big house all by himself. And his family . . . he was so disappointed . . ."

"Disappointed about what?"

"His daughter has had drug problems and a boyfriend he couldn't stand. I think there was trouble there. And he wasn't happy with his son, though I don't really know why. But the *really* big thing—along with the separation from his wife—was that his practice was going downhill. His patients were older. Some had died, some retired and moved to Florida, and he'd been forced to cut back on his office hours. He wasn't even sure if he was going to renew the lease on his office. He didn't want to stop practicing and he didn't know how he'd fill his days."

Liz asks about neighbors, grudges, phone calls, if he seemed worried about anything; she asks if the doctor ever said anything more about Mike Brock; if there'd been any changes in his behavior, a host of questions, but nothing else of importance comes to light. "One other thing, Mrs. Donovan," Liz says, "do you think your husband knows about you and the doctor?"

Her eyes widen. "I can't imagine he does."

"Could he have even a hint of what's been going on?"

"Even if he did, I doubt he'd care."

"Okay, Mrs. Donovan," Nager cuts in, standing. "Thanks for your honesty." He hands her his card. "If you think of anything else, please give us a call."

They head toward the door.

Nager stops and turns to her. "Oh . . . and your husband's full name is . . .?"

"Brian Douglas Donovan."

"And the name of his bar?"

"Brian's Place on Emmons Avenue, down by Sheepshead Bay."

Mrs. Donovan wipes tears from her eyes, folds her arms across her chest, and steps closer. "You're going to talk with him?"

"Yes."

"Please don't tell him about . . . you know." More tears trickle down her cheeks.

Nager says, "You realize we have to go where the investigation takes us. But let me tell you something . . . if you call him before we get to see him, we'll know it and it'll look very bad for both of you."

She nods, fully understanding the implication of Nager's words.

Nager says, "Don't hesitate to call us if you think of something else."

CHAPTER ELEVEN

SHAKING HIS HEAD, the Shooter thinks, *How could I have made a mistake like that?*

I shot the wrong guy. Thought I had him in my sights but I blew it.

I should have scoped things out more carefully, made sure of the target. The guy looked just like Rick Shepherd. But on the street, with a cold wind whipping everywhere and people hustling along, there was no way to tell the difference.

Shit, I wanted to get the son first, then the father.

But it wasn't to be.

So, I got to the father first. It wasn't hard. There was a good chance he'd be leaving to make a house call, like he did all the time. That's the way the guy was: a man whose goodness was just a veneer, a thin layer of deceit covering over his vileness. He hid his depravity from everyone, but not from me. Yeah, I knew better than to buy into his good-guy act, his compassion routine.

It was an easy kill. Followed him from the house on Cranberry Street to that building and shot the son of a bitch dead. Three slugs to the back. Blew out his heart.

If I'd killed the son first, he'd have suffered a greater agony. That would've been justice.

But you gotta go where the wind takes you.

James Shepherd deserved to die.
Yes, eventually payback comes.
It finds you and comes with no warning—like a sniper's bullet.
And soon, it'll be the son's turn to die.

CHAPTER TWELVE

AT FOUR THIRTY that afternoon, after having left the Donovan apartment, Liz parks the sedan in front of Randazzo's Clam Bar on Emmons Avenue.

After getting out of the car, Nager stands on the sidewalk and peers out over Sheepshead Bay. The water appears indigo as the late afternoon sun sets over Seagate and Bath Beach to the west.

He smells the bay's backwash of brine, fish, and a hint of diesel engine oil wafting shoreward from the water. The high-pitched cawing of seagulls carries on the breeze. The brackish odor and shrieking birds remind him of being a kid—maybe ten or eleven—when Dad took him fluke and flounder fishing on the *Chief*, the largest fishing boat berthed at the Emmons Avenue side of the Bay. A momentary wash of sadness flows over him. Those were days when the world felt different, when so much seemed possible, days that're gone forever.

Walking toward Brian's Place, they pass a Russian restaurant, Patrushka, and a Greek diner, The Acropolis, where Nager occasionally stops for a cup of coffee and a toasted bran muffin.

"The Bay's changed," Nager says. "When I was a kid, none of these places were around."

"Yeah, Lundy's is gone," Liz adds. "Best clam chowder in the world. And the steamers were to die for."

"Ever wonder about your memories from when you were a kid, Liz? If you've reworked them . . . made things seem better than they really were?"

"Yeah, that's nostalgia for you. It always makes the past seem better than it actually was. But when I think about it, I had maybe five or six good days in my life."

"Wow. Where'd that come from?"

"From living my life," she says, casting a quick glance his way, then averting her eyes.

"You unhappy, Liz?"

Am I getting too personal?

"I gave up on happy. These days I just shoot for content."

Nager knows her words are an invitation to ask more, but he's not gonna push those buttons. *Keep it business. Don't let it get personal.*

"I was locked into a lousy relationship . . ." she says.

"I know all about those . . ." he says, aware they're each offering a glimpse into their private lives. But he won't let his curiosity take him any further. Not as her rabbi in the Bureau. Not now, not ever.

"I got out of it six months ago . . ." she says.

Another hint?

"Still in recovery?" he asks.

"Yeah," she says with a laugh. "It takes time."

Nearing Brian's Place, Nager knows he's gotta change the subject. "It's nearly five," he says. "I'll bet some hard-core juicers have been there for hours."

"You think Donovan's wife called to tell him we'd be paying a visit?" she asks.

"We'll have the DA subpoena her phone records and see if she did. But I don't think she'd take a chance on doing that after what I said. Of course, you never know."

"Do we tell him what his wife's been up to?"

"Let's see where he takes us," he says. "One thing's certain: the doctor was having an affair with a married woman, which could put things in a different light."

"An affair always does."

*   *   *

Liz notices that Brian's Place looks like it's been around since Jesus walked the earth. Reminds her of Paddy's where Dad would drink the nights away.

The tavern has a black and white checkered tile floor and a coffered tin ceiling and is so redolent of cigarette smoke, you could get lung cancer just walking into the place. Liz detects a hint of sweat in the air, mixed with the odors of urine and malt. Framed photos of early-era Irish boxers adorn one wall: John L. Sullivan, Jack Dempsey, Gene Tunney, along with some lesser known palookas.

From the look of the place, Liz is certain of one thing: no fancy-ass French wines or California chardonnays are served in this saloon. It's a Four Roses and Old Crow crowd and whatever watered-down suds the barkeep has on tap. Memories of Paddy's flow through her mind. And of Dad, who is certainly going to drink himself into liver problems.

The bar—on the right side as you walk in—curves around to the wall near the entrance. The barstools have cracked vinyl seats set in front of a long brass footrail. Dishes of peanuts are strategically placed along the bar top—enough salt to keep the thirst going and the beer flowing.

As Liz unbuttons her coat, she sees what she knows is a strained cliché: at four thirty in the afternoon, four rheumy guys are slouched reverently over their whiskies—their Milk of Amnesia as she likes to call the drinks. These guys are sitting in a row, elbow to elbow, barely talking to each other. Hard-core drinkers, drowning their misery in booze. Median age sixty, same as Dad's crowd. These guys suck down the juice to quell the loneliness of their lives. Cigarette smoke rises, then flattens on the ceiling.

The barkeeper is an overweight fifty-something guy with a bulbous nose and drooping earlobes. His face reminds Liz of a bloodhound. His beer gut's big enough to have its own zip code. A soiled apron is draped over it. He sucks on an unlit cigar. "Gentlemen . . ." the bartender bellows in a deep whisky voice as Liz and Art approach the bar. "Or is it gentleman and *lady*?" he calls, his tone ripe with insinuation. His eyes loiter on Liz.

I've gone through this shit a thousand times in my life.

Liz is certain this guy's made them as cops. It happens so often, she wonders if detectives—even women detectives—send out a subliminal signal, maybe a musk-like odor that perps sniff out in a heartbeat.

"Brian Donovan here?" Liz asks.

"That's me," the barkeep says. Wide-eyed, he looks expectant, like maybe he knows why they're here. Actually, the more she thinks about it, the man appears stunned. Liz is certain the wife didn't call to let him know they'd be coming. Donovan's hands come off the bar top and drop to his hips.

Jesus, how does a slob like this snag a woman like Catherine Donovan? Liz wonders.

She reminds herself not to jump to *concussions*, as Art would say. It could be that Donovan's a nice guy who just got lucky when he met Catherine Donovan; but now, the marriage has soured like a carton of milk that's passed its sell-by date.

Leaning across the bar, Nager lowers his voice to a near-whisper. "Detectives Nager and Callaghan, NYPD, Mr. Donovan. We'd like to ask you a few questions." Nager tilts his head toward the other end of the bar.

Donovan glances at the tipplers. "Excuse me, fellas. I gotta talk with this gentleman."

"And lady . . ." Nager adds.

Donovan nods and lets out a soft snort. "Be back in a minute," he says to the drinkers.

They let loose with a collective grunt, never bothering to look up. Just lift their glasses and suck down the booze. One guy coughs; it sounds like a rattle, like he's got lung problems from years of smoking.

Donovan drops his cigar in an ashtray, lumbers toward the far end of the bar.

Liz and Nager walk in the same direction, sit on the two stools closest to the entrance.

*   *   *

Donovan spreads his hands on the bar top, leans forward, eyeballs Liz again, then turns to Nager. Nager smells the fucking guy's breath—a combination of beer, liverwurst, and cigars. The odor nearly makes him recoil in disgust. So Nager breathes through his mouth. It helps a little.

"Can I get you a drink . . . on the house?" Donovan asks, his eyes flitting back and forth, first to Nager, then to Liz where they again linger.

"No thanks," Nager says. It's obvious to him that Donovan's not thrilled by their presence. But then, it isn't every day two detectives walk into your place of business to talk to you after a homicide went down in your building. Especially when the victim was on his way to see your wife.

"Of course, you know about the shooting that happened last night," Nager says.

Donovan's eyes narrow. He's taking Nager's temperature. "Yeah, sure," Donovan says, then shrugs, feigning indifference. *Same deal as with the wife*, Nager thinks. "What can I say," Donovan says in a casual tone. "It's a goddamned shame. Brooklyn's turning to shit, if ya ask me."

"The doctor was on his way to see your wife when it happened," Nager says, wondering if Donovan is clued into his wife's extracurricular activities.

Donovan stares at Nager with his head canted and a bored look on his jowly face.

"What's her problem?" Nager asks.

Donovan sighs. "If ya ask me, it's all in her head."

"What makes you say that?"

"A lotta years ago, we lost our son . . . leukemia." There's a slight hitch in Donovan's voice. And his eyes appear unfocused—distant—for just a moment. "Ever since then, she thinks she's sick. It's always one thing or another . . . palpitations, stomach pains, headaches. You name it. Get the picture? She's a goddamned hypo, thinks what happened to the kid is somehow her fault . . . because her brother died from the same thing. She thinks it's in her genes, and feels guilty as hell. It's a bitch tryin' to live with this shit."

"When did you lose your son?"

"Maybe fourteen, fifteen years ago. I don't remember. I don't *wanna* remember."

"Who was the doctor taking care of him?"

"Some guy at Woodlawn Hospital. I don't remember his name. I don't wanna remember that either."

Nager nods. "I'm sorry about that." He knows the expression is a hollow one; it's standard when you hear about a loved one's death. The only one that's more perfunctory is *I'm sorry for your loss*.

"Yeah, yeah . . . shit happens," Donovan says, shakes his head, then glances down at his feet.

Poor guy has his own brand of misery.

Donovan lifts his head, tries for a subtle peek at Liz's breasts, but it's as obvious as his halitosis.

A stab of annoyance pierces Nager. Unlucky son of a bitch lost a son . . . but his ogling Liz shreds any sympathy Nager feels for him. Jesus, what's going on? Does Nager have some proprietary feeling about her? Is he jealous? Shit, this is like being back in high school. *Just do your fucking job. Liz can take care of herself.*

"You ever meet Dr. Shepherd?" Nager asks.

"Wouldn't know him if I bumped into him. I stay away from doctors. Give 'em a chance they'll give ya a pill that'll make your dick go limp."

Joker's trying to embarrass Liz.

"Where were you last night?"

"*Me*? I was here. Why, am *I* a suspect?" His eyebrows shoot up toward his thinning hairline.

"No, but we gotta rule people out."

"Just like on TV, huh?"

"Yeah, just like on TV."

Donovan shakes his head and sighs, then says, "Jesus Christ, what a fuckin' world."

He's a world-weary guy, knows the ropes. We'll get nothing worthwhile out of him.

"When'd you leave here?"

"We close at two. Then I take care of the register, add up the receipts, shit like that."

"A long day, huh?"

"Yup. And I have only one employee, a part-timer. A real dickweed. Makes my life tougher than it already is. Guy's a thief. I'm tryin' to sell the goddamned place. Fact is, I'm talkin' with a lawyer. The bastard blinks twice, he sends me a bill."

"Can anyone vouch for you being here last night?"

"My part-time guy can. He's here three evenings a week. My regulars, too. They know I was here."

"What's your part-time guy's name?"

"Richie Hall. I gotta watch the register, or he'll steal me blind like every bartender who ever lived."

"His address?"

"Somewhere on Sheepshead Bay Road. I don't know the exact number."

"You don't keep records?"

"I pay him in cash. You're not from the IRS, so it isn't a problem, is it?" He lets out a quick laugh, then snorts.

Nager whips out his pocket-sized notebook, jots the name down. "And you were behind the bar the whole time?"

"Not always . . ."

"Whaddaya mean?"

"I got a room with a cot in the back. Sometimes I throw myself down and grab a nap, ya know? Standin' on your feet all the time takes its toll. So Richie covers the bar while I lie down. Then I check the till to make sure he didn't take a taste, know what I mean?"

"You won't mind showing me the room, will you?"

"Nah. Follow me."

Donovan lifts the bar hatch, leads Nager along the outside of the bar past the drinkers, and heads toward the back of the tavern. Liz stays perched on her stool. Nager and Donovan walk down a dimly lit hallway with walls painted battleship gray. Before they get to the men's room—Nager's certain it reeks—Donovan opens a door on the right.

Nager peers into a musty room only slightly bigger than a closet. An Army-style cot, side table, and lamp are squeezed inside.

A steel door with an EXIT sign stands at the end of the corridor.

"Where does that lead?"

"Out back to the Dumpster. There's an alleyway out to the street."

Back in the barroom, Donovan lifts the hatch, repositions himself behind the bar.

"Mr. Donovan. You own a gun?" Nager asks.

"Yeah, and as long as you're askin', I got a permit."

"You keep it on the premises?"

"Yup. And I got a baseball bat under the bar."

"May we see the gun?"

Donovan heaves a sigh, turns and bear-walks down the bar, stops in front of the cash register, reaches behind it, removes what must be a pistol wrapped in a dish towel, trudges back toward Liz and Nager. He unwraps the weapon, sets it on the bar top. It's a fully loaded .38 Taurus six-shot revolver.

*   *   *

Liz feels a slight nudge from Nager's knee.

It's the signal for her to take over the questioning.

"This the only gun you own, Mr. Donovan?" she asks.

"That's it."

"So if we get a search warrant, we won't find another one?"

"You can search your pretty little ass off, missy. You won't find anything else."

What a gorilla. I'd love to shoot a knee into his crotch.

"You have one at home?" she asks.

"Nah, only here."

"Ever been held up?"

"Once, eleven, twelve years ago. That's why I got it."

"What about your Wilson Pro?"

"My what?"

"Your Wilson Pro. Your other handgun."

"Whaddaya talking about?" Donovan's face doesn't flush. His voice is steady, no quivering of his chin or lips, no wavering of his eyes. He finally fastens his eyes on Liz's and for once holds her stare, doesn't try sneaking a peek at her chest. His brow furrows in perplexity.

Liz leans back.

This guy's breath smells like a sewer.

"I don't *have* another gun, missy. What you're lookin' at is it."

"Any other employees besides Richie Hall?"

"Nope."

"Anyone you know own a handgun?"

"How should *I* know?"

"So if I get a search warrant for your apartment and this place, we won't find a Wilson Pro handgun?"

"What's a Wilson Pro?"

"You know what it is."

"I don't know, and what's more, I don't give a shit. Now if you'll excuse me, I got a business to run . . ."

"One other thing, Mr. Donovan . . ."

He looks questioningly at Liz, then averts his eyes, peers down at the bar; now he can't hold her stare.

"How're things between you and your wife?"

"We're fine." He grabs a glimpse at Liz's breasts, then averts his eyes. When he rotates them back to her to peer directly at her face, he has a steely stare.

"How's your intimate life?"

Donovan's face goes bone white. "None of your fuckin' business," he growls in a voice loud enough for the guys down at the other end of the bar to look up momentarily from their drinks.

"We're through talkin'," Donovan snarls and picks up the pistol, rewraps it in the towel, and begins to turn away.

"Thanks for your cooperation, Mr. Donovan," Liz says, setting a card on the bar top. "Give us a shout if you think of anything."

"Yeah, sure..." Donovan mutters as he heads back toward the juicers.

*   *   *

On the street Nager says, "He didn't like you asking about his sex life."

"He's not getting any at home, that's for sure."

"You notice there was only one time when he looked directly at you?"

"He sure checked out my boobs."

Nager feels a twinge of discomfort. For sure, Liz isn't shy.

About to get behind the wheel, she says, "You don't like him for the shooting, do you?"

"I'd put him pretty far down on the list."

"One thing's certain," Liz says, "that marriage's headed for the Dumpster."

"Losing a child is tough," Nager says. "That kind of thing can make a marriage go south."

"You think he knows about the affair?" Liz asks.

"If he does, you think he cares?"

"Nope. And that might take away from any motive he'd have to off the good doctor."

In the sedan, Nager says, "Even with a reason to shoot the doc, there's only a small window of time when he could've been away. He smells pretty clean, despite the halitosis. We'll see if this Richie Hall character confirms Donovan's alibi. And maybe we'll talk with a few of his nighttime regulars."

She chortles. "Like *they'll* be reliable."

She turns the ignition key. The engine comes to life.

"And we'll go through the doctor's records . . ." he says. "Let's see if there's a possible somewhere in those notes. If it's not Brian Donovan or that Mike Brock character, it's an open field. But it sure looks like a targeted killing."

"The question is, *why.*"

"In this crazy world, who knows?"

Nager realizes this could end up being one of the many unsolved homicides he's seen on the job. He says, "Frankly, Liz, I don't have a good feeling about this one."

CHAPTER THIRTEEN

AFTER ANOTHER SLEEPLESS night, Rick finds himself feeling woozy as he rides the elevator down to the basement.

In the building's indoor garage, he gets into the Chevy Malibu, turns the ignition key, and backs the car out of the parking space.

The garage is always damp and reeks of exhaust fumes. And it means a hefty fee tacked onto the monthly rent for a parking spot barely big enough to park a sub-compact. He maneuvers the car up the ramp and presses the remote button on the visor. The overhead door clatters upward and he rolls out onto East Eighty-Fourth Street.

At nine in the morning, rush-hour traffic has eased, so he can avoid the usual snarl heading into Brooklyn. Rick gets to the FDR Drive and heads south toward the Brooklyn Bridge. He's going to Brooklyn to close down his father's office. Once over the bridge, he gets on the Brooklyn-Queens Expressway leading to the Prospect Expressway which empties into Ocean Parkway, a wide north–south boulevard with grassy medians on each side.

Driving south on Ocean Parkway, he glances into the rearview mirror. A dark blue Ford Granada is directly behind him. Only five minutes earlier, he'd seen it on the Prospect Expressway, a few car lengths behind. Is he being tailed? He knows he's been overly vigilant since the shootings. Actually, he's primed, completely jacked, so it could be he's reading ominous intent into the most innocuous circumstances.

Shifting into the right lane, he thinks it's ridiculous to assume he's being followed. Only moments later, the Granada swerves into the space immediately behind him. The thing's tailgating him. It's so close he can't even see its front grill. The sun's reflection on the car's tinted windshield makes it impossible to see the driver.

The guy edges his car so close he's nearly touching Rick's rear bumper. He's a macho jackass busting balls for no reason.

Or is there more to it? Rick's pulse begins galloping. Is he being paranoid? Maybe, but the hang-ups have gotten more frequent. Yesterday there were three, and there was one at six this morning. There's never been a hang-up so early in the day. Hearing the click on the answering machine caused that feeling of dread to return. In spades.

His life is being invaded by an unseen caller who seems to know his routines: when he'll be home, probably knows where he lives and works. There's little doubt about it: someone is lurking at the edges of his life. Maybe he should call Howell, but for sure, that'll go nowhere.

Catching the traffic light wave, he drives steadily. Now back in the middle lane, he glances into the rearview mirror.

The Granada's gone.

Don't let suspicion take over. Howell's probably right. The Harper shooting has nothing to do with me.

A teacher in medical school once said, *If I ask you to examine your skin for purple spots, you'll eventually find them. Look hard enough for anything and you'll find it.*

* * *

The streets of his childhood neighborhood look familiar, yet somehow they appear strange, even foreign. Kings Highway—a main commercial hub in the Midwood section of Brooklyn—is lined with retail stores, food markets, and banks. It looks far less impressive to the eyes of a thirty-four-year-old man than it did to a kid. A strange feeling pervades him—it's a blend of nostalgia, and now there's also fear. Because his father was killed only three blocks from here. The savagery of it is stunning, still seems unreal because murder just doesn't happen in your own life.

So, after finding a parking place, he sets the Club steering wheel lock into place, slips the No Radio sign onto the dashboard.

Goddamned city. People steal cars or break a side window to steal the radio.

* * *

Entering the office, an undertow of wistfulness tugs at him.

His father's presence in the office feels like a ghosting. The walls are covered with diplomas, certificates, honoraria, and sepia photos of Dad's heroes: Pasteur, Lister, and Salk. Two empty file cabinets stand with their drawers partially open. The police were here and took all the patients' records. What will the cops find when they comb through the handwritten notes and lab reports in those folders? Will the records lead them to the killer?

Only a short while ago, his father had been in this room, dispensing advice and reassurance to his patients. He'd never had a nurse, a receptionist, a technician, or an employee of any kind other than a housekeeper who came in every evening after office hours to clean the place. His practice was a one-man show. He didn't run a multi-specialty, high-tech operation anything like the sophisticated practice of East Side Medical Associates.

Sitting at his desk, the smell and feel of his father's leather chair are strangely comforting. Rick's thoughts return to the times he sat in this room when Dad offered advice, often unsolicited.

Forget baseball, Rick. A sports career is over by the time you're in your thirties.

A handwritten note to the landlord sits on the desk. His father wanted to renew the lease for one year, not the usual three-year arrangement. He knew his practice was approaching its endpoint. The note—scripted in black ink with swooping cursive letters—was done with his Parker fountain pen, which he'd had for at least twenty years. Yes, he kept things forever. He'd grown up during the Depression and never forgot the lessons learned from those days of deprivation. In fact, when Rick was a kid, his father would go around the house on Cranberry Street and turn off the lights. *I don't own stock in the electric company*, he'd say.

Rick slides open a desk drawer. It releases the aroma of the tobacco his father used when he smoked a pipe sitting at home, reading his medical journals.

Two framed photographs stand on the desktop next to the black rotary phone: one is a picture of Mom from years ago. The other is of Rick and Kate, ages twelve and ten, sitting together.

Despite the separation, he'd kept Mom's photo on the desk. She appears to be about thirty years old in the picture.

"Meeting your mother was the luckiest day of my life," his father said many times over the years. "We accidentally bumped into each other in the lobby of the Met Life building. I fell in love at that moment. Just her name—Claire, such a beautiful French name even though she was Irish—seemed like magic to me. I convinced her to join me for coffee across the street at Schraft's."

A mahogany bookcase is laden with old medical texts. And a stack of recent journals. Yes, he kept up with the latest medical literature.

In the examination room, an ancient monocular Leitz microscope stands beneath a glass bell jar. How many times had Dad stared through those lenses, examining slides? Rick knows he'll take the microscope home.

Back in the consultation room, a radio sits on top of a file cabinet. Rick turns it on. It's set to WQXR. His father loved classical music, could name the composer of virtually any symphony after hearing just a few bars. Rick adjusts the tuning knob and the elegiac strains of Barber's *Adagio* seeps into the room. A swell of sorrow cascades over him. It feels like his father is present everywhere—and yet, he's gone.

He snaps off the radio, plops into the chair, leans back and closes his eyes.

He's jolted by the telephone ringing.

He reaches for the receiver.

Then hesitates.

Who could be calling his father's office now? A patient who hasn't yet learned he's dead?

"Hello . . ."

He hears a shallow intake of breath, then an exhalation. Nothing else.

"Who's this?"

Silence.

Rick's stomach churns.

He slams down the receiver.

That sense of dread bleeds through him.

None of this is coincidence. Something terrible is going on and he doesn't know why. Or who's behind it.

And there's no way of stopping it.

CHAPTER FOURTEEN

LIZ AND NAGER climb the stairs to the fourth floor of the brownstone on East Eighty-First Street.

"When I tried to talk with her the other day, she couldn't handle it," Nager says. "I hope she's doing better now."

"You always say dealing with the victim's family's the worst part of the job."

"For sure it is."

When the apartment door opens, Liz notices Kate Shepherd's eyelids are red and swollen. Her face has a bluish skim-milk hue and puffy bags are slung beneath her bloodshot eyes. She's a good-looking young woman, but grief, and possibly drugs, have obviously taken their toll.

"Thanks for agreeing to see us," Liz says as they enter the apartment. "I'm Liz Callaghan, Detective Nager's partner."

The apartment's a cramped studio. Liz and Nager take seats on a sofa while Kate sits facing them in an overstuffed chair.

Kate wears a tie-dyed t-shirt and faded blue jeans. Liz notices Kate's blond hair is disheveled and her fingernails are bitten down to the quick. Her cuticles are red, raw-looking; they've been chewed to bits.

Liz gets a certain vibe from Kate; she senses this young woman could unravel in a heartbeat if the questioning gets too aggressive. So, she'll tread lightly. "Kate, I hope you're feeling well enough to talk now."

She nods, makes brief eye contact, then averts her gaze.

"Rick told Detective Nager about Mike Brock. We'd like to speak with him, but we're having trouble locating him. We're hoping you can help us?"

She shakes her head. "He's out of my life now, and I want it to stay that way."

"We'd just like to get an idea of where to find him."

"He could be anywhere for all I know," she says in a trembling voice.

"Does he have family, mother, father . . . any relatives you know about?"

"No. He bounced around from one foster home to another since he was five years old. I don't think he even knows who his parents are."

"Are you worried he'll come back?" Liz asks.

"I don't want to see him or any of his friends. Ever."

"Kate, are you afraid of him?" Liz presses.

She nods while looking down.

"We understand your father didn't like him."

"Yeah, that goes back a long time. I hated his criticisms of Mike, so I moved out."

"Your brother once had a run-in with him, right?"

"Yeah . . . after Mike hit me."

"Kate, we really need to find him."

Kate's knee begins dancing up and down. It's obvious this is hitting a raw nerve. "I broke up with him a month ago."

"Do you know where he might be now?"

"No idea. I don't want him thinking I put you guys on to him."

"Can you tell us who can put us in touch with him?" Liz asks. "We won't mention your name."

"You promise?" Kate's eyes narrow.

"Yes. We'll keep you out of this, completely."

Poor woman, she's still a victim of this guy even though he's not in her life . . . for now.

"Okay, there's a guy by the name of Knucks. Mike hangs out with him."

"Knucks?"

"Yeah, because he has tattoos on his knuckles. And he's huge, weighs over three hundred pounds."

"Where can we find him?"

"He might be at CBGB down on the Bowery. He's always with his crew and they hang there pretty often."

Liz jots something in her pocket pad.

"Does Mike still get gigs at clubs in the East Village?"

"He sometimes fills in when some guitar player doesn't show up."

Her eyes swerve back and forth between Nager and Liz. "I hope I didn't make a mistake by talking to you."

"We'll keep you out of this. We promise," Liz says, wondering if Brock hated Doc Shepherd enough to blow him away. And had he tried to take Rick Shepherd out the day Harper went down?

Father and son. Is there a connection?

CHAPTER FIFTEEN

ALL FAITHS CEMETERY, a sprawling forest of the dead, looks like an endless vista of headstones spread across an expanse near the Long Island Expressway in the Maspeth section of Queens.

There was no service at the funeral home. "Your father had little use for formalities," Mom said. "And we don't need all those patients paying their respects. It's too depressing."

At her request, Rick arranged for a minister to say a few words at the graveside. He's thankful there was no formal ceremony, no chapel crowd with the well-intentioned platitudes, the air-kisses and hugs, the mournful faces, along with the obligatory condolences—words spoken even though the speakers know there's no way to soothe the raw wound to the soul suffered by the family. And there would be the inevitable, *James was blessed to have a son who became a doctor, just like his father.*

The whole cloying, annoying, syrupy death ritual would drive him batshit.

And now sitting with Mom, Kate, and Jackie in the back seat of a Lincoln town car, he peers at endless rows of tombstones. Uncle Harry follows in his car.

The bleakness of it all is soul-crushing.

*   *   *

The three-car procession arrives at the grave site.

Uncle Harry looks wasted. His face is gaunt and pale. He walks slowly, nearly bent over, as though he has a spinal problem; he's sixty-four but looks much older. Losing his fraternal twin brother has got to be yet another shock to him in his blighted life. Poor guy: lost his wife and unborn child nearly thirty years ago and has been living a sad and lonely existence ever since.

Black-suited funeral employees stand behind the hearse; they're trained in the morbid rites of the profession. They open the vehicle's rear gate. A platform swings down.

"I'm sorry to bother you, Dr. Shepherd," says an undertaker, "but I have to ask you to identify your father. It's standard procedure nowadays."

"I understand."

"You want me to do it?" Harry asks. His voice sounds thick, phlegmy, clogged with grief.

"Thanks, Harry. I'll take care of it."

Rick walks over to the hearse and stands behind it.

The coffin rolls onto the rear platform.

The upper portion of the casket lid has been lifted and is held by one of the undertakers. His father can be viewed from the chest up. Looking at the remains, tears roll down Rick's cheeks. Dad's face is flaccid, masklike, frozen in death. He's gone, violently, exists no more. Will this last sight of his father remain lodged in his mind for the rest of his life?

Remorse stabs him as he realizes that for the last two years, he'd paid little attention to his father's lousy situation; he'd shunted him aside, thinking of his own petty concerns.

Rick recalls an old Sicilian saying: *Two parents can raise ten kids, but ten kids are too busy to take care of one elderly parent.*

"It's him . . ." Rick murmurs through a cloud of misery.

* * *

At the graveside, Rick sees a yellow backhoe looming nearby. It was used to gouge out the earth for the grave. The sight of it sends a chill through his flesh.

Watching Mom, Katie, Jackie, and Uncle Harry at the graveside, Rick wonders what goes through their minds. Does Mom regret having left him? She knows the separation caused him pain. He begged her to return, but she wouldn't do it. Rick is certain she now feels guilty.

Clinging to Mom's arm, Kate seems so childlike, so fragile. Poor Kate, always craving Dad's attention. Resenting him, rebelling in any way she could, even living with Mike Brock just to make him notice her. And now, she's drowning in grief.

And there's Uncle Harry. As fraternal twins, he and Dad were part of each other's lives—beginning in the womb. His brother's death must be like losing part of himself. It's another loss for Harry, one that'll sink him even lower into the depths of his misery.

The minister is a hollow-cheeked stranger with white hair, rimless glasses, and a mellifluous voice. He recites incantations from the Old and New Testaments. As poetically profound as they are, Rick can barely listen to the words. He's too consumed by sadness.

A cemetery worker turns a winch handle and supporting straps lower the coffin slowly into the grave.

Mom picks up a handful of soil from the waist-high pyramid piled beside the plot, lets it sift through her fingers onto the casket below. Katie does the same thing. Then, they each drop a red rose into the hole.

The minister nods; Rick picks up a shovel. After slicing the blade into the earthen pile, he pours a shovelful of it—soil, loam, and pebbles—onto the casket. The mixture thumps onto the coffin lid, sends a shivery sensation through Rick. He hands the shovel to Harry who, with tears rolling down his cheeks, does the same thing.

Rick turns away; he can't bear watching the coffin disappear beneath the earth. His father will be buried—out of sight and gone for good—and Rick feels the loss of him anew. The finality of it is wrenching and he's beset by a sense of sadness so profound, it weakens him.

Looking out at the cemetery, it's so somber, so eerie: this expanse of grass and granite, these lichen-covered tombstones, endless in their granite configurations, and the elaborate mausoleums all beneath the darkness of a winter sky. There's silence but for the whooshing of cars on the Long Island Expressway amid the bleak industrial lowlands of Maspeth. Gazing into the overcast distance, Rick sees the Elmhurst gas tanks, as a freight train moves along the Long Island Railroad's Montauk Branch.

Only a few days ago, Rick could never have imagined his father being murdered while he wonders if he's in some maniac's crosshairs.

When is murder part of anyone's life?

CHAPTER SIXTEEN

AFTER CLIMBING UP the subway steps, the shooter begins winding his way through a warren of Manhattan streets.

The lawyer's waiting in his office at the Woolworth Building. Fucking guy's a thief; he's a member of the bar in three states, steals from people all over the country. He wants to discuss a deal with the government. Can you ever trust those so-called officials? Of course not. They're a duly elected coven of crooks and connivers. They're only interested in lining their pockets at the expense of taxpayers.

Is there anyone I don't loathe?

No, not really.

The world is an ugly, evil, and corrupt place. It's filled with treachery and deceit.

And that goddamned subway—the back-to-belly squeeze of a rush-hour crowd, the dirty platforms, the graffiti-covered subway cars, the smells, sights, and sounds of it, all disgusting. The streets are no better: honking horns, shrieking sirens, panhandlers scrounging through garbage. The tumult, fumes, and filth.

Why do I feel such rage, such hatred?

It's an unjust world, where no one cares about you from the moment you're born until you're dropped into the ground. Like old Doc Shepherd was.

But right now, what counts most is where and when Rick Shepherd will take his last breath.

CHAPTER SEVENTEEN

STANDING BENEATH A cascade of water, Rick luxuriates in an early morning shower.

Steam billows through the bathroom as pulsating needles of water buffet his back and shoulders, slosh over him and sluice down his skin. He'd love to stay in this cocoonlike wrap until his finger pads are puckered and wrinkled. But there's no sense in delaying the inevitable: getting back to the office after a full week away.

Today, he's returning to the insane circus of the practice. Fortunately, Dave and Phil have been covering for him. The three of them will try to see the flood of patients Kurt Messner's lined up for the internists. Burying himself in work—examinations, chart entries, even the mind-numbing minutiae of insurance forms—will make it seem like some semblance of normality has returned.

His thoughts drift to choices he could have made besides medicine. As an eighteen-year-old All-City center fielder at St. Ann's High School, he consistently hammered baseballs over the outfield fences. When an offer came from the Columbus Confederate Yankees, a Double-A team in the Yankee farm system, the fatherly mantras—always part of his father's repertoire—intensified to the point of exhaustion.

You're only eighteen, Rick. Any sport's a young man's game. Medicine is an honorable way to spend your entire working life.

Though he was offered baseball scholarships to Louisiana State and the University of Miami, he turned them down and went to NYU, his father's alma mater. As a pre-med student.

Then, medical school at Manhattan Medical College. Also Dad's alma mater.

Yes, he chose his father's way—the prudent, comfortable, predictable life.

*   *   *

This morning, he shares the elevator with an elderly man who lives on the fourteenth floor. An inveterate busybody, the guy's long since retired, sits for hours each day in the lobby, and gabs his ass off with tenants passing by or talks with any doormen willing to share the building's scuttlebutt.

"Sorry about your father. I heard he was a fine man," says the gossiper.

"Thank you," Rick responds, staring at the elevator door and wishing this guy would just disappear.

"A goddamned shame," the man mutters. "There's so much violence in the city. You hear about that poor guy on Seventy-Ninth Street? Shot dead in broad daylight. Three times, right in the back, for no reason. The city's going to the dogs."

Rick's pulse ramps up with the mention of Robert Harper. He feels like turning to the guy and shouting *Shut the fuck up, asshole.* But it's not his style. Besides, silence is the best way to shut this guy down as he prattles on about crime, the shitty mayor, and the city's steady deterioration.

At the lobby floor, Rick mumbles, "Have a good day," and heads for the building's outer door.

Roberto, the daytime doorman, shoots Rick a solace-laden look. Rick wonders how long he'll be known as the tenant whose father was shot down in the night. For how long will he be seen as the poor bastard burdened by the yoke of tragedy clamped around his neck? He's become an object of whispered comments each time he enters or leaves the building.

*   *   *

It's a short walk from the apartment to the East Seventy-Ninth Street office of East Side Medical Associates. Before last week, Rick's always loved walking the city streets. He'd get into a rhythm where his mind drifted to a million things as he hustled along in a nearly trancelike state.

But this morning, he's vigilant and his mind teems with thoughts of what he's done over the last few days: he'd placed a death notice in the *Times*, terminated the office lease, took some mementos from the office, got hold of his father's lawyer regarding his Will, contacted the utility companies, and made an appointment with the Salvation Army to haul away the office furniture. He got hold of a real estate agent to sell the house in Brooklyn and took his father's Buick to a storage facility on Furman Street near the Brooklyn docks.

Rush hour brings a roar of cars, trucks, and taxis streaming north on Third Avenue. Horns honk and brakes squeal as a phalanx of vehicles rushes uptown on this cold, sunny morning. The sidewalk teems with glassy-eyed people bundled against a cutting November wind. Swarms of them head toward Lexington Avenue and East Eighty-Sixth Street to catch the number 4, 5, or 6 train.

Between Eightieth and Eighty-First Streets, he sees him—stepping out from the entrance of a four-story walk-up next door to a gourmet take-out store.

Holy shit, it's *Dad*.

The sight of him brings a lurch to Rick's step. It's a momentary flash. This tall man in his sixties with white hair brings a shock wave of recognition, which hits him like a punch in the gut.

The man turns at the next corner and heads toward Lexington.

Rick's heard patients tell him of "seeing" a dead loved one on the streets, and now his mind is playing that same painful trick on him.

Nearing Eightieth Street, Rick's aware of a guy walking behind him. He virtually *feels* him closing in. *Jesus, is this it?* Glancing back, he sees a young man striding quickly toward him, head down, pushing against the wind. Barely watching where he's going, the guy nearly slams into Rick, then mumbles, "Excuse me," steps around him, and moves on.

Rick can't banish the thought of someone coming up behind him and pumping him with bullets.

A little farther on, an ominous feeling creeps up Rick's back, slithers into his neck. He stops in front of Parma restaurant and, gazing into the window, scans the street's reflection in the plate glass.

Nobody's following.

He's almost sure of that.

From now on, I'll take a taxi or a car service to work each morning.

*   *   *

Approaching the office entrance on Seventy-Ninth Street, he can practically see Robert Harper's tarp-covered body lying there, the estuary of blood glistening on the sidewalk. That sight will plague him every time he approaches the outer office door. And now it triggers his fears of all those hang-ups.

As Rick enters the office, Carla, the head receptionist, says, "Rick, it's good to see you. I'm so sorry about what happened . . ."

He nods, shoots her a wan smile. "Thanks, Carla. Appreciate it."

Heading toward his consultation room, he stops at Jill Kotch's office. She's a fifty-year-old, silver-haired office manager whose finger rests on the pulse of the practice—the people, the problems, the politics. Jill tells it like it is. And she's the only person in the office who doesn't tolerate Kurt Messner's shit.

Her lips flare into a smile. "Welcome back, Rick . . ."

Since his father's death, they've talked a few times on the phone. Condolences are no longer necessary.

"Glad to be back," he says.

"You sure?"

He laughs, "As sure as I can be."

"Kurt's on the warpath again."

"What's up now?"

"He was pissed you took a week off . . ."

"I guess I should apologize for the inconvenience of my father's murder."

"I set him straight on that," she says, brushing back a stray lock of hair. "But there's something new . . . he says the internists are taking too much time with patients, that it's affecting the *bottom line*." She makes air quotes with her fingers. "On top of that, he wants more in-house referrals for procedures like colonoscopies, you know, the big-ticket items."

"Incestuous referrals," Rick mutters.

A twinge of irritation seizes him. "The surgeons are a one-shot deal," he says. "Most of their patients are unconscious when they're treating them. When the surgery's over, they see the patient once for a post-op evaluation and that's it."

"Of course," she says. "It's different with the internists."

There are examinations, telephone calls, lab reports, talking with family members, pharmacy calls, the whole office practice thing.

Jill closes her door. "I've done some arithmetic," she says. "You, Dave, and Phil—three out of the nine partners—account for sixty-five percent of our office visits. And the reimbursements for the internists are the lowest of all the specialties. Kurt says he can't run a business this way."

"So now we're a business?"

Rick is aware that Messner's always rushed patients. Years ago, when he worked as an emergency room physician, his penchant for discharging patients too quickly only to have them return hours later earned him the moniker Dr. Bounce-Back by the ER nurses and aides.

Jill says, "If you, Dave, and Phil ever leave, just let me know. I'll be out the door with you."

*   *   *

Rick sits at his desk. He has fifteen minutes before the first appointment of the day.

The last time I was in this room, Dad was alive. It still seems so unreal. And why do I feel that returning to work makes me feel like I'm betraying him?

It suddenly crosses his mind that he thought of his father infrequently while he was alive; now that he's dead, Rick misses him every day.

Phil Lauria pokes his head into the office. He's cardiologist-thin— hasn't consumed an ounce of saturated fat in decades, wouldn't know a prime cut of beef if it slapped him in the face. But he's a great guy. "Good to see you back, Rick."

Aside from having a common enemy in Messner, Phil, Dave, and Rick are friends outside the office. Their histories go back to medical school; they occasionally get together at restaurants; know each other's families, and visit each other's homes.

"It's good to be back," Rick says. "I hear we're busy."

"Kurt's at it again. Let's talk about it at lunch."

"You got it."

"The Skyline?"

"See you there at twelve."

Alone now, Rick's thoughts ricochet back to one still-unanswered question about Dad's role in his acceptance to medical school. He recalls one evening when his father was trying to convince him to apply to Manhattan Medical College, his alma mater, in addition to the four other medical schools to which Rick had applied.

"Why, so you can pull some strings? Listen, Dad, I want to make it on my own."

Finally, Rick said, "Okay, I'll apply there, but it's my last choice."

Weeks later, when four rejection notices arrived, a deep sense of unease gnawed through Rick.

One week later, an acceptance letter from Manhattan Medical College arrived.

If not for Dad's Good Old Boys Club, would I ever have gotten into medical school?

CHAPTER EIGHTEEN

THE DAY HAS been so busy, lunch with Phil was canceled.

Exhausted at five, Rick sits alone in his consultation room wondering if he returned to work too soon. The examining room with its fluorescent lighting appeared unreal, as did the glass jars stuffed with cotton balls and tongue depressors, while the patients were like a never-ending carousel of complaints and illness. He feels like trudging back to the apartment, sucking down some wine, then dropping onto the sofa, zoning out, and falling asleep. Just shutting out the world.

Today, he's reminded of his father by nearly everything he sees or hears—when a patient calls him *Dr. Shepherd*, when he listens to someone's heart or lungs, when he sees a medical journal lying on a desk.

When the desk telephone rings, his gut lurches. He thinks of those hang-ups. Is it now happening at the office, too? He reminds himself to call Howell. And the telephone company. It's time to change their number or find out if the calls can be traced.

"Rick, Detectives Nager and Callaghan are here to see you," says the receptionist.

A needle of dread pierces him. *What's up now?*

* * *

Nager's standing in the waiting room with an attractive woman. She wears stonewashed jeans tucked into knee-high black leather boots and an oxford blue shirt beneath a black leather jacket. Her strawberry blond hair is pulled back in a ponytail. Her height—looks like she's close to six feet tall—and coloring are similar to Jackie's.

"Rick," says Nager, "this is Detective Liz Callaghan, my partner."

They shake hands. Her grip is firm and she makes direct eye contact. Rick reads her as a tough woman whose beauty camouflages a core of grit. It must work to her advantage when she questions suspects.

In the consultation room, Nager and Callaghan sit in chairs facing the desk.

"Has there been any progress?" Rick asks.

"We've gathered some more evidence," Nager says, "but nothing close to solving the case." He pauses. "We have a few more questions for you. And, Rick, thanks for taking the time to see us."

"Ask away." Rick suddenly feels sweat varnishing his cheeks. With two detectives sitting in his consultation room, Dad's death feels even more visceral, more immediate.

Nager says, "I spared you some of these details when we first spoke because I didn't want to overload you at the time."

Now droplets of sweat are blistering Rick's forehead. "Understood," he says, wondering what's coming. It can't be good.

"We've pretty much ruled out a drug-related motive," Nager continues. "It's far down the list of possibilities. The ballistics people ID'd the type of pistol used. It was a high-end piece."

"A 'high-end piece'?"

"Yes. A Wilson Professional; it runs a few thousand, retail."

"Professional? Are you saying the killer was a professional, a *hit man*?"

"Not necessarily," Nager says, raising both hands with his palms facing outward. "Gangbangers and muggers mostly use Saturday

Night Specials, stuff they buy on the street. This one had to have cost big bucks and makes us think this was more of a targeted situation."

"Targeted?"

"Yes, we think your father was being stalked. But that doesn't mean it was a professional killer."

"Can you trace the gun?"

"Not yet. The recovered bullets tell us the *kind* of gun used—but not the *specific* weapon. If we had the actual piece, we might be able to track down where the gun was purchased and by whom. But that's a long shot. It could've been bought at a gun show or changed hands a dozen times over the years. Or, it might've been stolen. Without the actual pistol, we can only ID the make and model."

"What about sporting shops?"

"We're asking around at local gun shops and gunsmiths. And we've contacted the ATF."

"The ATF? Why?"

"Because every licensed gun dealer's required to have a federal firearms license, an FFL. When any legitimate dealer sells a gun, he has to fill out a government form; it's called Form 4473—also known as the *Yellow Form*. It has information about the buyer. The dealer has to keep this form on file for twenty years, and it can be inspected by the ATF at any time. So in theory, we may be able to track down the weapon that way."

"What if the dealer goes out of business?"

"If the dealer closes up shop, the form's gotta be handed over to the ATF. These records are stored at a warehouse down in Maryland. Finding that form, if it's around, could take a while."

"Understood."

"We're thinking the shooter had something personal against your father."

"What about Mike Brock?"

"We haven't been able to locate him, at least not yet. I'm sure you know we've talked with Kate and we're checking out clubs around the East Village. It might take some time before we snag him."

"What about my father's telephone and office records?" Rick hears himself ask.

This all feels so unreal.

"We're still going through them. There are years of records and we have to be thorough, so it'll take time. We also want to go through the records of any patients who might have been hospitalized over the last year or two."

"Give it to me straight, Detective. Is this case gonna be a dead end?"

"I don't think so."

Rick notices that Liz Callaghan maintains a blank expression. It tells him more than anything Nager says. There have got to be some uncomfortable things they'll bring up, which, no doubt, is why they're here.

"We've been going through everything," Nager says. "Your father's financial records and his appointment book. It's clear he wasn't working very much. What can you tell us about that?"

"His practice had slowed down over the last couple of years. Basically, he was being forced into a retirement he didn't want and hadn't planned for." Rick feels his throat constricting. He coughs and swallows hard.

I could have done more to help him out.

Nager nods. "Yeah, retirement can be a bitch." He pauses, then says, "So, Rick, lemme ask you again, is there anyone who might've had a problem with your father? Someone who wasn't part of his practice, someone like . . . for instance, a loan shark . . . ?"

"A *loan shark*? No way. He never borrowed a nickel in his life. He never bought stuff frivolously or spent money he didn't have. He never even bought anything on time."

"You understand, we have to ask these kinds of questions."

"Sure, I get it."

"Is there a chance he gambled, maybe went to Atlantic City, or played the horses? Do you know if he bet on sports?"

Jesus, loan sharks, gamblers, playing the horses? Was there a secret part of Dad's life?

"No. He was never in a casino in his life and never bet on any sport."

"I have to ask this, Rick . . . do you know if your father wrote lots of prescriptions for drugs?"

"No way. Only what was necessary."

"Did he occasionally prescribe stuff like Valium?"

"I guess so. But it wasn't a big part of his practice."

"How about codeine or barbiturates? Or amphetamines?"

"You have his records so you can see if he prescribed them. I'm sure there was the occasional prescription for pain or sleep, but he didn't treat addicts."

Rick knows that some doctors truck in Medicaid and Medicare fraud. Others sell prescriptions for opiates, tranquilizers, uppers, downers, even anesthetics to patients; you name it; they'll fill out an Rx for anyone who'll pay the price.

The possibility of *Dad* selling drugs? Not a chance, especially since he saw what drugs did to Kate. But it hits him at that moment: you know only what your parents *let* you see of themselves. They had lives before you were born and you have no idea what those lives were about. Their earlier years, along with the good and the bad they may have done, didn't vanish simply because you came into the world.

"Your mother told us he wasn't very good with money," Nager says. "What about that?"

"I think she meant he didn't care much about money. He treated some poor patients and never charged them a penny. My mother sometimes said, 'Your father has a big heart . . . sometimes it's *too* big.' He always said, 'I don't sell healthcare.'"

"Any chance he might've kept a secret bank account?"

"He and my mother had joint accounts. After she left, she opened her own account. But something secret? I don't think so, but then if it was secret, I wouldn't know about it."

This is unreal. I can't believe we're talking about this.

"How about a safe deposit box?"

"They had a joint box at a Manufacturers Hanover branch in Brooklyn. I guess he could've opened another one after they separated, but I don't know."

"We've gone through his personal effects but haven't found any safe deposit keys. And Manny-Hanny has no record of one in his name alone. We're checking with other local banks." Nager pauses, then adds, "One other thing, Rick . . . did your father ever mention knowing anyone with shady connections?"

"No. Do you think he was involved with *criminals*?" Rick doesn't want to sound incredulous, but he's aware of a quivering quality seeping into his speech. And he knows he's blinking rapidly.

"No, there's nothing to suggest that, but we've gotta think of every angle. I hope you understand."

"Yeah, I get it."

Nager turns to Callaghan. "You have any questions for Rick, Liz?"

She's gonna ask some hard-core shit. That pretty face hides a tough cookie.

"Rick," she says, "I don't mean to make you feel uncomfortable but I have to ask some other questions."

"Ask away."

"Was there a woman in his life?"

"Not that I know of."

Rick thinks he sees Callaghan and Nager share a barely perceptible glance.

What the fuck do they know about Dad? How much was I kept in the dark about him? Did he have a secret life?

"I mean after he and your mother separated," Liz adds.

"I guess it's possible but I think he'd have mentioned it if he was seeing someone."

"But your mother left him after he had an affair, right?"

"That was about two years ago. I think it happened because his practice was slowing down, and he was trying to boost his ego. His practice was very important to him, maybe *too* important. I know that's a big part of why my mother left; she felt he had very little time for her and the family. The truth is, I haven't kept up with his life all that much, which I regret."

Jesus, I was a lousy son.

"Please excuse my asking," Callaghan says, "but is there a chance he visited massage parlors or prostitutes?"

An adrenaline-laced jolt streaks through him.

Dad? Hookers or rub-and-tug parlors?

"I have no idea." But then, Rick thinks if you scrape away a man's outer crust, you might find all sorts of urges and predilections. Was there a seedy underbelly to his father's life? Were there prostitutes, loan sharks, even mob ties?

Don't most of us think we're basically good? Okay, maybe you run a red light or skim a few bucks on your tax return. But you don't see yourself as a sneak, a liar, a cheater, or a fraudster. Aren't we all the heroes of our autobiographies? What the fuck? Has he been a naïve kid who could never imagine anything shady about his mother or father?

One thing's certain: his father's dying practice shook him to his foundation. His definition of himself was circling the drain. With that reality, he must have been starving for some kind of human contact. So what if he *did* pay for the comfort of a woman, even if it was counterfeit caring? After all, the guy was human; he had urges that couldn't be smothered.

Dad visiting hookers? Why not? He wasn't a eunuch.

"I apologize again," Callaghan says, "but we've got to cover all the bases. I hope you're not offended."

"No, no, of course not," he hears himself say even though his underarms are soaked and his scalp tingles. What a shitty situation: his father's in the ground, and for these detectives he's just another fucking case in a roster that's probably thicker than the Manhattan phone book. And they're wondering if James Shepherd swam among bottom-feeders—with mobsters, hookers, and drug dealers.

But it's a wake-up call. Violent death brings a hard look under the hood of someone's life.

And who knows what kind of ugly shit waits to be discovered.

Callaghan says, "Have you ever heard of a Mrs. Catherine Donovan or her husband, Brian?"

"No. Detective Nager asked me that a while back. Why? Was something going on there?"

"She was the patient your father was going to see the night he was attacked."

Attacked. A fucking euphemism.

"Do you think this Donovan woman was involved in the . . . in what happened?"

"There's no evidence of that," Callaghan says, "but we've gotta be flexible in our thinking. We're just trying to touch every base."

Just as Rick had expected, Callaghan asks the tough questions, does the heavy lifting. And she's good at it. In her sweet, feminine way, she gets right down in the mud.

Callaghan turns to Nager. "Art, do you have any more questions for Rick?"

After clearing his throat, Nager says, "One more thing, Rick. Your father's funeral . . . did you notice anyone unexpected at the cemetery—a stranger, someone who didn't belong?"

"No. Only my family—my mother, me, Kate, Jackie, the undertakers, and my Uncle Harry—and of course the cemetery workers were there." He shakes his head. *This is unbelievable . . . like the crime shows on TV.* "But I wasn't looking around for anything like that."

Maybe that's the problem: I hadn't really looked at Dad's situation. I was too goddamned selfish to pay attention. And now it's too late.

At the door Nager says, "We'll do everything we can to find whoever did this."

Rick nods and hears himself thanking the detectives for stopping by.

When they're gone, he realizes he was so shook up that he'd forgotten to ask them if it's possible to trace those hang-ups. And he'd meant to contact the telephone company about changing their number. But that's a whole different ball game.

CHAPTER NINETEEN

SO FAR, HE'S been lucky.

He still walks the earth, but not for long. It's only a matter of time and one thing's certain: his time will run out.

Like most people, his day-to-day life is predictable. Those hang-ups have provided a road map of his life, gave me a basic outline of his regular activities. Makes it easier for a kill shot. He's home most evenings by five thirty or six. It's a steady routine, unlike what his father had.

There's gotta be a way to get to him, one that guarantees he joins his father.

A good kill can only happen after you've reconnoitered the terrain, when you can be sure the target will be out in the open, going about his daily schedule, completely unsuspecting.

The trouble is . . . a rifle can't be used, so there's no way to make a head shot from a distance. Not in Manhattan. It has to be done with a pistol, close up.

And to be sure he dies, I won't go for a head shot. The head is a small target, and unless you're only a few feet away, it can be tough to do it right with a pistol. So you go for body shots, a much bigger target; you pump at least two or three into the heart like what I did to James Shepherd. The bastard had an evil heart. He bled out like the pig he was.

Though it would have been better to have gotten the son first, it's good to know James Shepherd got what he deserved. He's rotting in his grave. And he'll stay there for an eternity.

And soon, Rick Shepherd will join his father.

CHAPTER TWENTY

CERTAIN THINGS ABOUT his mother's apartment remind Rick of the house on Cranberry Street.

When she left his father, she took her favorite furniture pieces with her. The Chesterfield sofa and club-style chairs are arranged similarly to when she lived in the house on Cranberry Street.

Entering the apartment, the cooking aroma—roast chicken in the oven—reminds him of his childhood. When Mom cooks, it smells like home.

Sitting at the dining table, Rick notices her face looks milky white and her fingers tremble. Her hair's white roots are showing. It's obvious that she hasn't been to the hair salon for a while. Her teacup rattles as she sets it down and some tea spills into the saucer.

She's still trapped in the blast radius of her husband's death.

Rick feels saddened to see her looking so bereft.

Sighing, she says, "Rick, dear, I want to tell you something important."

"What, Mom?"

"You know, your father was never good with money."

Has Mom discovered a secret stash? An account of Dad's that had been hidden, possibly with money made illegally?

"You know how he was . . . sometimes, he'd charge only two dollars for a house call if a patient couldn't afford more. And there were some people he never charged."

One of Dad's mantras: "Medicine's a calling, not a business." It was right up there with his other refrain, *I don't sell healthcare.*

"But now, Rick, I have to think about my future."

"Mom, you don't have to worry about—"

"Rick, listen to me. You know your sister's had her problems. Ever since she left school, we've been giving her a monthly stipend."

"Mom, I can—"

"Just listen," she says, setting her hand on his wrist. "Over the last two years, your father's practice was draining away. I'm sure you knew that. In fact, I'm sure that within a year or so he'd have no patients left. But he still sent me a check every month. He never missed a payment. But now with him gone, there's very little to fall back on."

Rick's always assumed living comfortably was a fact of his parents' lives. He knew very little about their financial affairs. And his mother being close to broke was never something he'd have considered.

She peers into Rick's eyes. "But, there's something else . . ." She pauses.

"What, Mom?"

"You know that years ago, your father gave money to his brother, Harrison," she says, using Harry's formal name, which she's always done.

"Yes, it was seed money for his business."

Rick recalls having overheard his parents arguing when he was very young.

James, why give Harrison every cent we have?

Claire . . . he's my brother. I owe him.

What on earth do you owe him?

Loyalty.

"I was furious," Mom says. "He was going to give his brother almost everything we'd managed to save. We argued about it every day. I even thought of leaving your father but didn't because you and Kate were so young." She shakes her head and sighs. "Harrison was a car mechanic, and I couldn't see how that qualified him to start an auto parts company." Tears perch on her lower eyelids. "Well, he went behind my back and gave Harrison *every* penny of our savings without asking to be paid back. Of all things, it was a *gift*.

"I know twins can have a special bond, that it can be unlike any other relationship between people," she says as her lips pull back into a thin line, "and I really felt at the time, his brother meant more to your father than I did. I also was certain Harrison played on your father's sympathy . . . that he was taking advantage of what happened to Andrea."

"You mean when she died."

"Yes. The poor woman . . . pregnant and falling down a flight of stairs, breaking her neck. And with the baby dying, too." Mom sighs and shakes her head. "That poor man's been a miserable soul ever since. So when Harrison asked him for money, your father, who always had a big heart, just couldn't refuse him."

She raises her teacup, sips, then lowers the cup with a shaky hand.

"Mom, why are you telling me this?"

"You know the business has been a success. And Harrison never stopped repaying us."

"If it was a gift, why did he *repay* you?"

"In exchange for the money, Harrison made your father a silent partner in the business . . . he gave him fifteen percent of the company. *That* was the payback, even though your father never asked for it. Harrison sent us a check every month as part of a profit sharing arrangement. It's kept up over all these years. And for the last two years, that check's been our main source of income."

"I never knew any of this," Rick says as the conversation with Nager and Callaghan comes to mind. *You look under the hood, and you find things you never knew.*

"Your father would have been embarrassed for you to know we depended on Harrison for our income." The trembling of her hands worsens. "Now, your father's share of the business passes to me."

"So you'll still have a steady income."

"Yes. It's ironic, isn't it? The business proposal that nearly ended our marriage ensures my future now that your father's gone." Leaning her elbows on the table, she clasps her hands. "Now, the house is up for sale and Harrison's checks are keeping me afloat."

"It sounds like you should be fine financially."

"Rick. I'm sixty-two years old. You never know what life has in store. I'm so aware of that since what happened to your father."

That sign in the diner: LIFE IS UNCERTAIN. EAT DESSERT FIRST.

"My rent goes up every two years, but I don't want to move. And I still have to think about your sister. She's only beginning to get her life together."

"Mom, I—"

"*No.*" Her hand slams onto the table with such force the saltshaker pops into the air.

"At my age, I don't want to be in a business, in *any* business. So, I called Harrison and asked him to buy me out. He agreed . . . he'll buy out my share . . . for two million dollars."

"*Two million?*"

"Yes. It'll take care of me for the rest of my life . . . *if* it's invested wisely."

"You'll be set."

"Mr. Cirone, the accountant, suggested an appraisal of the business to see if that money actually represents fifteen percent of its value, but

I'm not going to look a gift horse in the mouth. I'm accepting Harrison's offer. And believe me, I'm grateful to him."

Rick nods, knowing Harry's offer is a no-brainer. It's the one good thing that's happened since his father was murdered.

CHAPTER TWENTY-ONE

LIZ DRIVES ALONG Cortelyou Road in Brooklyn's Ditmas Park section.

It's a residential street lined by Tudor and Victorian homes situated behind spacious, well-kept lawns. Old-growth sycamore trees create an arcade of leafless branches over the road.

Turning onto Rugby Road, she says, "This is the most beautiful neighborhood in Brooklyn."

"I grew up in an attached house in Flatbush," Nager says. "An evening out meant going to Ocean Parkway to watch the drag races."

She laughs. "We used to go to the bowling alley on Neptune Avenue."

"Yup, Neptune Lanes. I went there, too."

"Funny . . . we never ran into each other," she says.

It's strange, Nager thinks. He's never asked Liz anything personal. He knows she was on the Honor Roll at Lincoln High School and then went to Brooklyn College where she graduated Summa. That stuff's in her personnel file, which he sneaked a look at a few months ago. But asking about anything beyond that could be taken as too intrusive, even inappropriate.

She mentioned having recently gotten out of a lousy relationship. Now that she's free, is she looking for someone new? Does she date? Is

there anyone special? That's doubtful from what she said about looking for nothing more than contentment. How come she's never mentioned a thing about her social life? Ah, it's none of his business.
Besides, he never talks to her about his nonexistent social life. *What's
good for the goose . . .*

Just keep things to yourself and do your job.

Despite himself, he glances at her out of the corner of his eye. Her
lips—full, but not that bee-stung, trout-pout look—seem to be in a perpetual smile, never far from a kiss. Or is it his imagination? Sometimes
his fantasies go off the deep end; he's gotta keep them under wraps.

For shit's sake, Nager, just focus on the job.

She pulls over to the curb at the intersection of Rugby Road and
Ditmas Avenue.

The house is a well-kept Victorian, painted yellow with white trim,
has a slate roof, a veranda-style porch, two rounded turrets and
stained-glass windows. The front of the house is bordered by rows of
yews and boxwood shrubs. It's primo real estate in what might be considered one of the best neighborhoods in Brooklyn.

"So, this guy McHugh calls in a stolen pistol," Liz says. "A Wilson
Professional. Interesting."

"It could be important," he says as they walk toward the steps leading to the front door. "But my gut tells me it's just a coincidence."

"You believe in coincidences?"

"After all these years working Homicide, I guess not."

"He lives large," she says as they climb the steps.

"He owns McHugh Opticians . . . a huge chain of optical stores.
Guy's a widower; spends most of his time at his Bedford estate. Sometimes he's at his condo in Manhattan."

"You have book on him?"

"Yup."

"Are you going to question him?" she asks.

"No, you will. We'll get more out of him that way."

Nager rings the bell. Westminster chimes sound from inside.

A man who looks to be in his sixties opens the door. Sporting a well-coifed mane of white hair, he has a ruddy complexion and watery, gray eyes. Casually dressed in slacks, a sports shirt, and a cardigan sweater, he wears high-end, gold wire-framed glasses that would probably set you back a few hundred bucks. "Detectives, I'm Kevin McHugh. Thanks for coming so quickly. Please come in."

The house is impressive if you're into Brooklyn Victorian, Nager thinks. *Or am I just a jealous bastard?* Beyond an expansive parlor, McHugh's home office sports lots of dark woods—acres of mahogany—large furniture pieces, elaborate wainscoting, and rough-hewn chestnut ceiling beams.

Facing McHugh's desk, Nager and Liz sit in old-fashioned wing-back chairs.

"I called as soon as I realized the pistol was missing," McHugh says.

"Robbery's handling the burglary," Liz says. "We're from Homicide."

"Yes, they said you would be coming . . . I understand there's been a murder in the area and it was done with a Wilson Professional."

"Yes," Liz says. "When did you realize the pistol was missing?"

"Yesterday. You see, I was in Italy looking at a new line of frames. I got back to the States a couple of weeks ago, but stayed at my Manhattan apartment, then went up to the Bedford house. My housekeeper here has been on vacation, so no one was watching the place."

*   *   *

Life's tough for the super-rich, Liz thinks. *It's gotta be tough finding a good chef.*

"You don't have an alarm system?" she asks.

"I do, but it malfunctioned. I've called the alarm company. They'll be here later today. When I got back here yesterday, I realized the house had been burglarized. They took silverware and a coin collection along with the pistol."

"How long were you away?"

"Nearly three weeks."

"So there's no way we can put an exact time on when the pistol was stolen."

"Unfortunately, that's right."

"Is it possible the pistol was stolen even before you went to Italy?"

"I guess so. I'm not here that often. I usually stay at the Bedford house. I really keep this house for sentimental reasons. It's where my wife and I brought up the kids."

"Other than your housekeeper, does anyone else have access to the house?"

"No. She's the only other person with a key and she only comes twice a week."

"Is the pistol registered?"

"I don't really know. It was a gift from a friend."

"Who's the friend?"

"Alfred Mayweather."

"How can we get in touch with him?"

"Unfortunately, he died about five years ago."

"Do you know where he bought it?"

"No, I never asked. So I don't know its provenance."

"When did he give it to you?"

"Let's see," McHugh murmurs, "it would have been about six years ago."

"Can you describe the piece?"

"It's a chrome-plated Wilson Professional with a pearl handle. And it's a nine-millimeter, but that's all I really know about the gun."

Liz jots down a few notes. "And it was in firing condition?"

"I assume so."

"Did you ever fire it?"

"No. It wasn't something I would ever do."

"Did you have bullets for it?"

"No."

"Where did you keep it?"

"In my upstairs study, in a desk drawer."

Liz cants her head. "Mr. McHugh, do you know a Dr. James Shepherd?"

McHugh's brow wrinkles. "No, I don't. Should I?"

"Not unless you have a medical condition and were looking for an old-fashioned physician who makes house calls."

"I'm perfectly healthy," he says, knocking a thin fist twice on the desktop.

"Do you have any relatives who might be in treatment with a Dr. Shepherd here in Brooklyn?"

"No. I never even heard the name."

He may be one of the few people in New York who hasn't heard about the Shepherd murder, Liz thinks. *And the guy looks genuinely befuddled. He's not putting on an act. As Art would say, the man doesn't show a scintilla of a tell. And besides, why would he want to kill the doctor? The guy's a law-abiding citizen, a straight arrow.*

"Dr. Shepherd was shot dead not far from here," Liz says, "with a Wilson Professional."

"So, *my* pistol could have been used?"

"Yes."

McHugh's mouth drops open as his face blanches.

"Mr. McHugh . . . where were you on November fifteenth?" Liz asks.

He closes his eyes, looks lost in thought, then says, "I'd have been in Milan on that date."

"And you can verify that?"

"Certainly. Why? Am I a suspect?" He smothers a burgeoning smirk.

"No, sir, you're not. But we have to be thorough. I'm sure you understand."

Nager cuts in. "Will you show us your passport?"

"Of course," McHugh says, shaking his head as he gets up from his chair.

Leaving the room, he says, "I'll be back in a moment."

Liz shoots Art a glance. "Do you really suspect *him*?" she whispers.

He shakes his head. "Nah, just busting balls."

Liz's lips spread into a smile.

McHugh returns and hands his passport to Liz. She opens it and flips through the pages. Sure enough, the stamps confirm he'd been in Italy at the time Dr. Shepherd was killed.

Liz asks a few more questions, tries to get more details about the Wilson Pro, but nothing significant comes of it.

"Thanks, Mr. McHugh," she says. "In case we need to call you, can you give us your numbers both in Manhattan and Bedford?"

"Of course." As McHugh recites them, Liz jots them down.

"Thanks for your help, Mr. McHugh," Liz says as she and Nager get up and head for the door.

CHAPTER TWENTY-TWO

"LET'S CONTACT ATF about Alfred Mayweather purchasing a Wilson Pro," Nager says as he settles back into the passenger seat.

"That won't tell us whose hands it's in now," Liz says.

"True, but you never know . . . it might be the start of a trail that leads somewhere."

She turns the ignition key; the Crown Vic roars to life. "Brooklyn Command, here we come."

"Meanwhile," Nager says, "let's check the doctor's telephone records again for any calls made from McHugh's house in Brooklyn, the Bedford place, or the Manhattan apartment."

"You don't really like *this* guy for the homicide, do you?"

"Never trust a man who owns three homes."

"C'mon, Art, he called in the missing pistol."

"Like in the movies, Liz, always suspect the one who calls the cops."

"You don't trust anyone, do you?" she says with a smile.

"That's what eighteen years of being a cop have taught me."

Without turning toward him, she asks, "Do you trust *me*?"

"You, I trust," he answers in a near-whisper.

He sneaks a sidelong glimpse at Liz. Her eyes are on the road, but he thinks her lips have curled into a subtle smile. It seems mysterious, and it's beguiling.

Is she toying with him? Flirting? Hinting? Or is that his impression because he's seeing her through a lens of desire? He can't interpret these little gestures—a semi-smile, a raised eyebrow, pursed lips, or if she stands so close he can smell her hair's floral scent—as though these things have some hidden meaning. Is he reading too much into these moment-to-moment non-events? Jesus, he's even doubting his own perceptions.

Right then, Nager's aware how this woman makes his blood hum. It's like electricity vibrates through his body when he's with her. If he had any brains, he'd ask Pildes for a change of partners. If the Chief *did* switch her out, there'd be plenty of watercooler bullshit about it. Especially between Miller and Moreno, those jackals. He can imagine them huddled together, talking.

How come Nager and Callaghan aren't working together anymore?

It was too hot to handle. I'll bet they were bumpin' uglies. How could a guy resist?

And if he *did* try to unload her on someone else, wouldn't Pildes ask "why"?

He can't even *hint* at the reason. Jesus, he's locked in a honey trap.

Get her assigned to another detective? Hell no. Why deprive himself of the most delicious moments of his day? Except for a few harmless asides nothing out of line is going on, and he'll keep it that way. Besides, if these little things do mean something, there's nothing he can do about it. Not a goddamned thing. Because he's her rabbi and anything beyond a professional relationships could be seen as his taking advantage of a subordinate and the power disparity between them.

What the hell is he anyway? A fourteen-year-old kid who knows shit about the world? Forget about it. Anything beyond the job is *verboten*. Besides, she's so far out of his league, they're not even in the same ballpark.

He should be thinking about a hundred other things—like tracking down that Wilson Pro, putting word out with every snitch he knows—even the street-guys in the Bronx where he once worked at the Four-Nine. They still have at least a dozen gun stores in the metropolitan area to check for those Yellow Forms. He should be tapping every pawnshop in the city, phoning every bank manager in all five boroughs, looking for an account or safe deposit box in the doctor's name because that might throw some light on what was really going on in the guy's life.

The bottom line's simple: you never know what's *really* happening in anyone's life. Don't we all carry our little secrets around with us? Don't we all have some sub rosa shit in our lives? For all Nager knows, the doc was into some illegal crap that could've cost him his life.

Nager knows he should be checking the tip-line, weeding out the cranks from a caller who might lead them somewhere. He should be combing through everything not just once, but twice, and then again. After all, there's a murder book screaming to be closed, and what's he doing? He's toying with some bullshit fantasies about Liz Callaghan.

Why is that? Because he's living in a shitty two-room apartment and has nothing besides every other weekend with Bobby. Thank God for the kid. He's a lifesaver. He's the one great thing salvaged from that disastrous marriage to Ellen.

What else is there to look forward to? Bullshit sessions with the guys at Brooklyn Command? Hearing them whine about their pensions, their wives and girlfriends, or listening to their complaints about their commutes from the burbs to Brooklyn, or the cost of sending their kids to private schools?

Other than the job, how does he spend his spare time? There're the penny ante poker games with some high school buddies who knock down beers and bum cigarettes off each other—all married and out of circulation. They bullshit about their lives and gripe their assess off.

Christ on a bike, what does he have besides feeling drag-ass tired at the end of the day?

And what does he do most evenings? He sits in that apartment and after scarfing down some shit from a deli on Flatbush Avenue, he reads a thriller, then guzzles a can or two of Bud—not that he likes the taste of it, but it takes the edge off things. What things? Ellen and Bobby and the disaster his marriage turned out to be, that's what. With barely a beer buzz on, he watches a Knicks or Rangers game—the Mets or the Yankees during baseball season—and nods out in his easy chair. Like the Donovan woman did the night the doc was murdered.

What else is there? There's his fantasy life about Liz Callaghan whose eyes are fixed on the road after she asked a loaded question. *Do you trust me?*

Do I trust you? Of course, I do. I have to. My life might depend on you if push comes to shove.

Except for Bobby, all he really has is the job. It not only pays the bills, but it's who he's been for eighteen years and he can't fuck it up with an office romance. If it were even *possible*, which it isn't. And if it happened and the Chief learned about it, Nager would be toast. What could he do without the job? What qualifications does he have to do anything else? Besides, with her brains, personality, and looks, Liz Callaghan could land any guy she wants. In a heartbeat. Why would she *ever* have him on her radar screen?

So, Nager, you sappy asshole, just keep your eyes on the case and don't get distracted. Finding out who killed Doc Shepherd is what counts right now. Nothing else. Think with your head, not your dick. And don't say a word that could be misconstrued by Liz Callaghan or anyone else.

That's right, Nager, don't be a worldclass schmuck. Just do what you can to help solve the Shepherd murder and go on with your shitty little life.

CHAPTER TWENTY-THREE

IT'S SEVEN THIRTY p.m. and Jackie's still at the office.

She's working on a corporate mega-merger. "It's a marathon nego-tiation because big money—more than a billion—is at stake," she'd said. "I swear, Rick, being a lawyer is no more than arguing for a living. Sometimes I get the feeling it's modern-day gladiatorial combat."

He laughed at the analogy but understands where she's coming from. Much of her work is adversarial.

They agreed they'd grab dinner later at Harper's on Third Avenue. He'll limit himself to one glass of the house red. And he won't drop a Xanax at bedtime. He's gotta stop taking that shit.

The telephone rings.

It'll be Jackie saying she's on her way uptown.

He picks up the receiver. "Hello."

No response. He listens for sounds coming through the earpiece—traffic noise, a background voice, music, anything—but there's only dense silence broken by the soft sibilance of someone breathing.

With the receiver to his ear, Rick's suddenly aware of a visceral urge to shout, *Hey, asshole, the cops're on the line and they're gonna nab your ass*, but before he can utter a word, there's a click, then a dial tone.

It's the third hang-up in the last two days.

Someone is out there.

His pulse quickens as a sense of danger leaches through him; it feels like electrodes are taped to his chest and voltage sears his skin, then goes straight to his heart. Shit. He forgot to contact the telephone company, but maybe there's a better way to handle this. Nager and Callaghan might know if there's a way to trace these calls and nail the bastard. He'll give them a call tomorrow and find out.

The television is on. It's the evening news.

NBC News reports a manhole cover exploded on Fourteenth Street, killing a hot dog vendor whose cart was nearby. Poor guy was decapitated.

Another report: a deranged man pushed a woman from the subway platform onto the tracks as the Number 6 train roared into the Forty-Second Street Station. The assailant ran up the stairs and was lost in the crowd in the main concourse of Grand Central Terminal.

Life in the city can be treacherous. It feels like death is everywhere, especially when you least expect it. No matter where you are, or what you're doing, it can all come crashing down on you in a moment, and your time on this planet is over.

Anything can happen.

Like what happened to Robert Harper.

And to Dad.

A wave of melancholy washes over him. A moment later the sadness is replaced by a nervous sense of exhaustion. Rick's brain hums like an overloaded circuit. He *knows* these hang-ups are more than some crank getting his jollies. And Jackie's right: he should contact the telephone company and change their number.

The telephone rings again.

A spike of alarm stabs him. His pulse goes thready.

He clicks off the TV.

He'll let the answering machine record a message. If there is one.

After the fourth ring, the answering machine activates and he hears a voice on the speaker. "Rick, it's Mother. I just want—"

He picks up the phone.

"Hi, Mom." His heart begins decelerating.

"Mom, did you try calling me a few minutes ago?"

"No, dear . . ." Her voice sounds reedy. "I just want to double-check that you and Jackie are coming over Friday evening at seven. Your Uncle Harrison is driving into the city, and we'll finalize everything."

"Of course. We'll be there."

"I'm going to ask him to stay for dinner. And I'm inviting Katie. We'll be together as a family. I'm so glad you thought of having the papers signed at my place, instead of at some lawyer's office."

"It'll all work out fine, Mom."

When they hang up, Rick realizes his mother's financial windfall is the last link in a decades-long chain of events—one in which his father's brother was able to turn axle grease into gold. The circle culminated years later with Harry ensuring that Mom will never have to worry about money for the rest of her life.

Sometimes, it's true: what goes around comes around.

The telephone rings.

Rick waits.

After the fourth ring, the outgoing message begins.

There's a click.

Another hang-up.

CHAPTER TWENTY-FOUR

IT'S JUST PAST six the next evening. Rick is back at the apartment after an insanely busy day.

The answering machine's recorded two more hang-ups. Both after five p.m. Glancing at the telephone, Rick feels his heart begin a slow crawl into his throat. And going to Howell will be a waste of time. He'll call the telephone company and have the number changed. And he'll make sure it's unlisted.

He picks up the telephone to dial Ma Bell's customer service when "Eye of the Tiger" begins pulsing through the living room wall. It's the next-door neighbor's stereo turned up loud enough that a physical sensation radiates through the walls and into his feet. A prickle of annoyance surges through him as he drops the receiver back onto the base. The neighbor does this every evening, then lowers the volume after a while. He'll call the phone company when the din dies down.

It's Manhattan apartment living—the sounds and smells of nearby lives intrude: doors slamming, cooking odors in the hallways, restaurant menus being slipped under their door, and a shitload of other intrusions.

The intercom's buzz jolts him like his finger is inside an electrical socket.

"Dr. Shepherd," says Angel, the evening doorman, "two detectives are here to see you."

That voltage sizzles its way through his chest. "Thanks, Angel, send them up." It seems Nager and Callaghan are in Manhattan as often as they're in Brooklyn. At least they're working the case. He breathes deeply; sucks in a lungful of air to calm himself down.

Standing at the open door, he hears the neighbor's music lower in volume. Peering down the hallway, he sees the detectives walking toward the apartment.

"We were in the neighborhood," Nager says. "We took a chance you might be home."

*   *   *

Callaghan and Nager sit on the sofa. Rick settles into an Eames chair facing them.

Nager obviously reads the befuddled look on Rick's face. "Let me explain why we're here, Rick. We talked with your sister again. We'd like to confirm some things she told us."

Katie's wrecked over Dad's death. She probably contradicted herself with every other word. She might be using again.

Nager says, "We're still trying to locate Mike Brock. Can you tell us anything else about him?"

"The guy's a leech. He'll stay with anyone so long as it's rent-free. He crashes at friends' places. That's probably why you're having a tough time finding him."

"Let me tell you why we're here," Nager says. "A Wilson Pro was stolen in Brooklyn just before your father's . . . just before what happened on November fifteenth. The Robbery Division turned up information that the house from which it was stolen was painted in

October. We telephoned your sister and she told us that Brock sometimes took temporary jobs with a house painting crew in Brooklyn.
We contacted the company and it turns out Brock was on the crew
that painted *that* house."

"My *God*. That could connect the bastard to that gun, right?"

Rick's heartbeat ramps up.

"Yes, it's possible."

Another image of Mike Brock comes to Rick—an array of tattoos
on his arms, faded jeans, motorcycle boots, and a Nazi-style brain
bucket on his head.

I'd like to shoot that bastard dead, just put an end to his life.

"Anything else you can tell us about him?"

"Nothing more than what I told you. He really hated our father."

Nager pauses a moment, then continues, "The home that was burglarized belongs to a man named Kevin McHugh. Ever hear of
him?"

"No."

"Okay, Rick. Thanks for your help."

"Detectives . . . anything new on the Harper case?"

"Oh yeah . . . glad you asked," Nager says. "The slugs were ID'd as
being thirty-two-caliber bullets fired from a Smith & Wesson revolver
so there were no shell casings, but the rounds were identified. There's
no information about the provenance of the weapon. The bullets are
nothing like the ones used in this case."

At the apartment door, Nager says, "We'll let you know if anything
new develops."

Even though I was gonna forget about it, they're here so why not ask?

"Detectives, before you go . . . quick question."

"Sure," Nager says. "What is it?"

"Can you put a trace on my phone?"

"You getting more of those hang-ups?" Nager asks.

"They're happening almost every day now. At night, too."

"Does the caller say anything?"

"After I pick up, there's a pause and then a hang-up."

"You have an answering machine?"

"Yeah."

"Any messages?"

"Just the hang-ups."

"And you have no idea who it might be?"

"None at all."

"A colleague? A patient? Former patient?"

Same questions Howell asked.

"None of the above."

"When did this begin?"

"A little before what happened to my father."

"The best thing to do is to change your number and make sure it's unlisted."

"If you change the number and the calls continue, then it's someone who knows you," Callaghan says.

"Is there any way to trace the calls?"

Nager shakes his head. "I know the movies show it all the time. But it's not easy. The phone circuits are connected mechanically; believe it or not, some are still done manually. It takes a long time for Ma Bell to pinpoint a caller's location through the switching stations. *That's* just like in the movies. The caller has to stay on for a while for the call to be traced. The telephone company's started installing electronic switching systems; in a year or so it'll all be computerized and we'll be able to match a caller with a location instantly, but not now."

"Got it. Thanks."

"Just change the number and see what happens," Nager says.

*   *   *

Sitting alone, Rick's thoughts race to the possibility that Mike Brock murdered his father. He's a much more likely suspect than a patient or former patient. Mike Brock—that son of a bitch—and his motorcycle friends, a pack of feral-looking bikers throttling down city streets on their crotch-rockets, revving their Harleys and spitting out bone-jarring back-blasts, scaring the shit out of people as they pass by them on city streets.

And whoever's calling him and Jackie is probably trying to find out when they're home. He wonders if it's safe to walk anywhere in Manhattan. And now, he's taking a car service to the office each morning. And he convinced Jackie to take one to work every day.

Is he being tracked by the guy who killed his look-alike, Robert Harper?

He used a different gun, but so what? He could have an arsenal of weapons for all I know. Mike Brock has those biker friends. They have plenty of guns.

Is there a game plan this bastard is using? Like first try to hit the son, then get the father.

It could definitely be Brock. It could be payback for the scuffle they had. Or maybe the guy's so doped up he's lost his mind.

A deep sense of foreboding shudders through him, right down to his bones.

CHAPTER TWENTY-FIVE

KATE'S APARTMENT IS on the third floor of a four-story townhouse on East Eighty-First Street.

Rick's certain the building, now divided into eight rental apartments, will soon be converted into a co-op. The tenants will be forced to make a choice: you either buy your apartment or move out and hope you're lucky enough to find another affordable rental. Or you're shit outta luck. It's a good thing Mom's coming into that windfall. She'll put up the money for Kate to buy her place.

Walking into her apartment always seems like a glimpse of earlier times—the place is furnished with stuff Kate appropriated from the house on Cranberry Street. It's like Mom's apartment. Dad was left with only the bare essentials.

"Don't worry, Rick. I'm not using," she says, eyeing him as she settles onto the sofa.

"Hey, Katie, I'm not judging you."

But he *was* judging her. Really, *pre*-judging her. He'd sniffed for the resinous odor of weed as he entered the apartment. But there's none.

"I still can't believe Dad's dead," she says in a quivering voice as her lips twist into a pink knot.

"I know. It still seems unreal."

"The detectives came to see me about Mike," she continues. "Then they called and asked even more questions about him."

"That's why I'm here, Katie. Did the detectives tell you about the missing gun from that house in Brooklyn, the one where Mike was on that painting crew?"

"Yeah, they told me."

"Do you have any idea where he might be now?"

"No. Like I told the cops, he could be anywhere."

"How about when you were hanging with him. Where did he stay then?"

"Lots of different places. I don't remember them."

"Were you stoned then?"

"Probably. Back then I spent half my life stoned and out of it. That's over, too. Mike and I are history. I kicked him out. For good this time. And I'm not using anymore."

"C'mon, Katie, think about it. You must remember something about his friends and where they hung out."

"I already told the cops as much as I can remember, including about his friend Knucks."

"Where did they buy their dope?"

"I don't know. I just smoked a lot of it."

"Was there a dealer you heard about?"

"I don't remember. I was stoned most of the time. If I could remember, I'd tell you. Believe me, I want to find out who killed Dad as much as you do."

"Katie, I don't want to frighten you, but have you been getting any hang-ups lately?"

"No. Why do you ask?"

"Because I've been getting them—and they've been increasing since Dad was killed. So, let's try to nail this down. Where would Mike be staying now? And where does he hang out?"

"You know as much as I do. He gets temporary gigs in the East Village. His whole life is temporary. He and I were on and off again a hundred times. That's just the way he is. And I'm so over that. For once, I have a decent job and I'm gonna stay with it."

"You mean walking the dogs?"

"Yes, I love doing it, and I'm getting paid good money. Maybe I'll get off the dole with Mom. Mike's out of the picture." She shakes her head, then says, "I finally realized something . . ."

Rick waits; he won't take a chance being overly inquisitive. Katie's always resented questions about her lifestyle and choices.

"All those years with Mike . . . I just wanted Dad to notice me."

"You mean the drugs and your unemployment . . . and Mike?"

"Yeah, Dad never had time for me. He was always too busy."

"Kate, Dad noticed you and loved you . . . a lot more than you think."

"Oh, Rick, don't kid yourself. You were his *Golden Boy*," she says, making air quotes. "It was written in the stars. You were going to be a doctor." She stifles a sob.

He gets up and sits next to her, then drapes an arm over her shoulders.

"Kate, Dad loved you. He was just so busy he didn't have time to pay much attention to any of us."

She shrugs.

At the door, they embrace.

Holding her close, he knows Kate's take on him was on the mark. He was the *Golden Boy*, destined to follow Dad into medicine. He recalls the few times his father took him on house calls when he was six years old. Rick carried his toy doctor's bag. And there was that question the patients asked: *Are you going to be a doctor like your daddy?*

There's no doubt about it. Kate is right—he was the *Golden Boy*.

CHAPTER TWENTY-SIX

NAGER AND LIZ sit facing Assistant Chief Dan Pildes, a thick-chested bull of a man.

Pildes's office furniture—New York City municipal issue—reminds Nager of elementary school at P.S. 197. Jesus, he can almost smell the chalk dust on the ledge beneath the blackboard. And the wardrobe, too—that enclosure with heavy sliding doors jammed with coats reeking of damp wool and kids' bodies. And there was the boys' bathroom where they flipped Topps bubble gum baseball cards or rolled dice for nickels. In those days, the teachers were older spinsters, mostly Irish. Dad called them "battle-axes."

So here he is, sitting across the desk from the Command Center Chief—like a kid who'd behaved badly and has been called into the principal's office. Except now, Liz, sitting beside him, is watching the shitshow that's gonna start up.

If things don't turn around, Pildes will assign him the Brownsville projects with their graffiti-covered buildings and burned-out rubble, where bummed-out junkies lurk in piss-stinking stairwells, and the gangbangers have more firepower than the cops.

"Art, I need some good ink on this thing," Pildes says, slamming a heavy hand onto his desktop. Nager knows he looks like a dickweed in front of Liz.

"Bob McGuire's all over the Chief of D's butt," says Pildes, "and then *he* goes heavy on *my* ass."

Pildes only refers to the Chief of D's, Jim Sullivan, when he feels industrial-strength frustration. And Pildes's irritation has been building on this case for two weeks.

Nager brings him up-to-date on the autopsy report, ballistics, forensic details, what they've learned so far. He also explains how they're contacting gun dealers, and the talk about the Mike Brock situation.

"You mean to tell me you can't find this guy? A guy who plays backup in rock bands?"

"We'll find him, Chief. It's just taking a little time. He floats around, has no permanent address."

Pildes snorts, then begins tapping a pencil on his desktop. Other than the *tap, tap, tap*, the room stays in a conversational vacuum. Suddenly, Nager's gut growls like a junkyard dog. He shifts in his seat, tries to cover over the belly-rumble with the chair's creaking.

Jesus, is Liz hearing this? Did she just glance my way?

"Anything else?" Pildes asks.

Tap, tap, tap.

"Chief, we've followed up on every lead," Nager says, glad for the question. If he keeps talking, his voice might mask the boiler factory in his bowels. "Everyone talks about the doctor like he was a saint."

"What about this Donovan character?"

"We checked him thoroughly. He can account for his time at the bar. And it's confirmed by four other people."

Pildes turns to Liz. "Did you confront him about his wife's affair?"

"We didn't want to tell him unless we had to."

"Bullshit," the Chief shouts. Pildes's eyes look like they'll pop out of his head. "The guy could've known about the affair and hired some goon to go after the Doc. Your job is to solve a *murder*, not save a marriage." He turns back to Nager. "Get back there and grill that son of a bitch like a club steak."

Fucking Chief . . . always with the food references.

"Okay, Chief, will do."

"I'll bet this Donovan character has some seedy connections. Look into it."

"Got it, Chief."

"And for the love of Christ, go back and question every tenant in that building. Do it again. I don't care if it's some *yenta* who talks a blue streak about her grandchildren. Those crones see *everything* and they gab like a buncha crows." Pildes's nostrils flare. "What else ya got?"

Nager goes over everything: he gives the Chief a rundown of the medical files, phone records, the bank and financial transactions, the medical society, the insurance carrier, and doctor's friends. Some they've already interviewed; others are on their to-do list. He and Liz have been lint-picking their way through the man's life like a pair of scavengers. And they've come up with squat, except for the Brock lead, which is turning out to be its own kind of nightmare.

Nager's face feels hot. He's certain it's flushed, and it's happening in front of Liz.

Pop, pop, pop . . . Pildes cracks his knuckles; they sound like a kettle drum. Guy's always pulling on those fingers like he wants to pop them from their sockets. The Chief shoots a look at Liz. A half-smile breaks out on his face, like he's softening because she's so damned good looking. Nager feels a pang of jealously.

Looking at Liz, Pildes says, "You telling me a guy's been practicing all those years and didn't have *one* lousy outcome? Not *one*? Someone's gotta blame him for *something*. Hit those files again, every word, every syllable, every comma."

Liz nods and folds her arms across her chest.

"And what about that Wilson Pro . . . is the ATF on it?"

"They're going through their records down in Maryland, looking for a 4473," Liz says. "I've called them three times. They're tired of me hassling them."

"Hassle the *shit* out of 'em." Pildes leans back in his chair, clasps his hands behind his head, gazes briefly at the ceiling. Then he straightens up and again pulls on his fingers, but they're all popped out.

"We agree this wasn't a random homicide, right, Liz?" Pildes asks.

"We're working on that assumption," she says.

"So, the Doc may've been set up, yes?"

"Set up?" Liz asks, her voice rising. "Meaning what?"

"Meaning by someone who knew him well . . . like the estranged wife."

"*Really*?" Liz says.

Nager thinks Pildes is off the charts on this one, but won't contradict him. Why get the Chief even more agitated?

"Yes, *really*, goddammit," Pildes roars. "She left the Doc because he had no time for her. But he had time to take up with the *Donovan* lady."

"But, Chief . . . that was *after* his wife left him," Nager interjects.

"Sure, but he had an affair *before* that, right? *C'mon*, Art, for Crissake." Pildes almost rockets out of his chair. "This case stinks out loud," he mutters. "The wife coulda hired someone. Maybe there's a lotta dough she comes into after the doc's takin' a dirt nap. Maybe there was an insurance policy, so a dead doc would set her up for life. Don't let her take you on a chump-walk. Money always moves the needle."

Nager knows there's more than a modicum of truth in the Chief's speculation. Money—that green elixir—can tip the scales to the darkest of the dark sides.

"How come they separated two years ago and the wife never filed for divorce?" Pildes asks. "Who knows what fantasies she cooked up about her husband? I want you to work this case like pizza dough."

CHAPTER TWENTY-SEVEN

Rick and Jackie get out of the taxi and enter Lombardi's, a trendy new eatery on Third Avenue. The restaurant is so packed, the body heat in the place could bake a loaf of bread.

"It's gotten rave reviews in *New York Magazine*," Jackie says.

"Yeah, let's see if they honor our reservation."

"Rick, I can see it's really crowded, but let's try to enjoy ourselves."

She's right. I have to get out of this funk and try harder. And it's probably safe to be in this big crowd.

"Seriously, honey," he says, "I'm sorry I was such a drag at Thanksgiving."

"I thought going to my parents' place made it a little easier this year. You, Mom, and Katie did fine. My folks were happy to host the dinner. And my sister wasn't her usual princess self. She was actually pleasant."

"You know what?" he says. "I don't appreciate you enough."

"Stop blowing it out your ass, Rick." She gives him a playful slap on his arm.

The restaurant's entrance is jammed with would-be diners. The hostess, besieged by a trilling telephone and a horde of impatient patrons, shouts at Rick, "We can't seat you until nine fifteen. Please take seats at the bar."

Rick laughs to himself. Fucking place doesn't respect its clientele. Even with 8:30 reservations, they have to wait until 9:15 . . . if they're lucky.

Rick eyes the bar crowd. After about five minutes, a couple abandons two barstools; he and Jackie grab their seats. When the barkeep finally approaches, Rick asks for club soda in a wine glass, no ice. Jackie orders a glass of Chardonnay.

Drinkers are bellied-up to the bar, three-deep—Upper East-Siders in all their varied types, from coupon clippers to newbies who'd just moved from the outer boroughs and burbs—wearing fancy-ass threads from Barney's and Bloomie's. Melding with the crowd's choral roar, music seeps through the sound system. But Rick hears only the thump of the bass as it adds to the ear-bleeding noise level of the place. To his left, a guy's voice is thick with alcohol as he shouts over the noise. He drinks his scotch, straight-up. Rick catches a whiff. It smells like gasoline.

People are making Friday night connections: flirtation, frivolity, and pheromones swirl through the air.

With Christmas approaching, Rick pictures the stone fireplace in the house on Cranberry Street; there were always scarlet-colored poinsettias and the fresh scent of a scotch pine Christmas tree as the holiday approached. And right now, as they sit here in this overcrowded trattoria, the house is up for sale. It's demoralizing, but life moves on.

Feeling as he does, Rick can barely tolerate the holiday atmosphere. He recalls his father looking at the house across from theirs. Each Christmas it was festooned with multi-colored decorative lights. His father always commented, "That place looks like a pizza parlor." Whenever his father heard Alvin and the Chipmunks warbling their "Christmas Song," he'd remark, "Those chipmunks could use some Sudafed."

Suddenly, Rick spies a steep-jawed guy sitting at the far end of the bar where it curves toward the wall. He has dark, slicked-back hair combed in a John Gotti style, wears a black leather car coat, black shirt, no tie. A lit cigarette dangles from his lips. It's a hard look, the look of a predator.

Holy shit, is this guy staring at me?

Rick feels a Stone Age kind of wariness, something primal, the way dogs sensing danger look away when challenged. The guy looks like some punk out of *Mean Streets*. Rick's body begins humming. This is unfuckingbelievable. He can't let his imagination overheat. He's gotta focus on something besides thugs and murder. He tells himself to be in the moment with Jackie; to try to have a good time; to do his best to forget the horror of the last few weeks—and calm the fuck down.

*   *   *

Luckily, a couple with a prior reservation hasn't shown; they probably booked tables at three different places and went to the one that suited their mood. So, Rick and Jackie are seated earlier than expected. It's a checkerboard-sized table beneath harsh lighting.

Rick grabs the seat facing the front of the restaurant so he can watch the thug at the bar.

Why? Because in this city anything can happen. Like what happened to the woman who was pushed in front of a subway train.

Jesus, I'm getting paranoid. Or is it just an awareness of my shitty reality?

As for the restaurant: high prices, high noise level, high turnover, that's the name of the game. Rick *knows* the portions will be miniscule. And they'll be rushed through the dinner.

An aproned twenty-something waiter drops two menus on their table.

"I'm Darren and I'll be your server tonight," he shouts, then promptly disappears.

When Darren returns, he refers to a cheat sheet and rattles off the specials in a voice virtually drowned out by the crowd's roar. Bending down to hear their orders, he scribbles them on a pad.

When their dishes arrive, Rick begins picking at his rigatoni. He has zero appetite, but he would love to order a glass of wine and guzzle it down. From what he's seen, the place serves a short-pour—at most, a shitty three ounces. It'd be great to feel alcohol soak into his brain and bring on that soothing indifference, even apathy. *Jesus, I can't enjoy anything right now.*

He knows he's gotta fight off the bleakness that's taken over since his father's murder. One thing's certain: he'd never have gotten through the last few weeks without Jackie. Over their two years together, their relationship's been a progression of intimacies, a slow reveal of each to the other. He meant it when he said he doesn't appreciate her enough. If not for this beautiful, intelligent, and understanding woman, his life would be dismal.

What the hell am I waiting for? Why not get married?

But not when you're feeling sad and vulnerable, not when you think you're being targeted by the madman who killed your father. *Is this all temporary? I hope so.* Amid the crowd's cacophony he mouths, "I love you." He really feels it. Deeply. He can't imagine life without Jackie.

Smiling, she whispers the same words back.

* * *

When the table is cleared, he tilts his head toward the door and says, "How 'bout we grab the check and get outta here."

Jackie says nothing. He wonders if the restaurant din is getting to her, too.

Jackie's eyebrows arch. "Rick, you're so uptight. I can see it in your body. If your shoulders were hunched any higher they'd be at your ears. I know you've been going through hell lately, but you're as taut as a wire."

"You're right. I'm not just worried about myself. I'm worried about you, too. And Katie. Maybe even my mother. We don't know who's behind those hang-ups."

"Honey, we still haven't changed the number."

"I know. I'll call the telephone company tomorrow. But we shouldn't be out tonight. Not until the cops locate Mike Brock."

"Rick, we don't even know if it's him. And we can't stop living because someone's been calling and hanging up on us."

"We have to do everything we can to stay safe."

"Like what? You wanted me to take a taxi to work every day and I'm doing that. You're taking a car service to the office. What else can we do? Go back to that detective . . . Howell?"

"It's too dangerous being out tonight. We could have ordered in some food. We're taking an unnecessary chance. And it's Saturday night. We'll never catch a cab to get back home."

"Rick, I know this has all been horrible . . . your father and that Harper thing. Believe me, I appreciate how it's affecting you. I really do. Anything that troubles you gets to me, too. But you've got to try to get a better handle on this. I know you're not sleeping."

"I'm fine."

"I know you get out of bed at two or three in the morning. I hear the medicine cabinet open. I know you're taking those pills."

"It's just to get some sleep."

"Honey, those things are addictive. Don't you think you ought to see someone?"

"Who?"

"You know a few psychiatrists at the hospital. I think you ought to be under supervision to help with your sleep."

"I don't want to do the Rent-a-Friend thing. I can medicate myself."

"And you've been so edgy. I think you need a little help, at least for a while. Maybe we can both see someone."

"Honey, it's nothing that can't be handled ourselves. And it's only a matter of time until the detectives locate Brock."

The muscles along her jawline tighten. She's annoyed.

Another glance at the bar area.

The thug turns away.

Was he just looking this way? But if someone's gunning for me, would he look so obvious? Wouldn't it be someone who fits in, a guy who looks harmless?

"Okay, Rick, let's leave."

He knows he's been straining Jackie's tolerance.

I gotta straighten up and fly right.

Catching the waiter's attention, Rick makes the air-scribble sign for the check.

Darren nods, reaches for his pad.

Rick grabs another peek at the bar.

The barstool is empty, and Rick catches a glimpse of the guy heading for the door.

* * *

Walking back to the apartment, Rick feels like he's trudging through a blurred nightscape. Is someone lurking nearby, waiting to gun him down the way Robert Harper was taken out? A river of people flows along the avenue—in both directions—but there's not a hint of anyone with bad intentions.

Passing restaurants and storefronts on Second Avenue, Rick scans every passerby. *Yes, Robert Harper and Dad were gunned down from behind.* He realizes he's amped beyond anything even remotely rational. *Am I going nuts, getting paranoid? No, that bastard Mike Brock is out there and if it's not him, it's someone else . . . just waiting.*

Now Rick just wants to get back to the apartment where he won't feel exposed. He's momentarily overcome by the strangest feeling; it's as though he's outside himself, floating high above the crowd streaming along Third Avenue.

When they get home, he nearly collapses on the couch from tension.

He knows there's no way to beat back the dismal reality of things right now. The last few weeks have told him all he needs to know: his life is in danger. Maybe Jackie's, too. And if it's Mike Brock or one of his cronies, Katie's in danger, too.

And that son of a bitch Mike Brock is walking around a free man. Somewhere. And Nager and Callaghan can't find him.

CHAPTER TWENTY-EIGHT

ON SUNDAY, RICK and Jackie join her Scarsdale cousins, Mindi and Alan, for a late afternoon dinner at Crabtree's Kittle House in Chappaqua.

The dining room is spacious with tables set far apart and napped with heavy linen. The place settings are tasteful and elegant. It's a telling contrast to Lombardi's and the glut of eateries dotting Manhattan's East Side. Many of those trendoid joints serve *Nouveau* American food composed of weird concoctions decked out in an "architectural" style that's just too pretty to eat.

Rick feels more at ease than he has at any time since his father's death. He realizes he's enjoying a leisurely meal—not the Eat-and-Get-Out tempo of Lombardi's and its ilk—amid a subdued Sunday afternoon suburban crowd.

He orders a thick slab of prime rib—medium-rare, red, and juicy—along with baked potato stuffed with sour cream and bacon bits and a Caesar salad to start, the whole cholesterol-laden, artery-clogging works. All followed by profiteroles and espresso. To hell with worrying about his coronary arteries or his blood sugar. Life's too short.

For a welcome change, his thoughts aren't fixated on Robert Harper, Nager, Callaghan, and murder. He's not even dwelling on thoughts about Mike Brock. There's no sense of menace thrumming through him as there had been at Lombardi's.

He didn't pop a Xanax last night, yet caught a half-decent night's sleep.

Driving home, Rick thinks maybe—just *maybe*—the shock of his father's death might be easing up. And Jackie's right: they're doing everything possible to stay safe. Maybe he can begin enjoying being with relatives and friends without wanting to sequester himself from the world. Cruising down the Henry Hudson Parkway, he's not holding the steering wheel in a death grip. He and Jackie sing along to Van Halen's "Right Now" blasting from the radio. For the first time in weeks, Rick hasn't thought of Dad's murder for the better part of an afternoon.

Exiting the West Side Highway at the Seventy-Ninth Street Boat Basin, he drives through Manhattan streets, entering the Eighty-Sixth Street Central Park transverse, and exiting at East Eighty-Fourth Street and Fifth Avenue. Nearing Lexington and East Eighty-Fourth, Jackie says, "While you park the car, I'll run into Gristede's and pick up something for dinner."

After dropping Jackie off, Rick cruises down the ramp to the building's underground garage. He presses the remote on the sun visor. The automatic door clatters upwards. An electric eye triggers it to close once the car's inside the garage. He drives to the far end of the enclosure, pulls into their reserved space, gets out of the car, and locks up. He glances about: lots of cars, no people.

The garage is dimly lit; the air is dank, smells of motor oil, exhaust fumes, and damp concrete. The Chevy's engine ticks steadily as it cools.

Walking toward the elevator, an eerie feeling invades him. It's like when he was six and imagined a monster lurking beneath his bed. If he slipped beneath the covers before the count of three, the thing couldn't drag him under. It was a kid's attempt to overcome imagined danger, but he nearly shudders at the recollection.

Striding toward the elevator, he hears a sound.

He stops, then turns and peers into the dim recess at the far end of the garage.

Nothing but rows of parked cars in the underground gloom.

About to turn toward the elevator, he hears a metallic clicking sound.

Is it the sound of the car cooling down or is it something else?

Now there's an eerie hush. Squinting, he peers into the semi-darkness. For a vertiginous moment, he hears only the thrumming of blood in his ears.

"Anyone there . . . ?" he calls. His voice echoes in the expanse.

Only shadows and silence.

It's a heart-freezing moment as a cold sensation seeps from his chest down his arms and into his fingers. He waits, hears nothing more.

About to turn and walk to the elevator, a pang of doubt seizes him. *Did I just hear something else?* A fluttering begins in the pit of his stomach. He wonders if he's so juiced he's now imagining things. Is he so primed, so charged he's magnifying ordinary sounds? Has stress sent his mind careening out of control? Maybe he *should* see a shrink.

Trust your gut. Always.

Now, the lighting seems brighter than it was a second ago. A power surge? In the middle of winter? That's ridiculous. And then, suddenly, he feels himself distant from his surroundings as though he's seeing things through binoculars turned backwards. Dread seeps through him.

He makes a visual sweep of the garage—cinderblock walls, overhead ductwork, a series of sprinkler outlets, crisscrossing pipes and cables, low-wattage light bulbs encased in wire cages, electric meters, no surveillance cameras. He hears only the barely detectible hum of a ventilator. Nothing else. But he can swear he heard something from behind.

He decides to wait.

He stands stock still, hovering between fear and calmness. An eddy of dank air wafts across his face and the little hairs on the back of his neck stand on end. His mouth goes dry, his scalp tingles.

A roar erupts behind him.

Panic—a neural blast floods him, and in that moment, there's an adrenaline-fueled priming of every nerve in his body making his heart jump, his muscles twitch, and his stomach drop.

The garage door ratchets upward with a rumble.

A tan sedan cruises down the ramp, eases its way into the garage. It's Warren and Nina, their neighbors from two floors below. The guy's a psychiatrist; she's a social worker. Nina waves as they pass him and Warren eases their Corolla into their assigned spot. They get out of their car.

In a state of gut-sick weakness, he greets the couple. Walking with them to the elevator, he feels drained; his legs are rubbery and his feet seem like they're miles from his body. The adrenaline surge is dissipating. He's depleted as though he can barely stand. Engaging the couple in conversation, Rick tries to tamp down the trembling in his voice, to act as though everything is normal. There's not a hint of anything said about his father's death. Trying to appear casual, Rick knows he's faking his way through the encounter.

Warren presses the elevator button. Nina's eyes narrow as she peers at Rick's sweat-slathered forehead.

The elevator stops at the tenth floor.

There's a mumbled goodbye as the couple gets off at their floor.

The elevator stops at the twelfth floor.
He steps into the hallway and heads toward the apartment.
What he's going through is beyond grief.
It's something else, and it's not going away.

CHAPTER TWENTY-NINE

When you're scoping out a kill, you familiarize yourself with the target and the terrain.

It takes a lot of groundwork. Lots of preparation for a surefire kill.

On a cold Sunday afternoon in December, East Eighty-Fourth Street was deserted—there was hardly a soul on the streets because of a nasty wind whipping in off the East River.

But it was a perfect day for reconnaissance.

The building is on the corner of East Eighty-Fourth and Third Avenue. It's a potential kill zone. While standing on the corner and scoping things out, a car turned onto the ramp leading to the below-ground garage. Moving down the ramp and getting into the garage before the corrugated door rolled back down was easy. Once in there, I crouched behind an already parked vehicle. The driver parked his car, got out, and walked to the elevator.

It looked like a perfect place for an ambush—dimly lit and deserted. Rick Shepherd has a reserved spot in the garage. But there was no sign of the blue Chevy Malibu. Meaning he was away, not in the building. There was no way to know when he'd get back. If his car had been in its parking spot, it would have been easy to take the elevator upstairs to his floor.

And then ring the apartment bell, wait until he opened the door.

And Boom.

But I purposely left the gun at home. This was a dry run. Preparation, preparation. That's key. It won't be like it was when I shot down that guy on Seventy-Ninth Street by mistake. This one will be planned, executed cleanly and accurately.

Suddenly, the garage door rose again.

Another car rolled down the ramp.

Ducking behind a parked vehicle was the only thing to do.

It was the Chevy Malibu.

And who got out of the car? Rick Shepherd. Alone. Not another soul in sight.

He was an easy target.

But without the gun, staying hidden was my only option.

By not having the gun, I blew my best chance of taking him down.

Forget a garage ambush. Too many unknowns that could prevent the kill.

The telephone calls have revealed a great deal about his schedule. But the problem is where to make it happen.

Tracking the father from Cranberry Street to East Nineteenth was easy. It just meant waiting outside the house until he left to make a house call. The kill was in the lobby of a building on a deserted street in Brooklyn. It was a piece of cake.

In Manhattan there are too many people, too much activity. It's not a good kill zone.

There has to be a better place to get him.

CHAPTER THIRTY

RICK KNOWS IT'S high time for him to do something.

No more sitting around, waiting for hang-ups. And no more wondering when the cops will locate Mike Brock or some other asshole who's targeting him.

He knows Jackie's putting the finishing touches on that mega-deal and won't be home until after eleven tonight. He has plenty of time to do what must be done.

Though traffic is heavy at five thirty on Third Avenue, Rick knows it shouldn't be hard to hail a taxi. He walks around the corner and waits in front of the sports bar, and it's only a few seconds later when a taxi pulls up and disgorges its passengers.

"Bleeker and the Bowery," he tells the driver.

He can't depend on Nager and Callaghan. For them, this is just another homicide. For Rick, it's his father. And possibly his own life is at stake. When he locates Brock, he'll phone it in to the detectives. *I know where that scumbag hangs out. When I find him, it'll be tough to keep myself from strangling that son of a bitch.*

* * *

Aside from the bone-chilling cold, the early darkness of December days is one of the main reasons Nager hates winter.

At nearly six in the evening, the streetlights at the intersection of Bleeker and the Bowery make for an eerie gloaming. Nager gazes at a row of four-story tenements—grime-laden, splotches of dried pigeon shit everywhere and with a latticework of fire escapes and graffiti-covered, gated storefronts. The sidewalks are littered with shattered glass, discarded candy wrappers, and cigarette butts. Black plastic garbage bags bulge near the curb. The air feels grimy. It's a city in senescence.

Liz parks the sedan on Bleeker next to a fire hydrant. She lowers the visor displaying the NYPD ID. They get out and walk toward the club located where Bleeker T-bones the Bowery. Except for a group of young people clustered in front of the place, the street is deserted, eerie-looking. Traffic is light on such a cold night.

"What the hell does that mean?" Nager asks, pointing at the white awning with red lettering.

"CBGB?" Callaghan asks with a laugh. "It stands for Country Blue Grass and Blues. This is the home of punk rock . . . you know, alternative music."

Nager laughs. "Alternative music? Jesus, I'm outta the loop. The doo-wop songs from the fifties are still my thing. You know . . . stuff with real melodies . . . like what the Platters used to sing."

"God, you're such a cornball," she says as her lips curl into that incredible smile.

"I plead guilty."

A bunch of grungy kids—late teens, early twenties—loiter near the club's entrance. Punk rockers sporting the expected ensemble: body piercings—in their ears, noses, and lips—studded belts, hair spiked with gel, and a guy with a Mohawk haircut. One kid has so many rings in his ear he looks like a fucking clarinet. The kids giggle, sniggle, and snort amid a cloud of smoke. They're stoners sucking on blunts, shit-faced, numbed-out.

Inside the club, the walls are awash in a garish veneer of graffiti. Every square inch is covered with multi-colored renderings of spray paint, Day-Glo stickers, Magic Marker scribbles, and brightly colored ink of every kind—most illegible, some profane—an insane mélange of etchings, scratchings, and scrawls.

The place is pretty much empty, probably won't start filling up for a few hours. Nightlife here begins late and lasts until early morning. Nager's certain that once the live music starts, the decibel level will be stratospheric. He wonders if he'd been born fifteen years later, would this be his thing—alternative music in all its discordantly raw power, hanging out in clubs like this and smoking dope, the whole punk rock-grunge-I-Don't-Give-a-Shit-and-Fuck-the-World thing? It's tough to imagine, but maybe if he'd inhabited a different time he'd be a different person today. Like so many things in life, it's unknowable. *What if . . . what if?*

Once past the entranceway, he's astounded. Someone familiar is approaching the bar. It's Rick Shepherd.

Liz sees him at the same time and raps her hand against Art's arm. "Look who's here," she says in a voice more laced with annoyance than with surprise.

Liz moves quickly toward the bar and intercepts Rick. "What're you doing here?" she asks.

"I thought . . . I'm asking around for Mike Brock," he says as his face pales. He's obviously surprised to see them.

"What're you, Columbo?" Liz says in a voice laced with sarcasm.

"I didn't think you guys would be here. I mean—"

"Listen, Rick," she says, "the next time we need help with a case we'll give you a call, got it?"

"Yes, but—"

"But *nothing*," she cuts in. "You're sticking your face where it doesn't belong. So get lost and let us do our job."

"I'm sorry . . ."

Nager takes Rick's arm and edges him toward the exit. "Listen to me, Rick," he says. "I know how you feel. I understand the pain you're in. Believe me, I do. I know you want us to nab this guy, but you're not helping. You're only getting in the way."

"I didn't think you guys would come here. After all, you're in Brooklyn. I'd have called you if I spotted Brock and—"

"I understand, but just go home," Nager says, setting a hand on Rick's shoulder. "We'll find him."

"I get it. Sorry for butting in."

"If we don't locate him in the next few days, we're gonna put more detectives on the case. Believe me, Rick, this one's high priority."

As they shake hands, Rick says, "You promise?"

"I promise. It's only a matter of time before we get to Brock."

Looking sheepish, Rick heads out the door.

*　*　*

Nager and Callaghan approach the bartender—a gaunt, young guy with gelled hair and a rhinestone embedded in the side of his nose. His matchstick-thin arms make circular movements as he wipes down the bar top.

"We're trying to locate Mike Brock or a guy named Knucks," Nager says, flashing his badge. "We understand that Brock sometimes has a gig here."

"Not anymore," says the barkeep. "He got into a huge argument with the manager. Last I heard, he might be at Alcatraz . . . St. Marks and Avenue A. Knucks should be there, too."

CHAPTER THIRTY-ONE

ALCATRAZ SITS ACROSS the street from Tompkins Square Park, ground zero for the East Village drug scene.

It's junkie turf where drunks, drifters, and addicts camp out, drink and shoot up, and lay waste to their bodies. Nager expects to see needles, syringes, and empty bottles littering the street. But there are none. The Sanitation Department must've made a recent sweep of the area.

A clutch of choppers is angle-parked beneath a NO PARKING sign. Yeah, Brock's posse is here. An offshoot of Hell's Angels, they think they own these streets; they're Rulers of the Road. Rumor has it these guys haul drugs down from Canada by crossing through Indian reservations near the U.S.-Canadian border, but that's for the State's Narcotics Division to deal with. Not NYPD homicide detectives.

Nager and Liz enter Alcatraz. It's dimly lit, dilapidated, and saturated by the sour smell of malt, sweat, and cigarettes. Willie Nelson's version of "Always on my Mind" plays on an old-fashioned jukebox. *What a dump*, Nager thinks.

A motley bunch of guys—maybe ten of them, with bushy beards, long hair, doo rags, and lots of leather—are bellied up to the bar. Rough-looking dudes, they're covered in ink—swastikas, skulls, dragons, axes, and crosses—the whole Nazi-biker thing.

Alcatraz . . . the right name for this fucking dungeon.

Nager's pulse ramps up to cheetah speed. For sure there's gonna be trouble with this crowd.

Heads turn in their direction. The bikers stand stock still, in silence.

A whole bunch of eyeballs laser in on them.

Especially on Liz.

In the midst of the hush comes a murmur. "Gimme some of *that* pussy."

* * *

Liz's eyes swerve left, then right. She's trying to pinpoint the coward who mumbled "pussy." She's sure these guys find their courage in a bottle. Or a joint. Any mind-altering substance will do. And when they outnumber you, ten against two, trouble is definitely brewing. Any one of them alone would cave like a whipped puppy. Just looking at these guys makes her skin crawl. But dealing with people like this goes with the territory.

* * *

Hearing "pussy," Nager feels his pulse throbbing down to his fingertips.

"Yeah, that's hot stuff," one biker mutters as he leers at Liz.

When Liz shoots the guy an icy stare, he averts his eyes.

The air thickens with hostility; Nager's heart batters his chest wall and his fingers begin curling into a fist.

Someone pulls the plug on the jukebox.

There's complete silence.

This is trouble. Liz knows what to do if things go south.

"Mike Brock here?" Nager asks, modulating his voice so it doesn't sound aggressive; no need to get into a pissing contest with these humps.

"Who wantsa know?" snarls a huge guy. He moves toward Nager. He's gotta be six-six, maybe taller, probably tips the scale at a good three bills. He has a mountain-man beard, reddish in color with dried egg yolk solidified in the hairs bristling near the left side of his mouth. He wears a camo doo rag and a military vest over a khaki-colored short-sleeved t-shirt. His slab-like arms sport a swarm of red and blue tattoos.

Gotta be Knucks, has tats on his knuckles. Fucking guy's elephantine.

Nager tries not to stare too intently. He knows he's gotta maintain an air of authority but can't let this morph into a testosterone tournament. Not with these shitweasels.

Knucks edges closer. The guy's breath reeks of booze and butts.

"I'm Detective Nager, NYPD," Art says, showing his badge.

"And who's this?" Knucks asks. His eyes do a slow crawl over Liz.

"This is Detective Callaghan," Nager replies. "Mike Brock here?"

"I'm Mike Brock," says a dope-thin guy with blondish hair pulled back into a skanky ponytail. No beard, just a four-day stubble, has pale blue eyes, long sideburns, and sharply etched features. He too is covered with Nazi ink. Spider webs are tattooed on his neck.

"Why don't we step outside, Mike?" Nager says.

"Whatever you gotta say to Mike, you say in here," Knucks growls.

Leaning in and down, Knucks's face is inches from Nager's. His nose is dotted with black pores; a nest of dark hairs protrudes from each nostril. Guy's like a fucking dog marking his territory.

"Back off," Nager says.

"You gonna make me?"

* * *

Liz feels the hairs at the back of her neck stand.

This is definitely going to be a problem.

Her eyes focus on both men. Knucks has shuffled so close to Art they can probably hear each other's heartbeats. Their eyes are locked in death stares. It's as though nothing else exists in each guy's world but the other one. Liz senses a charge in the air between them, the way it feels when a thunderstorm is on its way.

There's something hard about Art right now; she can almost feel a dark energy radiating from him; it reminds her of Dad when he told her about confrontations with perps. She realizes her right hand has moved closer to the service pistol sitting in the holster beneath her jacket. If it happens, this will be the first time in her career she's had to draw her gun.

There's a first for everything.

* * *

Holding Knucks's stare, Nager says, "Hey, big man, we can make life tough for you, but we'd rather not. It's up to you."

Knucks' face curdles into a frown. He's unsure how to play this but can't back down in front of his posse.

Nager feels a buzz in his chest. With this guy so close, he could headbutt the fucker, crack his nasal bones, send him to the floor with pulp for a nose. If the bastard makes the slightest move, Nager's knee'll shoot up into his nuts and this tub of shit will jackknife to the floor. If the others come at him, he'll whip out his service revolver and threaten to waste every one of them. And Liz will pull her weapon, too. He's sure of it.

Nager feels an almost irresistible urge to do something to this Knucks character. Is it because Liz is here and it's a chance to show her he's got a pair?

Doesn't matter; Liz or no Liz, this honcho needs a righteous beatdown. But in a tenuous act of self-control, Nager mutters, "Just back off, big guy."

Nager holds Knucks' glower, feels his own temperature rising. His eyes burn from the intensity of the stare-down. But he doesn't blink.

The air's so thick it feels like mucilage.

"Hey, guys . . ." says the bartender. "Let's just cool it."

"Yeah, Knucks . . ." Brock's voice borders on a wimpy whine. "Lemme talk with the cops."

Knucks ogles Liz. His eyes drop to her breasts. "What's your name, sweetheart?"

"You know my name," she says.

Nager's astonished by Liz's voice. It's steely; no quivering. She won't take any shit from this rancid side of beef. She's even tougher than he'd thought.

Feeling a stab of anger—or is it jealousy?—Nager stifles the urge to move closer and slam his skull into Knucks' nose, break open his face.

Jesus, am I insane? I'm a cop, not some punk looking for a brawl.

Knucks backs away. Gradually.

Now, Nager's in cool-down mode. His heart slows, his body uncoils.

Turning to Brock, he says, "Let's step outside, Mike."

Brock casts a questioning look at Knucks.

The big man nods his assent.

Walking out the door with Brock in the lead, Nager feels a bunch of eyes drilling into his back. If these guys come outside, he'll draw his pistol and threaten to shoot every one of them.

CHAPTER THIRTY-TWO

ONCE THEY'RE OUTSIDE, Nager says, "You're a tough guy to find, Mike."

"Here I am."

Nager senses Brock's trying to man up, like he can tough it out. But he's certain the guy's a wuss.

"Where're you staying now?"

"A friend's place on Avenue C."

"Where exactly on Avenue C?"

"One fifty-three. Why? What's up?"

"What's up is I wanna know where you were the night of November fifteenth."

"What's this about?" That semi-whine returns to his voice.

"As if *you* don't know . . . that's the night Dr. James Shepherd was shot dead."

"What the fuck *is* this? Am *I* a suspect? Ya gotta be shittin' me."

"I asked where you *were* that night." He slams a palm into Brock's chest. "Answer the fucking question."

Brock stumbles back, regains his balance. "What the *fuck*. You have no right—"

"Maybe you'd rather answer the question at Brooklyn Command," Nager cuts in. "We can head there right now."

"Hey, man . . . no need for that. Okay, okay. Where was I? Lemme see . . ." he murmurs, brings his hand to his chin, pretends he's retrieving a memory. "Oh yeah, I was playin' backup at the Mudd Club."

"Where's that?"

"White Street."

"You remember that night . . . specifically?"

"I had a gig the whole month. You can ask the manager."

"What's his name?"

"Joe Cantwell."

Liz scribbles the name in a small pad.

"How late did you work?"

"'Til two."

"Any breaks?"

"Twenty minutes here and there. What's goin' on? I had nothin' to do with—"

"You didn't like the doctor, did you?"

He shrugs, shakes his head. "Prick thought I wasn't good enough for his little princess. Oh, *now* I get it. That bitch Katie put you onto me, *right*?"

"Actually, Mike, a friend of yours at CBGB told us where to find you. Tell us about your trouble with the doc."

"I *had* no trouble with him. I had nothin' to do with the guy. In fact, when Katie was stayin' at her folks' place, I'd pull up on my bike and she'd meet me on the street."

Brock taps a cigarette out of a pack of Camels, slips it between his lips, thumbs the lid of a Zippo, and lights up. He sucks in a long draw, lets smoke out in a bluish cloud that's blown away by the wind.

"When was the last time you saw the doctor?"

"Who knows? Six months ago, maybe more. He was standin' in front of the house when I pulled up."

"Don't lie to me, Mike. We know where you've been," Nager says, hoping an insinuation will force Brock to walk back his denial.

"What the fuck. I been nowhere near the guy."

"What about that run-in with Kate's brother?"

"*That?* C'mon, man. It was a long time ago and it was nothin.'"

"Nothing?" Nager growls. "He pushed you around; said he'd beat the shit outta you if you ever touched his sister again. You call that *nothing?*"

"Shit, that was a couple a years ago. I ain't seen the guy since then. And like I said, I had nothin' to do with the father. What the *fuck* . . . ?"

"You get your jollies slapping women around, Mike?"

"I admit it . . . I lost my temper a few times. But I'm not a violent guy."

Brock sucks on his cigarette, expels another cloud of smoke, then tosses the butt to the ground, crushes it beneath a studded motorcycle boot.

"How about that job painting houses, Mike? The one in Brooklyn on Rugby Road."

"What about it?"

"Why'd you break into that house?"

"*What?* I didn't break into *nothin'.*"

"Don't bullshit me, Mike. We know what you did."

Brock's eyes widen. "I was never *in* that house. It was an outside job."

"We talked with the foreman. He told us how you'd show up stoned, that you were a shitty worker. Where'd you get that Wilson Pro?"

"Huh? Wilson . . . *what?* What's that?"

"You know what it is."

"I dunno what the fuck you're talkin' about." Brock's nose wrinkles and he shakes his head, looks genuinely confused.

"It's a pistol . . . chrome-plated, pearl handle, nine millimeters."

Brock's face crimps into a self-righteous scowl of confusion. "No way. This beats the shit outta me."

Nager peppers Brock with questions; it's machine-gun quick, a barrage of rapid-fire queries. It's clear the guy's gobsmacked by the implicit accusation that he murdered Dr. Shepherd. His eyes look like they're ready to pop from their red-rimmed sockets. Nager's certain the guy wouldn't know a Wilson Pro from a jackhammer. Unless he's another Laurence Olivier, he's as close to telling the truth as a shit-bucket like him can be. Maybe his denials are too vehement because he's such an over-virtuous motherfucker, but he looks genuinely befuddled. Just to be certain, Nager sniffs for the smallest whiff of bullshit.

But he can't pick up a scent.

Okay, maybe he's a hog-riding proto-Nazi who doesn't smell like Clorox, but no way is this guy a killer. Nager's been on the job long enough to know every tell in the book—a hitch in the voice, a dead-eye stare like the guy's a storefront mannequin, even a quivering eyelid— they're all giveaways. The face and voice betray even the most practiced bullshit artist. The eyes, too. The most telling things are hardly ever said with words. And he's seen that *Who me?* look a thousand times. Standing beneath the spill of light from a streetlamp, Nager's gut tells him Mike Brock's not the doc's killer. He's just a shithead who sucks up to that slab of beef, Knucks.

"All right, Mike," Nager says, "don't make yourself scarce, because if you do, we'll find you. And if it comes to that, it won't go well for you. With your pretty face, you'll be in demand at the Brooklyn House of Detention." Nager pokes an index finger into Brock's chest. "You got it?"

"Yeah. I got it."

"And, Mike, make sure that if you move, you let me know. If you don't, you'll be looking at some really bad shit." Nager reaches into his pocket and hands Brock his card.

Brock takes the card, shakes his head and puts out a whiney sigh—a last shot at conveying how insulted he feels—pockets the card, glances at Liz, turns, and heads back into Alcatraz.

*   *   *

Liz is impressed.

She's just witnessed a side of Art she'd never before seen. He's never gone as hard-ass on a suspect as he did on Brock. He doesn't play the good-cop, bad-cop routine where he verbally roughs up a suspect and leaves the more gentle questioning to her. That's stuff you see in the movies, not in real life, at least not with Art. He's a straight shooter. He knows how to question people and get them to open up. For the last couple of months, he's let her do most of the questioning; it's part of her on-the-job training.

But something set Art off tonight. His capacity for confrontation, for violence surfaced, big-time. For a second, she thought she saw his head lean back—slightly—as though he was about to headbutt that elephant, Knucks. If that had happened, the rest of those freaks would have come at them and they'd have been forced to draw their pistols. But Art seemed to know how to read the temperature of the place. He knew how far to push and when to pull back. And one thing's certain: he's definitely got a pair.

Approaching the car, Liz notices Art's breathing so heavily it almost sounds like he's snorting. The guy's pumped, probably from the confrontation with Knucks, and he's doing his best to cool down.

She says, "You don't like Brock for the homicide, do you?"

"Highly unlikely, but you gotta remember one thing about these guys . . ."

"What's that?"

"Bullshit's their first language."

CHAPTER THIRTY-THREE

THE TRAVESTY OF my life started right at the beginning. Father didn't want another kid.

Being born was a complete surprise. For Father.

And if Mom had cared, things might've been different. But she didn't and they weren't. It was like living in a slaughterhouse. Yes, it was emotional slaughter, but I lived through it.

One incident sums up everything. There was the new fish tank I'd bought with my own money—twenty gallons filled with guppies, angel fish, black mollies, and swordtails. It was such a peaceful little world the fish inhabited—far from the horror of everything else.

Then, it happened. Father came into the bedroom, stood at the doorway, and stared at the fish.

"You like them?"

"I love them."

He turned and left the bedroom.

Soon, he was back and stood at the doorway. "You love them . . . ?"

It would have been disastrous for our eyes to meet. Father would take it as a challenge and get violent. I looked down.

He stood next to the fish tank.

Suddenly, a strong odor filled the room.

I looked up. Turpentine was swirling through the water.

The fish shivered, rolled over, convulsed, and died.

I felt disbelief, horror.

The fish tank was another slaughterhouse.

But a single tear would mean a fist in my belly, hard enough to make me vomit. Father would then tell Mom I was sick.

"Remember this . . ." Father said. "Whatever's given can be taken away. That's the lesson of the fish."

The lesson of the fish. Whatever is given can be taken away.

Yes, even life can be taken.

Now, it's time to do what must be done.

James Shepherd is dead, rotting in the ground, and there's only one more thing to do: shoot Rick Shepard down.

CHAPTER THIRTY-FOUR

NAGER HALF-DOZES IN his overstuffed chair, one of the few items he salvaged after the breakup with Ellen.

The television is set at low volume, one step above being muted; *Trapper John, M.D.* is playing. Nager suddenly realizes he must've conked out—it seems like only a minute ago a Miller High Life commercial was playing.

He grabs the remote, turns the set off, glances at the apartment's clutter: a paperback copy of *First Blood* lying on the side table, a few magazines, a bulging laundry bag ready to be hauled to the Suds 'n Duds on Flatbush Avenue, and a cardboard container that once housed a bunch of Roach Motels. It's all flotsam and jetsam, part of the scrap heap that passes for his life.

Jesus, sometimes it feels like his whole existence is little more than just putting one foot in front of the other. He's gotta change things up, like get the hell out of this dump. He doesn't even cook his own meals. Instead, he brings home some take-out shit from any one of the local stores.

Yeah, it'd be healthier if he prepared meals for himself, but he can't worry about that. He'll just do what he does and keep doing it. So, he's living like a slob, the way every single guy lives.

When the telephone rings, he bolts upright.

He clears his throat, grabs the receiver. "Yeah . . ."

"Arthur, you're late again."

It's "Arthur," not "Art." Her voice has that pissed-off tone.

His hand clutches the receiver so tightly, it creaks. "I'm sorry, Ellen. I'll drop it in the mail first thing in the morning."

"That doesn't work, Arthur. Run the check by the apartment first thing in the morning."

"Ellen, I'm on this case. I gotta get to the—"

"Arthur, I need the money for Bobby."

"You know the kid means the world to me. But listen, Ellen, I—"

"Arthur, don't make me call the lawyer."

His pulse goes thready, feels like water's rushing through his veins. "Ellen . . . ?"

"Yeah?"

"When are we gonna stop hurting each other?"

A few moments of silence. He feels a drawing pain behind his eyes.

"Okay, Arthur. Drop it in the mail but *do* it. *Tonight.*"

"All right, Ellen." He lets out a sigh—it's really for her ears. "I'll take care of it."

After a few more words, they hang up. Nager wonders why they ever got married. Why? Because of those nights parked at Gerritsen Beach where they did it in the back seat of the Impala. And she got pregnant. Actually, thinking about it, Bobby was a godsend because the kid's the best thing in his life. How naïve it was to think the sparks with Ellen would last forever.

Bottom line: they stumbled into a marriage that should never have been. Divorce is a bitch. He knows lots of divorced cops. Most are miserable. But if you take a poll, most people are on the low end of the happiness spectrum. Especially cops and docs. Don't they have the highest suicide rates?

Happiness? An ever-receding horizon. Like hounds chasing the mechanical rabbit at the dog track. And what about old Doc Shepherd? When did the sizzle fade from his marriage? He had at least one affair before he met Catherine Donovan. There might've been dozens of liaisons before her. Maybe he ate lead thrown by a jealous husband, or a boyfriend. Catherine Donovan must've been important to him. After all, who else did he have? It had to have sucked—you're sixty-four and living alone, you're estranged from your wife, your daughter has drug problems, and your professional life's draining into the shit-fields. Yup, the doc was beyond a midlife crisis; he was headed for life's Dumpster.

And just who's *really* happy anyway?

Catherine Donovan isn't happy. Nor is Brian Donovan. A son dead from leukemia. That's some heavy shit to carry for the rest of your life. A dead child can toss a marriage on the rocks. God, what if that happened to Bobby? You never get past something like that, ever.

Liz Callaghan gave up on happiness. *I just shoot for content.* If a woman with her looks and brains isn't happy, who the hell is? Are any of the guys at Brooklyn Command happy? If so, it's a well-kept secret.

Maybe *happy*'s the wrong word.

Liz is right: you gotta go for contentment.

Life's about coming to terms with your limitations. You're never gonna pitch like Koufax, sing like Sinatra, or be a detective like Popeye Doyle. So just content yourself with who you are.

Contentment. Nager wonders if Rick Shepherd is content. Poor guy, trying to track down Mike Brock at CBGB. Nager really feels for the guy's agony. He'll be haunted by his father's death for the rest of his life. And how can he possibly feel content dealing with sick and dying patients and their families—all that pain and suffering? Jesus, it's no more than people trying to fight off the big sleep. Some move to Florida—God's waiting room—to spend their so-called Golden Years playing pinochle or going to the dog track or talking about their precious grandchildren. But in the end, they're just staving off the inevitable. Yeah, if you're a doctor, the funeral home's gotta be part of your business model.

But not Doc Shepherd, the father. His business has closed up shop and his troubles are over.

How do doctors—Rick Shepherd included—keep doing it?

How the fuck does Art Nager keep doing what *he* does?

Every day of his working life he rubs elbows with liars, suspects, and snitches—the underbelly of the human species. You lose faith. And if you're not careful, you lose your humanity.

The shit he sees most days is ugly. If it isn't a crack whore dead at the bottom of a stairway, it's some guy who's been blown away in a mob rubout, or a twelve-year-old girl who's been raped on a rooftop, then thrown down an air shaft.

Jesus, I see as much death as Rick Shepherd does. Probably more.

But the victims' families are the worst part of it. They're people collapsing beneath the weight of loss, the kind that'll stay with them for the rest of their lives. He and Liz were talking about it only this morning.

"A murder doesn't just happen to the victim," he'd said. "It happens to a family, too. It leaves a hole in their hearts. Forever."

And right now, it's about the Shepherd family and what they're going through. And he and Callaghan are treading water, just like Art Nager's doing with his life.

Only this evening, while Liz was driving back from Alcatraz, Nager said, "One thing's certain about this case . . ."

"What's that?"

"We're not even close to finding out who shot Doc Shepherd."

CHAPTER THIRTY-FIVE

RICK CAN SEE that Uncle Harry looks exhausted.

The death of his pregnant wife years earlier has taken its toll. And now, added to his despondency is the loss of his fraternal twin brother. The deep creases on his face bespeak years of grief, of sorrow, of resignation. He looks like he's aged even since the day at the cemetery. It's a Willy Loman look, for sure.

Rick's aware that as a fraternal twin, Harry always bore a striking resemblance to his brother who was a mere twenty-eight minutes older than he—two handsome men, tall and distinguished-looking. But not now. Poor guy looks like someone emptied him out. He's a lost soul.

The death of a twin must be tough—it's like a piece of yourself is gone.

"Harrison, won't you reconsider my invitation to stay for dinner?" Mom asks. As if to punctuate her offer, the aroma of roast beef and potatoes permeates the apartment.

"No thanks, Claire," Harry murmurs as he sheds his coat. "I'll have to be going. I've got plans."

Rick's certain Harry's bullshitting his way out of the invitation. He wants to get back to Connecticut where he can sink back into his hermit-like existence.

"What's going on with the business?" Rick asks just to make conversation.

"I'm getting rid of it," Harry answers in a weak voice.

This isn't good, Rick thinks. *The business has been his life since Andrea and the baby died.*

"When did you decide this, Harrison?" Mom asks.

"I thought about it a few months ago. I lost the taste for it . . . just can't do it anymore."

Rick knows when one thing has been the core of your existence, it's gotta be awful when it's gone. The brothers were cut from the same bolt of cloth: they lived lives of near-obsession—his father with his practice, and Harry with the auto parts business. It became his life. The business gave him a reason to put his feet on the floor each morning.

Regret seizes Rick. He should have asked Jackie to take this meeting at her office instead of at Mom's place. They'd have avoided this maudlin family gathering.

Just like I should've thought more about Dad's life draining away from him. Dripping, drop by drop, patient after patient. Headed into oblivion. Just like Harry's.

Idle conversation takes over for a while, then Jackie shoots him a barely noticeable shake of her head. She knows they're putting off what must be done. Finally, she says, "I think we should conclude the transaction."

She always cuts through the bullshit, Rick thinks.

"Oh, yes, I have it here." Harry pulls out an envelope.

Jackie takes the envelope. After extracting a piece of paper and reading it, she says, "It's a straightforward letter of agreement. It states that Claire Shepherd agrees to sell to Harry her interest in Shepherd Automotive for the sum of two million dollars."

With the papers signed, Rick realizes one of the few vestiges of Mom's connection to Dad is now gone. When the house is sold, the last link will be severed.

Harry pulls out another envelope. "I brought a certified check."

Jackie regards the check. "The deal is done."

Harry and Mom embrace and murmur a few words to each other. *It must feel so weird for Mom to be hugging Dad's twin brother.*

She again asks Harry to stay for dinner, but he says, "I can't, Claire . . . I just can't."

Rick walks him to the elevator. Standing in the hallway, Rick asks, "Harry, have you been getting any hang-ups lately?"

"No . . . why do you ask?"

"We've had a number of them lately, especially since what happened to my father, but it's probably nothing."

There's silence for what seems to Rick to be a long time. Harry's eyes are downcast. He finally says, "I wonder how we keep going in this life?"

"Harry . . . we're here for you." With his throat constricting, Rick is about to reach for him, but his uncle enters the elevator, presses the button for the lobby, and turns to Rick. Tears are dribbling down his uncle's cheeks.

The elevator door closes.

CHAPTER THIRTY-SIX

IT WAS ANOTHER long day at the office.

Sitting on the sofa, Rick's legs feel leaden, and he has a tension headache. It began as a feeling of pressure in his forehead, but now feels like a steel band is tightening around his skull.

Jackie's home early. "You look so tense," she says.

"I was thinking about how wrecked Harry looked the other night."

"Imagine losing your twin brother like that," she says, then sighs. "As twins they were together from the beginnings of their lives."

"My father did his best to stay close to Harry, but after Andrea and the baby died, he moved to Connecticut and became a recluse."

Jackie moves closer to him.

"You know what he said when I walked him to the elevator . . . ?"

"What . . . ?"

He repeats Harry's last words.

"My God. Do you think he's suicidal?"

"He just seems so lost."

"Let's face it, Rick, he hasn't been a well man for years."

He nods in agreement. "You know, seeing how down he was made me think of my father. I now realize how depressed he must have been. And I feel lousy about it because I didn't do enough to help him with his practice."

"Rick, your father was lucky to have you, Mom, and Katie. But let's face it, his practice was on life support. It couldn't survive in today's world."

"I could have done more."

"Honey, you tried getting him something with the group. What else could you have done?"

Rick thinks back to the partners' meeting when he asked if there was a way they could bring his father on board as a volunteer.

"How old is he?" Kurt Messner had asked with a smirk in his voice.

"Sixty-four," Rick said.

"Sixty-four? That's *retirement* age. He should be out on the golf course. What's next on the agenda?"

Sensing an impenetrable wall of resistance, Rick decided not to pursue it further.

But there was another way Rick failed his father, one far more telling.

It happened only one day before he was murdered.

And it will haunt Rick for the rest of his life.

CHAPTER THIRTY-SEVEN

LIZ GETS OUT of the sedan in front of 5 Montague Terrace, a four-story brownstone on a tree-lined street near the Brooklyn Heights promenade.

Pressing the doorbell, she hears a Westminster chime inside the house.

When the door opens, Liz sizes up Margaret Bradford. She's a sixty-something woman whose nose looks like it belongs on a mannequin in Bendel's. It's clear she's had plenty of work done. And her smile has probably financed some dentist's house in the Hamptons. She wears black slacks and a beige cable knit cashmere sweater.

The living room with its coffered ceiling has a marble fireplace and is filled with antique furniture. A hint of vanilla hangs in the air; makes Liz conclude a pipe-smoker lives in the house. The aroma is nothing like when her father smoked his Macanudo cigarillos.

When they're seated, Liz decides to ask an open-ended question, one that encourages a free-flowing answer. "Mrs. Bradford, what can you tell us about Dr. Shepherd?"

"It's all such a shock," she says. "My God, you never expect something like this. We socialized with the Shepherds for years. I can only say James was a very charismatic man."

"Meaning what?" Liz asks, hoping she'll ramble on.

"Oh, he could charm people."

"Can you tell me more?" Liz senses there's additional information waiting to surface.

"There was something seductive about him . . ."

"How so?"

"Oh, I don't mean in a *sexual* way," she says. "But . . . it's just that he was so *attractive*. He attracted people—women *and* men. I sometimes wondered if Claire ever got jealous."

"Was there any tension between Dr. Shepherd and the other men in your social circle?"

"Well, there were a few rumors about James . . . that perhaps he was a womanizer."

"Was he?"

"I know he had at least one affair. And some of the women in our group felt that James may have had an interest in them."

Mrs. Bradford spills more as Liz listens. The woman is essentially a back-fence gossip.

"I *do* suspect some of the women would have been happy to *take up* with him."

"To the best of your knowledge, did that ever happen?"

"I doubt it. But when he drank his scotch, he'd say things that could be misconstrued. Don't get me wrong; he was never inappropriate with me."

Liz waits for more.

"I don't want to give you the wrong impression," Mrs. Bradford adds as her eyelids flutter. "But a few years ago, I thought he might've had an interest in me."

"What led you to think that?"

"Oh, James had a way of looking at me. And that smile of his was something to die for."

Liz guesses that despite portraying herself as a model of propriety, Mrs. Bradford is lost in some erotic fantasy about the doctor. And maybe some of the other husbands had reason to resent Dr. Shepherd. But enough for murder? Who knows?

"How did Mrs. Shepherd react to his seductiveness?"

"To tell you the truth, there were times when you could see she hated it."

"Like when?"

"Certainly, after James had that affair."

"Who was that with?"

Mrs. Bradford inhales and shakes her head. "It became common knowledge in our group of friends that he was involved with Patricia Griffin, a neighbor here in Brooklyn Heights."

"Is Ms. Griffin married?"

"She's a divorcee."

"When did that happen?"

"Oh, about four or five years ago."

"Where's her ex?"

"He's in California. I believe in Santa Monica."

"Do you have her address here in the Heights?"

Mrs. Bradford goes to her Rolodex and recites it. Liz says nothing, again inviting Mrs. Bradford to elaborate.

"I'm certain his affair made Claire feel devastated. It was bad enough that he put his practice above his wife's happiness, but his cheating was the last straw. Claire could accept their never going on vacation, or all the times he went out at night on house calls, but the affair made her feel worthless, like she didn't measure up."

"Any idea why the Shepherds never got a divorce?"

"According to Claire, James wanted to reconcile, but she refused."

"Do you know if there was an inheritance Claire might have come into?"

"Exactly what are you implying, Detective?" She cants her head.

"I'm just being thorough, Mrs. Bradford. We have to look at every possibility."

"You'd have to ask Claire about that."

"Were there arguments about money?" Liz asks, sensing this question might open a door.

"None that I know of. Of course, I was never privy to their private conversations."

"Can anyone else give me more information about Dr. Shepherd? Friends, acquaintances?"

Mrs. Bradford mentions some names, which Liz writes in her pad. So maybe the doctor was a bedroom buccaneer, Liz thinks, realizing he was a good-looking man, as is the son.

Was one of the doctor's infidelities behind his murder, or was it something else? Liz doesn't have a clue or even the slightest hunch.

JANUARY 1983

CHAPTER THIRTY-EIGHT

OVER MESSNER'S OBJECTIONS, Rick is taking the morning off to get his father's Buick out of mothballs and sell it at a used car lot.

After taking the subway to Brooklyn Heights, he arrives at the storage facility on Furman Street. He retrieves the Buick and drives toward the dealership on Flatbush Avenue.

Rick's thought of keeping it, but the car's too drenched in meaning. His father drove it all over Brooklyn, including on the night of his murder. *His skin cells must be on the steering wheel; they're now pressed into mine.* It reminds Rick of holding his father's hand when they went to patients' homes.

There are so many regrets about what happened with his father. After Messner vetoed his volunteering at the office, Rick called Sean McCall, an administrator at Kings County Life. Would the company hire his father to examine applicants before issuing life insurance policies?

"How old's your father?" Sean had asked.

"Almost sixty-five."

"I'm sorry, Rick. We don't hire older doctors. They have subtle hearing deficits and miss low-level heart murmurs. Then we end up footing the bills down the road for deaths linked to heart failure."

A week later, a killer's bullets made it all a moot point.

*   *   *

The used car dealership's office is crowded with stacked *Car and Driver* magazines. The salesman, a potbellied guy with dropping jowls and wearing suspenders, clenches a cigar between yellow-stained teeth. After glad-handing Rick, the guy goes outside to take a look at the Buick.

"Gotta take her for a spin," the dealer says. Rick gives him the car key.

*   *   *

Having returned to the office, the salesman says, "This car ain't gonna be easy to sell. Not with that mileage and it feels like it needs a new suspension." He slips the saliva-stained perfecto past his wet lips and shakes his head.

The guy's full of shit. Rick's certain this swindler's gonna make a lowball offer.

"How's sixteen hunidt do ya?" says the dealer.

Rick's face launches into a mask of disbelief. "Forget it," he says and begins walking out.

The dealer clutches his arm. "Okay, let's make it twenty-two hunidt."

It's warmed-over crap—like the guy's making a major league concession.

"And to sweeten the deal . . . how 'bout we do it in Ben Franklins?"

So, in a cramped office redolent of cigar smoke, the dealer pulls a roll of hundred-dollar bills from his pocket and begins counting. Rick signs over the title.

"I'll take care of the paperwork, the plates, and registration," the dealer says.

Fucking crook.

Heading out the door, Rick knows he'll give Mom the blood money tonight.

*   *   *

Rick catches the Number 5 train back to Manhattan. As the train roars underground, he regrets having sold the car. *Life's too short for all these regrets. I gotta start thinking positively.*

There are the microscope, the fountain pen, the medical books, and the diplomas. They were more a part of his father's life than the Buick had been.

At least that's what Rick tries to tell himself.

CHAPTER THIRTY-NINE

IT'S EARLY MORNING and the squad room is deserted.

The empty coffee container sits on the desk. For sure, the heartburn's gonna kick in any minute. It's a real bummer because it can feel like his stomach's at war with his esophagus. And Nager read somewhere that acid reflux can lead to some lethal shit down the road, like what John Wayne called the Big C. For Art, it'll be esophageal cancer.

Shuddering at the thought, he reaches into his desk drawer, pulls out the roll of Tums, pops two in his mouth. Pildes isn't helping Nager's gut; he's busting ass over the Shepherd case and that can make for a tidal wave of stomach bilge.

Though he's fully caffeinated, Nager is blanketed by an early morning torpor. Without resorting to pills, there's gotta be a way to get a better night's sleep.

The phone rings.

"Detective Nager, Homicide."

"Art, it's me."

"Ellen, I put January's check in the mail."

"That's not why I'm calling..."

It's "Art," not "Arthur" and her voice doesn't have that pissed-off edge. Yup, she's got a favor to ask.

"Will you take Bobby this weekend?"

"So you can spend more time with *him*?" At the *thought* of her affair with Petey Glasses, that small-time hood, heat rises to Nager's face.

"Art, I know you love Bobby and he loves being with you. I promise we'll go back to alternating after this weekend. And you *know* Bobby wants and needs to spend more time with you."

Her voice is so cloying, he feels like throwing up. "You're right, Ellen. He *does* need more time with me, and I'd love to have him . . . more than I do with this shitty arrangement we have."

"Oh, no, Art. *I* have custody and it'll stay that way."

"I'm just asking you to think about it."

There's silence. Nager waits, imagines she's weighing the pros and cons. She'll do whatever's in her own best interest.

"So you'll pick him up on Friday . . . at five?"

"Yes, five sharp, but don't make me wait this time."

"I won't. And thanks, Art. I owe you."

Hanging up, Nager knows he'd love to have Bobby live with him. Pildes would accommodate the scheduling; he's good about those kinds of things.

Maybe this weekend they'll go to Coney Island. The kid loves the bumper cars. If it weren't so cold, they'd hop on the Cyclone with those stomach-turning dips and turns.

Clasping his hands behind his head, he leans back in his chair and plops his feet on the desk. Closing his eyes, he begins drifting away, nearing that sweet edge of sleep. Suddenly, a delightful scent seeps into his brain.

Opening his eyes, he sees Liz sitting at her desk; it's adjacent to his own. Her hair is tied back in a ponytail with a a Kelly-green scrunchie. A strand of hair trails down alongside her face. Is it a look she cultivates—a casual affectation—or was she running late this morning, got herself together quickly, and rushed to the command station? But why's he trying to dope out her routines? He drops his feet to the floor.

She swivels her chair and lasers him with those bottomless blues. "How're you doing this morning, Art?"

"Good, Liz . . . hey, I'm glad you're here. I meant to mention . . . I put in another call to Steve White at Manhattan North. There's no evidence yet linking the Harper homicide to the Shepherd case."

"And I called ATF again," she says. "There's still no Yellow Form for the Wilson Pro. They're wading through boxes of records. They need more time."

"It'll be a dead end."

Brushing that stray strand of hair from her face, she says, "Mrs. Shepherd and I had a long talk. And I went through her bank records. The doctor owned fifteen percent of his brother's auto parts business. She inherited it, and her brother-in-law just bought her out for two million dollars."

"Two *million*?" Nager is astounded. "That could be a game changer."

"So . . . like Pildes said, there *was* money to be made by the doctor's death," Liz says. "But the buyout seems to be completely aboveboard. There were no money issues between her and the doctor. She said he never cared much about making or keeping money."

"Consistent with what the son said."

"Mrs. Shepherd asked to be bought out because she didn't want to depend on her brother-in-law. Apparently, he's selling the business anyway, so it works out for everyone. Bottom line: I don't think she had a thing to do with the doctor's death."

Nager leans forward. "What about Margaret Bradford saying she resented her husband . . . even felt jealous?"

"So what? Is there *any* married couple without resentments?" Liz's eyebrows rise. "Besides, I'm not sure Margaret Bradford's a reliable historian. She had her own feelings about the doctor."

"True enough." Nager sighs and straightens his chair to an upright position. "This case is really getting to me," he murmurs.

"How come?"

"A violent death bums the family and this one's bumming *me* out."

"Art, how many times have you told me never to get personally involved in a case?"

He nods, then hesitates, unsure of what to say next. Then he blurts, "You know, Liz. I lost my father when I was fifteen. It was a violent death . . ." His throat tightens.

He hears Liz's intake of breath.

She fixes her eyes on him. "Art, I don't know a thing about your past."

He decides he's gone this far, so why not open up?

"Pop was into the horses, big-time," he says. "He always walked around with a few hundred bucks in his pocket. One Saturday afternoon, my mother gets a call from the police. Pop was on the subway coming home from Aqueduct.

"According to a witness, some guy comes out of nowhere, pulls a knife, and demands money. Pop was a ballsy guy, so he goes for the knife and the bastard stabs him in the heart. Pop bled out; died on the spot." Nager's voice thickens, then breaks. "It happened just as the train was pulling into the station. According to a witness, when the doors opened, the perp took off."

Nager's voice is quivering. *Jesus, I feel like I could cry. I don't want to do that in front of Liz.* "Later that day, Mom and I went to the morgue to ID the body and pick up his property. There was no cash in his wallet."

"Really?"

"Best guess . . . the uniforms took the money."

"That's terrible," she says as her eyes widen.

At this moment, Nager recalls how he held Mom up while they ID'd the body. And for years, the sight of his father's corpse has replayed in his thoughts. "My father died violently, like Doc Shepherd did. So, I can understand why Rick Shepherd was trying to track down Mike Brock."

She nods. "They ever catch your father's perp?"

"No. The witness barely saw the guy, couldn't give the cops a decent ID."

His thoughts drift to how after his father was gone, Mom's heart failed and despite all the medications, she passed away two years later. So relatives took him in until he was eighteen.

And Nager's kid brother, Paulie—only thirteen when their father was killed—quit school at sixteen. Now, he's a no-tell-motel manager of some dump near the Vegas strip, a minnow swimming with the sharks in Sin City.

Sometimes Nager imagines an alternate life for the family, one where his mother and father are living in Florida, where Pop plays pinochle with his old cronies and where his parents catch the early bird special a few nights each week. In this other universe, Paulie still lives in Brooklyn, is married, has a couple of kids, and works the store that his mother sold after their father died. Even thinking about it threatens to bring on that wave of teenage melancholia.

After the murder, Nager squeaked by in high school and managed to get into Brooklyn College where he graduated with a liberal arts degree. He then entered the Police Academy, became a beat cop, and then made detective.

"Like I said, Liz, murder upends a family."

Nager's gut begins a round of growls, gurgles, and squeaks, so he shifts in his chair to mask the noise. "Hey, Liz . . ."

"Yeah . . . ?"

"I never told that to anyone else, so keep it quiet, okay?"

"Sure, Art. I understand."

The silence seems to last a very long time.

Finally, Liz says, "Art . . . I've noticed that whenever we go to a crime scene, you look pale. Is it because of what happened to your father?"

He takes in a deep breath, then nods. "Yeah . . . it always kicks in and feels personal."

"And meeting with a vic's family . . . ?"

"That's even more personal. But I do it because I know how they feel."

An ache washes over him, but with it comes a strange sense of contentment. Why does he feel this way?

Ah, he knows why. It's now a shared intimacy with Liz, a closeness because he's given over a deeply held secret part of his life to her.

"Is it because of what happened to your father that you became a cop?"

"Yes, it's stayed with me all these years. It'll never go away."

*　　*　　*

Three hours later, Nager and Callaghan are leaving Pildes's office.

In the hallway, Liz says, "He was really tough on you."

"Par for the course," Nager says, nearly reeling from the acerbic tone of Pildes's questioning. "He's getting pressure from above, and the longer this thing goes unsolved, the worse he looks."

Back at the squad room, Nager says, "What really bothers me is the way he spoke to you . . ."

"So, he's a male chauvinist. What else is new?"

"Speaking of which, have you had any trouble with the guys?"

"Not really, at least not here at Command."

"That's a pleasant surprise."

Back at their desks, she says, "Before I made detective there was a problem . . . when I was on street patrol. It wasn't anything major but it was pretty obvious. Whenever a call came in, my sergeant would tell me to wait for backup before going in. So, I asked him, 'Would you tell me to wait for backup if I was a *man*?' He just shook his head and it dawned on him that he was treating me differently from the guys. After that, he stopped telling me to ask for backup."

Nager nods.

There's a moment of silence.

"Hey, Art . . ."

"Yeah?"

"Speaking of being treated differently, what about you and me."

"What do you mean?" His belly growls are suddenly an intestinal symphony.

"Don't partners sometimes go out for a beer?"

"I . . . uh, yeah, I guess . . ."

"Well, we've been together for six months and haven't had a single beer together."

Oh shit, what do I say here?

"If I was *Larry* Callaghan, wouldn't we've shared a few beers by now?"

"I don't know if it'd be appropriate." Nager's toes feel like they're starting to curl.

"What would be *inappropriate* about it?"

"I mean . . . I would . . . I don't know how you'd feel about it . . ."

"Okay, Art. You don't know how *I* might feel, but how would *you* feel?"

"I'd worry . . ."

"About what?"

"Our relationship."

Her eyes have this know-it-all look, like she can read his goddamned mind.

"What does *that* mean?"

"I . . . I'm not sure . . ."

"Why don't we find out?" she says.

Nager feels a wince-worthy fizz of arousal. "Liz, are you asking me out?"

"Don't overthink it, Art." She shakes her head. "Why don't we grab a few drinks sometime? I mean, if you're free."

Through the clog in his throat, he manages to say, "I'm free."

CHAPTER FORTY-

SEVEN OF THE nine partners sit around the conference room table.

Kurt Messner enters the room with his toady, Doug Richards, and drops his bulk into his chair. The air feels as though a fogbank has rolled in. To Rick, the ticking wall clock sounds like it's putting out rifle shots.

Messner's discarded his usual office attire—a white lab coat with his name stitched on the chest pocket. He's wearing a double-breasted suit—probably Armani or Hugo Boss. Messner has more money on his back than Rick spends on clothing in a year.

Scouring the partners with his eyes, Messner's forehead furrows in his signature frown.

Fucking guy burns calories just by scowling, Rick thinks.

"People, it's a new year," Messner says. "If we don't juice things up, we'll go belly-up."

Phil Lauria and Dave Copen shoot quick glances at each other, then at Rick.

"More than half our patients come to see our internists," Messner says, eyeballing Rick, Dave, and Phil. "The geriatric wellness exams are eating up time and money. And the reimbursements are paltry. I'll remind you people again that Ben Franklin said, 'Time is money.'"

Yeah, time is money so I went and bought a Rolex, Rick thinks, and snorts so loudly Kurt can hear him.

"We've gotta speed things up," Messner says, ignoring Rick. "The internists have gotta see four patients an hour."

"Four patients an *hour*?" Rick says, trying to modulate his voice. "It can't be done."

Phil and Dave voice their agreement with Rick.

"It's *completely* possible," Messner says. "We'll drop the prostate exam for men over seventy. Prostate cancer takes years to metastasize. Older men die of other causes anyway."

"We can't play *God*," Maryanne, the group's geriatrician, says.

Messner's face flushes. "Okay, Maryanne, if you want a prostate exam done, refer the patient to Doug. We'll get better reimbursements if our urologist does it."

"Kurt, we're not running an assembly line," Phil says.

Messner rivets Phil with his eyes—it's his Mussolini look. *Fucking Il Duce.*

Rick says, "Kurt, let's call in an engineer with a stopwatch to *really* speed things up."

As though Rick hasn't said a word, Messner turns to the others and continues, "As for women patients, the internists won't do vaginal exams. You'll refer the patients to Sarah. Reimbursements are higher if our Ob-Gyn does a gynecologic exam. We have to cross-refer."

"You mean we should run a self-pollinating practice," Rick calls out thinking, *This guy attended a dictator's workshop.*

"And there's something else," Messner adds, still ignoring Rick. "We won't do any more rectals . . . on *anyone* over sixty-five, male or female."

Phil bursts out, "There'll be lawsuits if a bowel cancer's diagnosed soon after that."

"Just recommend a colonoscopy. If the patients refuse, make 'em sign an AMA form. The reimbursement's higher for a colonoscopy than for a physical . . . *including* a rectal."

Rick says, "You want to put a patient under *general anesthesia* instead of doing a rectal?"

"Yes. And we'll improve things by cross-referring."

"You mean we'll improve our *cash flow*, right, Kurt?" Rick snaps as his stomach clenches.

"That's right. Our cash flow. After all, we're in *business*."

"I didn't become a doctor to maximize billing," Rick says. He knows he's running too hot, that he feels incendiary. But he can't eat this shit sandwich anymore.

"Getting paid is what puts food on the table," Messner says as his face turns venom red. "You'd better rethink your attitude if you wanna stay in this group, Dr. Shepherd."

"There's no need for threats," Phil says with an edge in his voice.

"This is how it's gonna be," Messner snarls. "Otherwise, you'll *both* be tossed."

"You don't get to kick anyone out," Rick calls, almost shouting. "Here, the *majority* rules."

"Okay," Messner says. "We'll vote right now. All in favor of my proposal, raise—"

"Hold on, Kurt," Rick cuts in. "This warrants a discussion. Let's—"

"No, I'm calling a vote, and I'm calling for it *now*."

Dad's voice sounds in his head: *Medicine is a calling, not just a job.*

Shit. Dad's dead and I'm in a practice that's turning into a money mill.

A second. Half-second. That's how long it'll be before Rick loses his shit.

Messner says, "All in favor of my proposal, raise—"

Rick rockets to his feet. His chair topples over and hits the floor and bounces.

Gasps explode from everyone around the table.

Messner's eyes widen in disbelief. "Where the hell do you think *you're* going, Shepherd?"

"This is bullshit. I'm outta here."

CHAPTER FORTY-ONE

GETTING INTO THE sedan, Nager watches as Liz turns the ignition key and heads west on DeKalb toward Flatbush Avenue.

"So we're gonna talk with yet another friend of the Shepherds," she says, glancing at him.

"Yup, and money says it'll get us nowhere."

She shoots him a smile so fleeting he's not sure it was there. Maybe he's reading too much into the most miniscule moments when they're together—an upturned lip, a half-smile, a quick laugh. That's what a promise can do—it raises expectations. Was her asking him out for drinks some kind of promise? Or something else?

When they get together, will it just be two coworkers sharing a few drinks, maybe burgers, some shop talk, the usual back-and-forth between cops away from the workplace? *What . . . were you born yesterday? Don't you see what's happening? One thing's certain: they have plenty in common.*

They both enjoy reading; he's seen paperback novels sticking out of her handbag. And she's a Mets fan—a huge plus. And he's seen her reading movie reviews in the *Post*. So, they both like reading, movies, and baseball. What if she met Bobby? Would the boy resent the fact that Nager's found another woman? Because no woman can compete with a mother.

Jesus, he's getting way ahead of himself. What is he, sixteen again? Excited about a date? That's what it is—a *date*. And he's been thinking about it for days.

It'll just be a casual evening out. What's the best restaurant in Brooklyn? Peter Luger near the Williamsburg Bridge? With all those meat-eating honchos bullshitting, and laughing, they won't be able to have a quiet one-on-one. When they were down at Sheepshead Bay, she mentioned Lundy's, so it's a good bet she's into seafood. Yeah, a fish house could be the way to go.

Enough, enough. Get your head outta your ass. Focus on work.

"So, Liz, where do we go from here?" he asks, staring out the Crown Vic's window.

"I don't know, Art," she says, turning onto Flatbush Avenue. "We have a murder book with the crime scene findings, autopsy report, photos, forensic evidence, a ballistic report, years of the doctor's records, and it all adds up to squat. The interviews have turned up nothing. Brock's a big zero. So far, nothing's come back about that Wilson Pro. I've called Maryland too many times to count. It's all up in the air."

"What about Patricia Griffin . . . the doc's affair?"

"She couldn't add a thing to what we know. That was two years ago."

"And her ex? There are plenty of angry and jealous exes out there."

"They were divorced long before her affair with the doctor," Liz says. "And it all checks out. He lives in California—Santa Monica—and he's a mid-level executive with Universal. And let's face it, Art, Catherine Donovan's a big *so-what*. So's her husband. As for the doctor, we have a wife who left him a couple of years ago. And she inherits a ton of money. But there's no way she's behind this."

"You're sure of that?" he asks.

"Yes, I am."

"Maybe she knew the business was gonna be sold," he says, "and she didn't want to split the money with the doctor. And don't downplay what infidelity can do to a relationship," he says, thinking of Ellen and Petey Glasses. "So maybe she made some kind of arrangement."

"Are you saying she hired some guy who offed him with a Wilson Pro?"

He laughs. "I guess it does sound absurd but aside from saying everyone lies, what else do I always say, Liz?"

"Follow the money."

"So let's do that."

"You think Claire Shepherd wanted the father of her children dead for the money from a business she didn't even know was going to be sold?"

"We don't know that she didn't know about it. After all, the doctor can't tell us what he said to his wife."

"It'll go nowhere. I'm sure of that," she says.

"Pildes will chew us out if we don't follow every possibility."

"My gut tells me it's a dead end." She lets out a quick laugh, then shakes her head.

"It's worth checking out. If she's clean, what are we left with?"

"Nothing," she says.

"And what then?"

"And I'm thinking this one's headed for the cold case file."

CHAPTER FORTY-TWO

THE SON SHOULD have been taken down before the father.

It would've been more traumatic that way. James Shepherd would've suffered and it would've been justice. Justice delayed, but still . . . justice. James Shepherd's in the ground, gone but not forgotten. Besides, it doesn't matter. The son's gonna go down. Soon.

And there's still that voice of Father in his head: "You're worthless. I wish you'd died in the womb. I'd never have been burdened by you." And those words: "Whatever's given to you can be taken away. It's the lesson of the fish."

Yes, nothing lasts forever. Life always ends.

These thoughts keep coming again and again. It's torture. Yes, the mind can be a slaughterhouse.

When Rick Shepherd's dead, it'll be over.

And there's a better way to make sure he dies.

It means a change in plans . . . a change in the killing zone.

It can't be on the street, and it won't be in his building; not in the garage or at his office. It won't be in Brooklyn or Manhattan or anywhere in the city. There's a better kill zone. After all the phone calls and hangups, after tailing him everywhere, there's a simple plan.

I'll lure him to the home of his beloved uncle.

CHAPTER FORTY-THREE

IT'S EIGHT O'CLOCK on Friday evening.

Earlier today, Rick spoke with Art Nager. It looks like Mike Brock's alibi checks out. He had a gig the night of his father's death and a dozen people confirm he was at the club until nearly two in the morning. And there's no evidence implicating any of his cronies. He's not a suspect or even a person of interest right now.

Since he and Jackie changed their telephone number, the hang-ups have stopped. They've only given the new number to Mom, Jackie's parents, and a few close friends.

Callaghan was right. It was a crank who called randomly and kept calling for some weird kind of satisfaction. It's strange how fear builds on itself, takes on an energy of its own. And as it grows, it makes you lose perspective. No matter who the caller was, it's ended.

Jackie's still at the office putting the finishing touches on that mega-merger she's been working on for the last few months. Big bucks, the whole M & A thing means tons of billable hours. That's where the money is—in the law.

Maybe Messner should have been a lawyer. There's that lawyer joke:

Q: Why won't a shark attack a lawyer?

A: Professional courtesy.

There's gotta be a better way to practice medicine than with this fucking group.

As intolerable as Messner was at the meeting, it was stupid to have walked out. Rick knows he'll be canned because Messner has a lock on the politics of the practice. He has five partners under his thumb.

Rick can almost hear Dad's voice: *Your practice is a perversion of medicine. It's time to get out and make your own decisions.*

Things are different from when his father became a doctor. Medicine's becoming corporate with large multi-specialty groups strapped with quotas for profits

Thinking about it is so fucking demoralizing. So he grabs the remote, turns on the television, and begins channel surfing. He's in luck. He finds *The Godfather*, his favorite movie of all time, is playing.

It's the scene where the Don and Michael Corleone are sitting in the garden. Brando and Pacino. Vito Corleone looks forlorn, has downcast eyes and a furrowed brow. His voice sounds weak, fatigued. Reminds Rick of his father's last months of life. And now, of Uncle Harry's dismal existence.

The theme music plays softly—mandolins, flutes, violins—so elegiac. That day at All Faiths Cemetery, with its memories, comes flooding back. A lump forms in his throat.

After the death of Sonny, Michael Corleone has returned to the States and is now a mafia kingpin. The Don's reign is done.

Rick *feels* the flow of emotion between them: the love a father and son have for each other.

Brando saying, *I never wanted this for you. I work my whole life, I don't apologize, to take care of my family. And I refused to be a fool dancing on the strings held by all of those big shots.*

It's sorrow about things done and not done; it's too painful to bear.

Rick grabs the remote, clicks "mute," and with tears welling in his eyes, stares up at the ceiling. The dreams a father has for his son. And the things a son should do for his father.

The lost opportunities, the doubts, the misgivings.

There was that phone conversation only one night before his father was gunned down. Rick aches with regret.

"How're you feeling, Dad?" he'd asked.

No response.

How Rick yearned for the soothing voice of the man who made house calls, night after, night, the father who was a role model, the one he thought of as *The Medicine Man of Brooklyn.*

"Dad, what're you doing these days?" he'd asked.

"Nothing..."

A lifeless voice.

"Dad, you have to get beyond this."

"No one wants to go to an older doctor," Dad said. "I'm an old horse put out to pasture."

"Dad, there's life after medicine. It can't be everything. Why not—"

"Rick, you don't understand..."

"What don't I understand?"

No response.

Rick's eyes filled with tears. At the same time, frustration and a simmering annoyance began mounting inside him. "C'mon, Dad, talk to me."

"There's nothing to say."

"Nothing...?"

Dad's breathing—uneven, labored—was coming in short spurts.

And more silence.

"C'mon, Dad, say something..."

"I have nothing to say, Rick."

"Hey, Dad... let's talk about—"

"There's nothing to talk about."

Frustration led to more than annoyance; it was anger at his father's nihilism, his helplessness, the hopelessness. *"Nothing?"* Rick said.

"Nothing."

"Fine, then we'll talk about *nothing.*"

Rick slammed the receiver down.

And now . . . there's so much regret.

Jesus, why didn't I pick up that phone and call him again?

A wave of anguish washes over him.

Fine, then we'll talk about nothing.

The last words he ever said to his father.

I could have been a better son.

If only there was a chance to redo that call.

But death means no do-overs.

CHAPTER FORTY-FOUR

NAGER MAY COME to regret having gotten what he thought he wanted.

Liz greets him at her apartment door. In contrast to her usual attire, she's wearing a mauve blouse, dark slacks, high heels, and a pearl choker necklace. Her hair is arranged in stunning Celtic braids looped around her head. As she slips into an overcoat, he realizes he's seeing her in a different light than ever before.

Gage and Tollner on Brooklyn's Fulton Street is a vintage fish house from a different era, with gas lamps on the walls, cherrywood framed mirrors, and mahogany tables.

As they talk about Brooklyn, the Mets—she's an even a bigger fan than he is—the beauty of Prospect Park, and their favorite foods, he's aware there's not been a single word between them about Pildes, the Shepherd case, or any other aspect of the job.

* * *

Liz is thoroughly enjoying being with Art in this totally different setting.

Sure, he's the same guy with the ruggedly handsome face, the guy she's been with five days a week for the last six months. Yet somehow, he looks different tonight. It's not just that he's dressed for an evening out, but he's much more animated and relaxed than he is on the job. And as she's always been aware, he's easy on the eyes, but even more so tonight.

Ever since he told her about how his father had died, she's seen him in a different light. He's not the uptight senior detective afraid to crack a joke, which was how she's thought of him. Now, Liz appreciates his vulnerability and knows he's a very complicated man capable of great sensitivity along with an equally strong toughness.

*   *   *

Nager takes in her smile, her laugh, and that profile is just amazing—her nose and that absolutely perfect chin. And those *eyes*—they're incredible: she can smile with them alone, and they have such depth he feels like he's falling into them.

Jesus, what am I getting into?

She says she loves white wine, so they order a bottle of sauvignon blanc.

After a few sips, he feels the beginning of a delightful buzz.

The waiter appears to take their orders.

"How about we share a dozen raw oysters?" Liz suggests.

He's heard somewhere that oysters are an aphrodisiac. Is she trying to hint at something? Art finds himself wondering as he readily agrees to sharing them with her.

He notices Liz has a hearty appetite, and Art enjoys watching her eat dinner with a gusto unusual for a woman with such a perfect figure. She's polished off the filet of red snapper, and is taking the last forkful of the roasted fingerling potatoes. For sure, she'd be a member of the "clean plate club," as his mother used to say when he was a boy.

Being with Liz, the thought of his mother, surprisingly, doesn't fill him with sadness, as it usually does. Instead, he feels an inner happiness, something he hasn't experienced in a very long time.

The combination of delicious food, a second glass of wine, and most especially, the pure pleasure of being with this woman he's fantasized about for months embolden him to ask questions he could never have imagined asking.

"That day we went to see Brian Donovan, you said something that made me wonder . . ." he begins.

"What was that?"

"You said you had only a few happy days and that now, you just shoot for contentment."

"I guess it's all about my never being able to please my father or get his attention. I don't need any shrink telling me what I've known most of my life, but can't seem to be able to do anything about."

She pauses.

He waits for her to say more.

"As you know, Art, my father was a big kahuna in the Detective Bureau. When he wasn't working, he was at a place called Paddy's, drinking. When he was home, he'd spend time with my two brothers. I can't remember ever having him take an interest in me or anything I did. It's fucked up, but that's why I joined the force. I desperately wanted him to *see* me."

"Did your joining the force change that?"

"Not really. But it's the best decision I've ever made. I love the job. I've always gone for guys who were either emotionally unavailable, or treated me like shit. Sometimes, I'd pick a real winner who'd be both. With my track record, I decided not to fool myself into thinking happiness is a possibility. Having a job I really love is good enough for me."

They fall silent.

Art is stunned by Liz's candor and equally by what she's just revealed.

But the silence isn't awkward. It feels right to have a few moments when this shared intimacy can be absorbed, each by the other.

* * *

Liz doesn't feel exposed or foolish, having just divulged as much as she did. Instead, she feels liberated. If she's being honest with herself, she's wanted to open up to Art for a while, especially after he shared the tragedy that changed his life. Intuitively, she knows he's very different from the men who've scarred her deeply.

This quiet moment between them feels like it could be the beginning of a monumental shift in their lives as partners, and possibly more. What started out as a pleasant dinner with a partner from the job has become something deeply personal.

* * *

Art knows not to trivialize what Liz has just shared, nor patronize her by expressing his surprise that any guy could treat her poorly. Instead of talking, he takes her hand in his.

"Let's get the check," Liz suggests, "and have a nightcap at my apartment."

It's only a few blocks from the restaurant to Liz's building.

Once inside her apartment, they move toward each other. They embrace and kiss, deeply, as if each is satisfying a hunger, not only in themselves, but in each other.

When they make love, it's exquisite.

Afterwards, they lie in an embrace, legs entangled, gazing into each other's eyes. Liz settles her cheek on the inside of his upper arm and they share more about their pasts, how they feel in this moment, and about what may come.

Amorously, they reconstruct their first impressions of each other. "I was attracted to you the moment you walked in the room," she whispers. "But of course, I couldn't show it . . ."

"And I thought you were the most lovely woman I'd ever seen. But I couldn't say a thing. I was afraid it would be . . ."

"Inappropriate?"

"Yes . . ."

Laughing, they draw even closer.

"Being your rabbi . . ."

"You might be accused of taking advantage . . ." she whispers.

"Yes. In fact, I thought about asking Pildes to assign you to someone else . . ."

"Because . . . ?"

"Because I was so attracted to you. But I didn't want to see you working with anyone else."

"I'm glad you didn't."

"I am too, but . . . this could be trouble if word spreads."

"So it won't," she murmurs and plants a kiss on his lips.

"It'll be our secret."

They whisper late into the night—the way new lovers do—and in the semi-darkness, he gazes at her face, strokes her hair, runs his fingers over her lips, along the line of her jaw, then kisses her, savors her taste, and the closeness.

He's never wanted to share as much as he does now.

And maybe, just maybe, there might be a future together.

CHAPTER FORTY-FIVE

RICK'S BEEN SPACED out.

He's fallen into a twilight realm, neither asleep nor awake, just seems to be floating in an ether of near-reality. Hearing a sound, he startles awake.

Peering at the muted TV, he realizes *The Godfather* has now moved to the scene where Vito Corleone will chase his little grandson around the sun-dappled tomato patch with an orange peel covering his teeth. Suddenly, the Don will falter, keel over, and die.

At least he wasn't shot down in the night.

Rick grabs the remote, clicks a button, and the screen darkens.

He glances at his watch. Jackie's late; the meeting's taking longer than expected.

When the telephone rings, he's certain it's Jackie.

"Hello."

Silence. Static, crackling, a bumble bee buzz, then a click.

A bad connection. Or is it the caller? Even after they've changed their number?

The receiver is scarcely back on its cradle when the phone rings again.

"Hello . . . ?"

"Rick, dear, it's me . . ." Her voice is quaking.

"Mom, did you try calling a minute ago?"

"Yes, it was a bad connection so I hung up and dialed again," she says in a quivering voice.

"Mom, what's going on?"

"That detective . . . Nager. He called today. He wants to talk to me. I've already gone over it all and it makes me sick."

"Mom, just answer any questions he has."

"I've told that Miss Callaghan everything. They may come to the wrong conclusions."

"The wrong *conclusions*? About what?"

"Let's face it, Rick, it doesn't look good that your father dies the way he did and I inherit his share of the business. Maybe they suspect I had something to do with what happened . . ."

"Oh, Mom, people die and their relatives inherit things."

"Who knows what the police think . . . after all, I've got all this money now."

It's so goddamned sad to hear this.

"Mom . . . they always talk with relatives. They came to my office and the apartment. Both of them . . . Nager and Callaghan. And after they went to see Katie, they telephoned her. It's routine."

He hears her take a trembling breath.

"What good will that do?" she asks. "Nothing will bring your father back."

She blows her nose, then clears her throat. "Actually, Rick, there's something else . . ."

"What's that?"

"I'm worried about your uncle."

"Harry? What's going on?"

"After seeing how dreadful he looked at the apartment, I've called him a few times. But there's been no answer. I've left messages, but he hasn't returned my calls. Something's wrong."

"Mom, something's been wrong with Harry for years."

"He's always reminded me of your father and that practice of his, how much it meant to him. After selling the business, what does *Harry* have?"

Rick recalls his uncle's last words before stepping into that elevator. The guy has a hollow existence.

She sighs. "Rick, please call him, and if you can't get hold of him, will you go up to Darien to see if he's all right?" Her voice is shaky. "Since this . . . this thing with your father . . . I'm so frightened. I just expect something terrible will happen again."

"Okay, Mom. I'll call. And if I can't get him, I'll go up there and check on him."

"I know you're busy, but Darien's not too far," she says.

"I'll go, Mom. But I'm worried about how *you're* doing."

"I'm doing . . . all right, all things considered. It's just . . ." She falls silent.

"Just what, Mom . . . ?"

The words come as though she's dredging them up from a deep well of guilt. "No matter what your father did, he was a good man. He never deserved to die the way he did."

CHAPTER FORTY-SIX

DRIVING TOWARD CONNECTICUT through the Bronx on the Major Deegan Expressway, Rick passes a series of rubble-strewn neighborhoods, with their boarded-up tenements, abandoned cars, wrecking yards, and chop shops.

Passing the looming bowl of Yankee Stadium off to his right, he's reminded of the offer he received after high school from their Double-A farm team, the Columbus Confederates. And of his father's words:

A million guys play baseball, Rick, and you're just one of them. Get a solid profession, not something that'll be over by the time you're thirty.

The road not taken.

Continuing north, the squalor eventually gives way to the pastoral beauty of Van Cortland Park off to his left, and the acre after acre of mausoleums and tombstones of Woodlawn Cemetery on his right.

He realizes his eyes and thoughts are fixated on the graveyard instead of on the handful of early-morning skaters enjoying the park's frozen lake.

It seems to Rick, no matter where he goes or what he's doing, reminders of death are now close at hand.

As a kid, he used to try holding his breath whenever he passed a cemetery. It made his father laugh, especially when Rick would turn blue in the face, as they drove past row after row of the dead, whose final resting places bordered a highway.

Now, his father rests forever, just like those other buried souls.

With the Bronx and the cemetery behind him, Rick approaches the Cross County Shopping Mall. He gets into the right-hand lane and swings off the Deegan and onto the Cross County Parkway, heading east.

He takes that road a short distance to the Hutchinson River Parkway-North. From there, it's a straight shot through Westchester into Connecticut and to his uncle's home in Darien.

Rick's thoughts turn to his uncle. He called him four times last night. There was no answer, not even at eleven o'clock. Each time the answering machine picked up, Rick left a message. "Harry, it's Rick. Please call me when you get this." Assuming Harry didn't know their new number, Rick recited it for him.

At one in the morning, with sleep a distant possibility, Rick slipped out of bed. Careful not to wake Jackie, he padded barefoot into the kitchen where he dialed Harry's number from the wall phone. Again, no answer, so he left another message.

An hour later, he telephoned again.

Something had changed: the answering machine no longer picked up. After ten rings, Rick hung up and dialed again, thinking he might have punched in the wrong number. Again, no pick up. Either the answering machine was out of commission or had been turned off.

He'd thought of calling the Darien Police. But he didn't, and now wonders what held him back. Was it a mistake that might have cost Harry his life? Maybe he'd had a heart attack or stroke. Or he might have tumbled down a flight of stairs and couldn't get to the telephone.

Rick recalls hearing about one of Phil's patients: an eighty-three-year-old widower who was living alone in a huge house. He wanted to stay where he and his wife had raised a family. His daughter called the police after he hadn't answered his phone for two days.

When the cops broke into the house, they found his corpse at the foot of the stairs amid a lake of dried blood. The poor guy fell down a flight of stairs. An autopsy showed he'd fractured his hip and lacerated his scalp. With his life's blood pouring from his scalp, he'd tried to crawl toward the wall phone, but couldn't reach it because of the broken hip. Lying helpless on the floor, the guy exsanguinated.

Bad shit happens when you get older—especially if you're living alone with no emotional supports or friends. Old age can be a slow-motion massacre.

Why hasn't Harry answered his phone? Has he committed the final act of a man who has no reason to go on living? Jesus, that was what he was hinting at when they said goodbye after he handed the check over to Mom. If Rick had called the police, what would they have found that might be different from whatever he'll discover when he gets to Harry's place? If he comes across a body, so be it. There's nothing that could've changed that.

One thing's certain: Harry's not basking in the sun on a chaise lounge at Cozumel. He's never taken a break from the office, not once in all the years since Andrea and the baby died. He and Dad were on the same wavelength: work was the spinal column of their lives. And with Harry selling the business, he has no reason to put his feet on the floor each morning. It's a recipe for disaster.

Those last words of his at the elevator keep playing in Rick's ears: *How do we keep going in this life?* If the guy isn't suicidal, he's damned close to it.

So now, Rick is cruising on the Hutchinson River Parkway, heading toward Darien.

He phoned Phil Lauria before leaving and arranged to have his patients covered both at the office and the hospital. He left word for

Messner: *Hello, Kurt. It's Rick. I'll be gone most of the day because of a family emergency. Phil's covering for me.*

It'll fuel Messner's animosity.

Too bad. Let him throw a shit fit. There are more important things to worry about than Kurt Messner's greed.

CHAPTER FORTY-SEVEN

IN CONNECTICUT, THE Hutchinson River Parkway becomes the Merritt.

The road heading toward Darien is lightly traveled so Rick picks up speed. Traffic heading toward New York City is bumper-to-bumper with commuters making tracks at the peak of rush hour. Gritty-eyed from lack of sleep, Rick negotiates the sharp curves, quick rises, and sudden dips as the Merritt meanders its way eastward through Fairfield County.

On this cloudy morning, the woodlands look bleak, ashen gray. The day is somber, overcast, dreary. It's a leafless winterscape. The air has a bitter January bite—even a wintery smell—as though it might soon begin snowing.

As the Malibu cruises through the slipstream with heat pouring from the vents, a swarm of thoughts streaks through Rick's mind. His staying power in the group is on the short side of fleeting. He'll be tossed from the practice—voted out by a two-thirds majority—that is, if he doesn't quit first. If he's ejected from the group, he can virtually hear the patients saying, *Did you hear about Dr. Shepherd? He was kicked out of the group. I wonder what he did that got him in trouble?*

And if Rick leaves, what kind of practice will he have? He can't work the way Dad did. Solo practitioners are fast becoming fossils buried in the La Brea Tar Pits of the profession. Nowadays, most older docs are retired; they're snowbirds wintering in Florida and returning each spring to be with their adult children and the grandkids.

He could join another group but that would be more of the same, a relentless treadmill of patients where billing and revenue are the driving forces behind everything.

So what does Rick do? Choices. We have choices in life. And there's a choice that must be made. How to practice medicine for the next thirty years?

The question nags at him like a splinter in his flesh.

And there's the other question, the one that eats away at him like acid eats limestone: Why did he become a doctor? Was it to please his father? Katie was right: he was the Golden Boy. Was his becoming a physician "written in the stars"? Was his future preordained?

And after what happened to his father and Robert Harper, will there even *be* a future. Because he can't rid his mind of the notion that some madman has targeted him for death.

As the Chevy's tires hum on the asphalt amid the wind rush, he realizes his thoughts have once again been ambushed by his father's murder. Thoughts of Nager and Callaghan and a Wilson Pro fill his mind along with ballistic tests and Robert Harper and secret safe deposit boxes and clandestine love affairs and Detective Howell and telephone hang-ups . . . they're all part of his life now. Death. Murder.

Yes, someone is still out there.

This shit happens to *other* people, not in your little corner of the world. And it never happens to your family. You watch these stories on the TV news broadcasts or read about them in the *Daily News* or the *Post*. They're on AM radio, 1010-WINS—*You give us twenty-two minutes, we'll give you the world.*

And here he is, driving at seventy miles an hour heading toward Darien to check on his uncle, a shell of a human being who's become even more bereft since his twin brother's life was snuffed out a few weeks ago. What's going on with Harry? One thing's certain: his life is now as dead as roadkill on the Merritt.

As he raises the volume on the radio, Rick can't block out the memories his mind keeps replaying about the arguments his parents had over the money Dad gave to his brother.

James, you went behind my back and gave Harrison all our savings. Why?

Loyalty. I owed him that. He's my brother.

And just what does Rick owe Harry? He owes him what he should have given Dad—attention.

Rick owes Harry commitment and caring, what this son should have given his father.

Yes, Rick wishes he'd been more attentive to Dad—and to his brother—and he regrets that this isn't an ordinary day where he'd be seeing patients while looking forward to an evening with Jackie, not where he's headed to Darien to check up on Harry.

Rick stomps on the gas pedal; the car surges ahead, shoots up to eighty miles an hour. If a cop stops him, he'll tell him he's a physician rushing to an emergency.

Maybe he'll wind up with a police escort.

If that happens, what will they find when they get there?

CHAPTER FORTY-EIGHT

Turning off the Merritt at Exit 37, he heads toward Darien.

Getting to Goodwives River Road, he recalls being on this road en route to visit Harry a few days before beginning medical school. Dad suggested that trip and was doing the driving.

The surroundings look familiar, yet somehow different; back then he saw everything in the hazy light of a late August afternoon. Now it's amid the bleakness of a frigid January morning when he's years older and making this trip alone.

Passing Gotham's Pond, he gets to Long Neck Point Road and continues south toward Long Island Sound. It's a desolate one-lane road situated on a peninsula jutting into the Sound.

He recalls Harry's place is located at the endpoint of Long Neck Point Road, sitting atop a bluff abutting Long Island Sound. There's not another dwelling nearby.

Passing a marsh sprouting tall cattails, he spies Harry's house at the top of a distant hill. The place is so isolated it looks like it's standing at the edge of the earth.

Fittingly, it's the hermitage of a lost soul.

Rick parks at the side of the road, maybe fifty yards from the house. He'll avoid the semi-circular driveway because it's filled with deep potholes.

Despite his sense of urgency, Rick finds himself frozen behind the wheel. It's fear of what he'll find in that house. Another death? At best, a sick and helpless Harry? Instead of jumping out of the car, he stares across the Sound where he makes out the contour of Long Island's north shore. A gray mist hangs over the water, nearly obscuring the coastline.

The sky has a sullen greenish-black hue. Dark clouds tumble in from the sky over Long Island, roil swiftly over the mist-shrouded water. Long Island Sound's choppy surface looks slate gray. The air smells of brine, fish, and seaweed. There's a strong wind and a wintery chill in the air. A few seagulls caw as they struggle against the wind; they're blown backwards and their shrieks dissipate in the air.

And based on the ominous look of the sky, a storm is coming.

Rick gets out of the car and begins walking toward Harry's house. It's a white Colonial with black shutters and a brick chimney at each end; no smoke rises from either one. The place is in terrible shape. Roof shingles are missing. Shutters are loose; two are angled and hang by a single hinge. The clapboard siding is speckled with black mold and strips of peeling paint. Neglect has taken its toll. On the house. Just like it has on Harry.

Rick raises his collar, zips up the jacket, and quickens his pace over frozen grass. For a moment, he's reminded of trotting out to center field during those high school baseball games.

Moving quickly toward the house, he sees cracked windows. A loose shutter on the upper story sways in the wind—first in one direction, then the other—slapping repeatedly against the clapboard siding. Jesus, what a place—right out of a horror movie. *How does someone's life funnel down to this?*

Climbing two steps, Rick stands beneath a small portico set above the front entrance.

The weathered oak front door is secured by rusted hinges. Huddling against the cold, Rick presses the doorbell. No chiming or ringing sound can be heard. Turning, he peers back at the Sound. Gray light plays eerily on the water against dark clouds stacked over the distant shore of Long Island. A far-off roar fills the air—the whine of wind whipping over the waves, speeding shoreward and causing the leafless trees to bend and sway.

Rick presses the doorbell and waits.

Nothing stirs.

He pushes the doorbell again.

Still no response.

The doorbell doesn't work.

He grabs the brass ring door-knocker. It creaks as he raises it and slams it against the door.

Three times.

He waits, listening. Still nothing.

His hand drops to the doorknob.

He's more aware than ever of his reluctance to find whatever's inside.

He twists the knob and pushes inward.

As the door swings open, his legs feel wobbly.

Why would this door be unlocked?

CHAPTER FORTY-NINE

ENTERING THE HOUSE, the door creaks loudly behind Rick as he closes it.

The sound of the wind is now muted to a low-level moan, an eerie backdrop that makes Rick feel even more wary than before. He stands in the entranceway, a rectangularly shaped foyer. The smell of mold is overwhelming. But there's no stench of a body decomposing. A tickle begins at the back of his throat. It intensifies. He gags, coughs up phlegm, swallows it, then clears his throat.

A dust bunny rolls over his shoes. The place is filthy, reeks of neglect.

"Harry?"

Rick's voice echoes off the bare walls.

No response.

"Harry, you home?"

There's silence, but for the muffled sound of the wind keening past the sides of the house. The place seems unoccupied, but Harry's gotta be here. It's inconceivable he'd go somewhere and leave the front door unlocked. And the house is heated. So it's obvious: someone's here.

"Anyone home?"

No answer.

Glancing up, Rick notices strips of peeled paint hanging from the ceiling; they look like stalactites. A jagged crack the color of tobacco juice traverses the ceiling's plaster, the sign of a leaking roof. The grass-weave wallpaper is old, cracked, faded, has separated at its seams; one section curls on itself. Dried brownish glue residue is visible on the wall.

The house is at the end stage of decay.

A noise comes from upstairs.

"Harry, you up there?"

Silence. There are no footsteps, no doors slamming, no sound of running water, or of a toilet flushing, or pipes knocking.

It's all wrong. Where the hell is Harry?

Rick unzips his jacket, then walks over creaking floorboards beyond the foyer.

Just beyond the entranceway, a dust-covered credenza is set against a wall. An eight-by-ten, black-and-white photograph in a tarnished frame sits on top of the piece.

He wipes away the coat of dust covering the glass.

It's a photo of Andrea reclining on an easy chair. She wears a flowing wedding gown with the hem spread on the floor before her. The bridal veil is draped behind her, falls over her shoulders. She holds a bouquet of lilies in her lap; her lips are curled in a Mona Lisa kind of smile. It's an idyllic picture of a long-dead woman moments before her wedding ceremony that took place more than thirty years ago.

Bronze candleholders stand on the credenza—one on either side of the framed picture. Each holds a tapered candle that's been burned nearly halfway down before the flame was extinguished. The arrangement looks like a mourner's shrine, a forlorn tribute to a long-ago tragedy and a woman many years gone. Harry's been living a life of perpetual mourning. And his brother's death may have sent him over the edge.

Rick peers into the living and dining rooms. Strips of peeling paint hang from the ceilings, as they did in the entranceway. The few pieces of furniture are covered with white sheets. Gray light washes in through the living room windows. Dust motes float in the air.

How does anyone live like this?

The tickle at the back of Rick's throat intensifies.

Where the hell is Harry? *I should have called the cops. Something's terribly wrong.*

Rick's now certain he'll find his uncle—possibly upstairs in bed— recently dead from a heart attack or stroke. Or maybe lying naked in a bathtub of blood-red water with his wrists or throat slashed by a razor. Or, hanging by a rope from a basement pipe, his neck broken, twisted to one side, feet swollen, eyes bulging in their sockets.

The thought of searching the rest of the house fills him with dread. But he's gotta do it.

He recalls the kitchen is at the rear of the house, behind the dining room.

"Harry?" he shouts.

No response.

Standing near the entrance to the kitchen, Rick's heartbeat drubs into his skull.

He'll likely have to go through the entire house to find Harry.

CHAPTER FIFTY-

THE KITCHEN REEKS of putrefaction.

Queasiness wells up from deep in Rick's stomach. It's a good thing he didn't eat this morning, or he'd be puking onto his shoes. The counters are littered with emptied cans that had contained Vienna sausage and beef ravioli. Food-encrusted dishes and knives and forks are piled in the sink and lie randomly about. A few houseflies buzz about the kitchen. Rick is certain they'll lay their eggs inside the meat residue and soon maggots will writhe inside each can.

Mouse droppings are everywhere—on the floor, the counters.

A scrabbling sound comes from behind the kitchen cabinets; it moves along the inside of the wall, then wends its way up toward the ceiling. Rats. Or mice are scurrying about inside the walls. And something—a rat or mouse, maybe a squirrel—has died in there; part of the stench comes from its carcass rotting in the space between the wall and the exterior wood.

Who would let a house deteriorate this way?

Rick moves back through the dining room, then stops at the bottom of the staircase. The newel post is cracked and leaning to one side. The handrail is covered with a patina of dust visible in the light filtering through an oval-shaped window at the second-floor landing.

Spider webs droop from the ceiling above the stairway, forming diaphanous canopies gleaming in the gray morning light.

How long has it been since Harry climbed those stairs?

Weeks? Months?

The dust on the handrail and those spider webs tell a bleak story: no one's gone up this stairway for a very long time. If Harry's still in the house, he's somewhere on the first floor or, more likely, in the basement.

From the bottom of the stairway, Rick looks up and calls for his uncle.

No response.

A sound comes from upstairs.

"Hello. Anyone up there?"

No answer.

Another sound.

A footstep?

A door closing?

Or is it his imagination?

No. It's that loose shutter slamming against the clapboard outside.

Apprehension seizes him, reminds him of that day in the garage. He listens for something, anything—creaking of the upstairs floorboards, the squeak of a door closing, the plunk of a pipe in a wall—but hears and feels only his heart thundering in his chest.

He's wired, completely jacked.

But he's gotta find Harry.

If he's here, he's dead.

A rumbling sound causes a vibrating sensation to course through his feet. He nearly jumps but realizes it's the furnace kicking in. Yes, he now feels hot air blowing through a register just above the baseboard. If this place has been abandoned, why is the heat still on? It's not a good sign.

About to head upstairs, he recalls an enclosed porch on the ground floor. It's at the rear of the house with a large window overlooking Long Island Sound. Harry had used it as a home office.

Rick heads back through the living room, moves across a threadbare carpet. The floorboards beneath it groan.

He stops, as though the floor's creaking will alert someone to his presence.

Get hold of yourself. No one's here except Harry. And he's probably dead. Just find him.

He moves toward a pair of French doors closing off Harry's home office.

Looking through the glass panes, he sees a worn leather chair and an ottoman. The rest of the room is off to the right, beyond his field of vision.

He has the strangest feeling Harry's in this room.

About to reach for the handle, he hesitates.

CHAPTER FIFTY-ONE

HE WAITS AT the French doors.

Why stand here? Why not open the door? And why do his arms feel so rubbery, so weak, as though he can't lift them? Why not press down on the handle, open the door, go into the room, and see what awaits him? Because the more he delays, the longer he puts off seeing whatever's inside.

C'mon, man, open the fucking door. Just do it.

With a deep breath, he presses the handle down and pushes.

The door opens inward.

He steps into the room. A noxious odor catches at the back of his throat. Is it mold—not mildew, but the kind Rick has smelled in a hospital room when a patient is at the end? Is it the smell of death? He gazes to his right, toward the far end of the room.

Slumped in a chair behind a large oak desk, backlit by the window behind him, Harry is motionless. His chin rests on his chest, his eyes are closed, and his arms dangle at his sides.

He's dead.

The sight nearly brings Rick to tears. And suddenly, deep in the privacy of his thoughts, he thinks, *I should have done more after hearing what he said at the elevator. This is the end stage of despair.*

Harry has neglected himself to death.

As Rick moves closer, the funk of an unwashed body assaults him. Or is it the smell of decaying flesh?

Suddenly, he sees it. Harry's chest rises and falls with each shallow breath. He's alive. But he's a pitiful sight. He wears wrinkled pajamas beneath a stained terry-cloth bathrobe. His face has a deathly pallor and is covered with a mottled growth of bristly beard. His mouth is agape. His lips look parched. His grayish hair is long, unkempt, hangs over his forehead and ears.

He could be in a stupor, maybe even falling into a coma.

"Harry . . . ?"

No response.

"Harry."

At the sound of Rick's voice, his uncle startles; his body jerks, his hands move to the chair's armrests, and he smacks his lips. But his eyes remain shut.

"Harry, it's Rick. Wake up."

His uncle's eyelids flutter, followed by a series of rapid blinks. Aroused from either sleep or stupor, he turns his head toward Rick but looks confused.

"C'mon, Harry, *wake up.*" Rick shoves his uncle's shoulder.

Harry grunts, nods his head, then pushes down on the armrests, slowly straightens himself into a sitting position. The man is responsive but seems barely aware of his surroundings. Or is it the confusion that can take hold when you're stirred from a deep sleep?

Licking his lips, Harry peers up at Rick, then whispers in a voice thick with phlegm, "Rick, it's you."

At least he recognizes his nephew.

A chill burrows down Rick's spine.

Has Harry eaten or had anything to drink? No water or food—especially lack of water—can send the body into sudden crisis. He'll need hospital care. Maybe it's best to pick up the telephone, dial 911, get him to a hospital where they can start an IV, hydrate and monitor him for some sort of metabolic imbalance.

Rick is about to reach for the desk phone, but Harry begins to mumble, "Rick . . . it's good to see you."

"Harry, what the fuck is going on? What're you doing to yourself?"

His uncle says nothing, rubs his eyes, coughs, shakes his head, and swivels the high-backed chair toward Rick. Thick white paste has formed at the corners of his mouth.

"Harry, what's happened to you?"

CHAPTER FIFTY-TWO

HARRY TRIES TO speak but manages only a hoarse croaking; his throat's dry.

"Wait, I'll get you some water."

Harry peers up at Rick, nods, smacks his lips. At least he understands what's being said to him. Maybe he's not on the verge of death, but he looks like he's in bad shape.

Rick notices a door off to the side of the room; when open, it reveals a half bathroom. Rick enters. There's a pedestal sink. Faucet drippings have left a coppery-blue stain in the basin; the toilet bowl has a brownish ring at the waterline. An empty glass sits on a ledge above the sink.

Rick turns the cold-water handle. Rust-tinged water spurts from the faucet. He waits for the water to clear, grabs the glass, rinses it, fills it, and returns to his uncle. Harry reaches for the glass; his hand isn't trembling, a good sign.

Harry takes the glass, tries to gulp the water. It dribbles over his chin.

"Slow down, Harry. Sip it."

Harry sips and swallows. Rick watches his Adam's apple bob up and down like a slow-moving piston. Harry tilts his head back, finishes the water, sets the glass on the desk.

He clears his throat and says, in a stronger voice, "Thank you, Rick. I needed that. I guess I fell asleep."

"Harry, let me find something else for you." With the glass in hand, Rick makes his way back to the kitchen. Opening the refrigerator door, he breathes in a putrid wave of stale air. Pieces of rotting meat sitting on wax paper are on the middle shelf alongside two unwrapped slices of bread, so covered in fuzz, they're growing penicillin. An unopened carton of orange juice stands on the top shelf. Rick grabs it and opens the carton. No sour smell, so he pours juice into the glass. The fluid will boost Harry's electrolytes.

Reentering the office, Rick notices the shabby furnishings—two club chairs face Harry's desk, a threadbare sofa sits off to the side of the room, a chipped coffee table stands in front of it, empty bookshelves line one wall, there's no drapery over the windows.

The desktop is in disarray: a box of tissues sits to Harry's left; papers are strewn everywhere; a letter opener lies next to the tissue box; a pile of auto catalogues sits at the edge of the desk, ready to topple to the floor.

Harry's eyes appear more focused than before. The water has helped. He looks reasonably hydrated; he's not about to fall into metabolic oblivion.

Harry takes the glass from Rick, brings it to his lips, sips the orange juice.

Sitting in a chair facing the desk, Rick makes a quick assessment of his uncle: his breathing is unlabored. The pallor of his face has begun lessening. He no longer looks confused. The confusion was because he'd been suddenly aroused from a deep sleep. Though he's not on the verge of being comatose or even stuporous, Harry looks like shit.

There's no need to get him to a hospital. Not yet. But he likely has a mental condition. He's been so neglectful of his own well-being that he could be a danger to himself. If he's suicidal, he might need psychiatric commitment. Where's the nearest hospital? Greenwich? Stamford?

Harry leans back, rests his head on the high-backed leather chair, closes his eyes, draws a deep breath. When he exhales, air whistles through the dryness of his nose.

He picks up the glass, drinks more juice.

That thumping sound comes from upstairs.

"Harry, is anyone else here?"

His uncle shakes his head. "No, just me . . ."

It's that upstairs shutter banging against the outer wall.

Harry finishes the orange juice, plops the glass onto the desktop, and stares into space.

"Harry, what's going on? You're not answering your phone."

"I turned off the answering machine."

"Why?"

"I don't need it. I got rid of the business, sold it . . . the warehouse and the land, too, fourteen acres," he murmurs in a lifeless voice. He exhales and closes his eyes. "I don't need a telephone. No one calls."

"My mother was calling and *I* called you. Why haven't you answered your phone?"

Harry waves his hand, dismissively. "Enough is enough. I don't care."

"When's the last time you ate?"

"It doesn't matter."

"Harry, are you trying to kill yourself?"

"In the end, everyone dies," he mutters.

"Harry, what the fuck's going on?"

His uncle rolls his chair closer to the desk, clasps his hands over his face, rubs his eyes, massages his forehead. In a voice ripe with fatigue, he says, "Getting rid of the business was a mistake. Now, I have nothing."

"Harry, you have family. You have us."

Rick knows his uncle sees everything through the veil of his sadness. His ability to think sensibly, to use logic, is impaired. He's been locked into a life of mourning, and it's worsened since his brother's death and now, after giving up the business. It's loss after loss. Way too much to bear.

He needs to go to the hospital. But he'll never go voluntarily.

A semi-smile suddenly appears on Harry's lips.

Rick recalls a psychiatrist once telling him that sometimes, when people decide to end their lives, a feeling of tranquility can take over.

"There's a final acceptance of the inevitable," the shrink had said. "For some people, a strange kind of euphoria supplants the depression, once the decision's been made to commit suicide. It's the calming realization that death will relieve the burden of living a life of misery, that peace will now come."

Is Harry at that point of hopelessness?

CHAPTER FIFTY-THREE

NAGER SLUGS THE last of his coffee.

He glances at the Dunkin' Donuts box on Zelnick's desk. He's already downed a powdered jelly donut—damned thing was delicious—and he's tempted to grab another. There's just something about sugar; you can never have enough of it. It's as potent as heroin but it's a sweet addiction.

It's absolutely amazing. He hasn't had a single episode of heartburn since the night with Liz. And he's downed plenty of donuts and slurped lots of office sludge passing itself off as coffee.

That evening with Liz changed things. Maybe it changed *everything*.

Even his lousy gut.

Okay, it's complicated, and their relationship will definitely cause an end to their partnership once they tell Pildes. One of them will be transferred, as department regulations require.

But maybe they can keep their "thing" under wraps for a while longer, at least until they can clear some of the cases they've been working on . . . especially the Shepherd one.

After all the crap with Ellen—the tension, arguments, and bitter resentments, except for the time spent with Bobby—Art's life had been the definition of "shitty existence," until that first night with Liz.

No matter what the future holds for them, Liz has given him the gift of hope.

Nager feels it in his soul. Something long dead has come alive.

But here in the squad room, he knows they have to play it cool.

They have to buy some time as partners, lest their lives as lovers be exposed.

He's never been very good at compartmentalizing things, and now he's gotta separate his love life from the job. He now lives in two worlds: one with Liz—away from the command station or the city-owned sedan—and the other at work, where Pildes is blowing steam out his ass over the Shepherd case. How long can these parallel lives be kept separate?

Liz approaches. "Art, I just got off the phone with Steve White at Manhattan North."

"What's up?"

"There are a few developments in the Harper case. They located the cab driver who picked up a fare fitting the description of the shooter," Liz says. "His trip sheet shows the perp wanted the taxi to take him from Seventy-Ninth and Third to Eighty-Sixth and Lexington. The cabbie distinctly remembers dropping him off in front of Gimbels. The guy headed down the steps to the southbound Lexington line."

"He have a description?"

"No. The guy was bundled up in an overcoat, scarf, and a hat. The cabbie said he was a white man but he couldn't even guess his age. It was only a seven-block trip but the cabbie remembers the guy dropped a ten-dollar bill onto the front seat, got out of the cab as it came to a stop, hustled to the subway entrance, and disappeared down the steps."

"Any evidence linking that shooting to our case?"

"Nope," she says. "Just what we already know . . . that the vic resembled Rick Shepherd and was shot in front of his office. And there were three slugs to the vic's back."

"So there's nothing else linking that case to ours."

"We already know the perp used a different handgun."

"The fact that the guy wanted to be dropped off at a main stop on the Lexington Line might mean he lives in the city and knows the subway system. Or he might have been headed for Grand Central Terminal. We have no way of knowing. But it's Manhattan North's case. We need a break on the *Shepherd* shooting."

Nager shifts his weight in the chair, then stretches. His back muscles are tight. With this workload, he hasn't seen the inside of a gym in a few weeks. Gotta get back in condition. Maybe Liz could join the gym; they could work out together. No, too great a chance they'd be seen. Maybe he can join her bike riding group? There's safety in numbers.

C'mon, man, focus on the job.

"Any word yet from ATF?" he asks.

"I spoke again with an agent yesterday afternoon," Liz says. "The Out-of-Business Records Center's been going through all their files. They're sifting through those 4473s, year-by-year. They're doing it by hand, so it's a slow process. They have only a few boxes left. If there's no Yellow Form for the Wilson Pro, we're out of luck. He said by next year, they should have the forms scanned and computerized."

"That'll be a whole new day for police work," Nager says, "but it doesn't help us now."

The fax machine rings, begins beeping.

A sheet of paper slides onto the receiving tray.

Snatching it, Liz scans the page.

She turns to Nager as her eyes widen. "Oh, *yes.*"

"What?"

"We got a hit on the Wilson Pro."

A surge of elation overtakes Nager as he shoots up from the chair.

Liz hands him the paper.

He notices her hand is shaking.

Peering at the printout, he feels his heart jump in his chest.

His hand begins trembling. "This is *huge*," he says. "We gotta make some calls, Liz, and let's get an all-points out. Include this . . . suspect is armed and dangerous."

CHAPTER FIFTY-FOUR

RICK WONDERS WHAT can be done for his uncle.

He's pretty sure the nearest hospital is in Stamford. He can't let Harry vegetate in his misery. It could be a death sentence. But he can't cart him off against his will.

A sudden flash brightens the sky. Metallic light rinses the room.

Rick squints in a blinding flare of brilliance.

A sharp crack sounds near the house. It's a lightning strike, very close.

The smell of voltage fills the air—it's ozone.

Rick feels the air pressure drop. He swallows; bubbles crackle in his ears.

A rare winter electrical storm is moving in over Long Island Sound; it's traveling northeast. It'll soon pass over the south shore of Connecticut.

Still sitting behind the desk, Harry's nostrils flare and his nose wrinkles as he inhales, looks like he's about to sneeze. His eyes close as he reaches for the tissue box on his desk, rips out a tissue, and brings it to his nose. His head lurches back, and is then thrust forward in a violent sneeze.

The sky brightens as another lightning flash washes the room in white light.

The air feels ionized. A static charge fills the room.

A jolt of thunder rocks the house in a percussive blast.

Suddenly, Rick sees it.

Sweat sheets down his forehead so fast, he's soaked.

Yet, his mouth goes dry.

"Harry . . ." he hears himself say as a metallic tang fills his mouth.

The tissue box and part of the pile of magazines were shoved aside when, moments before, Harry had reached for a tissue to cover the sneeze.

No longer hidden behind them, a pistol lies on the desktop.

CHAPTER FIFTY-FIVE

HARRY'S HAND IS only an inch away from the gun.

"Harry . . . why . . . why do you . . . ?" says a faraway voice.

"Why do I have a pistol?" Harry asks. His eyes look like they're on fire. "It's a Wilson Combat Professional, the finest handgun money can buy."

The room is etched in light—another lightning flash followed by the crack of thunder.

Stunned, Rick hears his own voice, small, distant. "Harry . . ."

"Yes . . . ?"

Sweat trickles from Rick's scalp, drizzles down his forehead.

"*You* killed my father."

A sickly smile forms on Harry's lips. He nods.

The moment feels otherworldly as everything in the room looks sharply etched.

"And that guy . . . Robert Harper . . . ? Did you kill him, too," says that same distant voice. "He was killed in front—"

"An unfortunate mistake."

Rick's thoughts swirl as he realizes the shootings weren't done by some crazed patient or a loan shark or street thug. His father's twin brother—Harry Shepherd, his own flesh and blood—shot Dad dead. And before he did it, he tried to kill Rick.

"I'm sure you're wondering why I would shoot my brother after try-ing to kill my nephew," Harry says in a voice tinged with menace.

A thought-storm spools through Rick's mind: *Dad, Harper, mur-der, Nager, Callaghan, the morgue . . . what the fuck is going on?*

Harry is silhouetted in gray light washing through the window be-hind him.

His uncle's hand—gnarled knuckles, mottled skin, liver spots—grabs the pistol. Fury pours from Harry's eyes. Spittle forms at the corners of his mouth. He looks like a rabid dog.

Rick spins a frenzied series of assessments—ponders time, distance, motion. He's always been an athlete, could swing at a pitch streaking toward the plate in a fraction of a second. And now he could launch himself across the desk, barrel into Harry with freight train power, send him to the floor, then pummel him until he's unconscious.

But Rick's too far away; there's no chance.

And now Harry raises the weapon, points it at Rick.

With a lightening-charged sky behind him, amid rolls of thunder, Harry explodes from the chair and stands behind the desk. He peers down the gun's sights.

The pistol points at Rick's heart.

CHAPTER FIFTY-SIX

RICK STARES AT the muzzle's opening, a looming black O.

"I knew if I didn't answer the phone, your mother would send you." Harry sits back down, rolls his chair forward, holds the weapon in a steady hand; his elbow rests on the desktop. His index finger is curled around the trigger. "I'm sure you'd like to know why, wouldn't you?"

As though removed from his own self, Rick feels his head nodding.

"You never knew your Grandfather Edward, did you?"

"I don't understand. Grandpa Shepherd's been dead for years. What's—"

"Or his wife, Pauline, your grandmother. Yes, they died before you were born. A car accident, in 1943, just before I was drafted."

Keep him talking, buy some time.

Through paste lining his mouth, Rick says, "I don't get it . . ."

"Your grandparents, your father and me . . . that's why we're here."

Rick notices a letter opener lying on the desk. He could try to snatch it and thrust the blade into Harry's throat. A quick stab to the carotid artery and he'll bleed out. Game over. But Harry's eyes are lasered on Rick. Harry can pull the trigger before Rick even begins to make a move. Harry's eyes glitter in the room's light.

"You know your father and I were business partners . . ."

"So, Harry, this is about *money*?"

"No."

"Then, why . . . ? *Why*, you son of a bitch?" Rick asks as the room brightens. He knows his pupils are dilated and his armpits are soaked. He knows his life is about to end.

"Your father knew being in business meant making payoffs. There were the Planning & Zoning people, those greedy bastards, crooks . . . every one of them. They wanted payoffs to approve the sale of the property so a developer could build a mall. But your father—the *Golden Boy* who owned part of the business—wouldn't go along with the payoffs. *Moral* man that he was. His honesty was flexible so long as he was getting my checks."

"So it *is* about money."

Harry shakes his head. "Oh no, it's bigger than that. *Much* bigger."

"Goddammit, Harry, my father gave you seed money for the business."

"But you don't know *why*, do you?"

"Because you were his *brother, that's* why."

Harry shakes his head. "It was because of what he *did* to me. And I finally took revenge."

"*Revenge?* For *what*? What the fuck did my father *ever* do to you that made you *murder* him, you miserable bastard?"

CHAPTER FIFTY-SEVEN

THE GUN HOLDS steady.

"He was the *good* twin," Harry murmurs.

"Whaddaya mean? Why'd you *murder* him?"

"Your grandfather *loathed* me. Why? Because I came along a few minutes after my brother. I was just another mouth to feed." Harry pauses, sucks in air, then says, "Can you imagine that? My crime was just being born."

"But what did my *father* ever do to you?"

"James was too busy being the Golden Boy. He never knew how our father would punch me in the belly so there'd be no bruises."

"But my father—"

"Your *father*? He was a *prince* and I was nothing. *Nothing.*" Harry's face contorts. His stare has a vocabulary all its own: rage, envy, sadness. "The hate our father had for me was . . . was . . . I can't describe it. There was a time . . . I had tropical fish; they were such beautiful creatures." Harry's voice now has a wistful tone and his eyes reflect the room's light like bits of shattered glass. "That bastard poisoned them with turpentine."

Tears trickle down Harry's face. "My son of a bitch father said 'whatever was given in this life can be taken away.' It was *the lesson of the fish.*"

The lesson of the fish? This is insane. He's a fucking madman.

"But . . . why'd you kill my father?"

Harry looks and sounds like he's in a feverish state. "Yes, you need to know why before you die."

My only chance is to see where this goes.

"It was years ago."

"*What* was years ago?"

"We were at a party . . . at a brownstone in Brooklyn Heights. After he'd had a few drinks, your father would always get flirtatious with the women. And of course, they swooned over him like lovesick children. Why? Because he was so charming and *so* kind, because he was the *Golden Boy.*"

"Harry, I don't understand a fucking thing you're saying. Why'd you—"

"It was at that party," Harry mutters in an acid-filled voice. "I'm sure he was embarrassed to have his grease monkey brother—a lowlife mechanic—mixing with his doctor friends.

"It was eleven o'clock and your mother was saying her goodbyes. Andrea and I were finally leaving so we could get away from them. Your father left, too, at the same time, said he was going to get their car.

"We were outside the house—the three of us—standing at the top of the stairway, and he turned to Andrea and said, 'Give me a goodnight kiss.' I'll never forget those words . . . *Give me a goodnight kiss.*

"Suddenly, he threw his arms around Andrea. She tried to push him away, but he'd trapped her in a bear hug, pressed himself against her pregnant belly. Then, he clamped his hands onto her face and forced her mouth open. He put his lips to hers. And he gave her a filthy, wet kiss. He was a hungry man, your father; he was ravenous. For my *wife.*"

This is the ranting of a maniac.

"In front of me . . . he did *that*. He was an animal, a beast, your fa-ther . . . and he was feeding on my *wife*." Harry's neck veins bulge like thick pipes. Tears slide down his face and drip from the edges of his chin. The pistol holds steady. "He had nothing but contempt for me, just like your grandfather did. And his hands . . . those hands . . . I saw them go to her breasts . . . and . . . he *fondled* them.

"Andrea tried to push him away, she fought him, and then . . . my God . . . she stumbled at the edge of the stairway . . ." Glistening tracks of mucous dribble from Harry's nose to his lips, mix with his tears. "She was off-balance and . . . she . . . she tumbled down the stairs and hit bottom."

An animal moan rises from deep in Harry's throat. His lips quiver but the pistol holds steady, points at Rick's chest.

"When she hit the bottom, I knew she was gone. My life ended that night. And for the last thirty years, I've cried for Andrea, and I cry for the boy we would have had; the boy I'd have loved . . . the son your father killed."

Rick is stunned, shakes his head, tries to process Harry's words but it all swirls in a thought-storm. *Could this be true? This is the tirade of an insane mind. Or did it happen the way Harry said it did?*

"So now you know why we're here."

CHAPTER FIFTY-EIGHT

RICK HAS NO words; he's mired in a bog of disbelief.

"Your father took what was precious from me . . . my wife and my son. And now, I'm going to take what was precious to him. I wanted *you* first, so my brother would know the agony of living beyond his own son. I'd have let him live for a few months knowing his only son was dead, that he'd died violently as mine did."

Harry moves the pistol closer to Rick.

"But I failed. I thought that man on the street was you. It was a mistake. But now I'll finish what I began."

Harry sucks in snot, swallows it as more tears drip down his flushed cheeks.

"It's the lesson of the *fish*. Whatever has been given in this life can be taken away."

As lightning flames through the sky, the room turns incandescent. A crack of thunder sounds and the house shudders. The storm descends in a violent downpour. The first solid patters are followed by pinging as rain and sleet slash against the window behind Harry. The sky flares; another spike of lightning makes the room blister in strobe-like luminescence.

"But . . . why now . . . ?" Rick asks in a voice that sounds distant.

"Yes, you should know why this is happening now."

Staring into his uncle's eyes, Rick sees madness.

"A few years after Andrea died, I went to my brother to borrow money. Your mother didn't want James to give me a *nickel*. She thought nothing of me, said I'd never make the business a success. So to keep what happened that night a secret, he gave the money to me behind her back and told her afterwards. Starting a business was the only dream I had left . . . and she, your mother, wanted to deny me that."

Harry keeps the pistol aimed at Rick.

"So I bought her out and gave her the money. Now, I want her to live a long life, the way I've lived mine. And now she can live knowing the agony of losing the life she brought into the world, her son's life. She'll suffer the way I've suffered. I lost my wife and child. She'll lose her husband and child. An eye for an eye. Isn't that what the bible says?"

Backlit by a greenish-black, end-of-the-world sky, Harry's eyes bulge and his face distorts into a mask of fury.

"So, dear nephew, this is the day you die."

CHAPTER FIFTY-NINE

THE SKY BRIGHTENS; the room blanches in the blinding brightness of a nearby lightning strike.

Afterimages of light play on Rick's retinas.

Another shock wave of thunder shakes the house.

Rick hears himself say, "And you told no one about what happened?"

Keep him talking . . . let him ramble on; it's my only chance.

"Who'd have believed me?" Harry mutters. "We were alone, just the three of us. Your father swore me to secrecy and told people that Andrea slipped and fell."

"And when you went to him for money . . . ?"

"Your father owed me *that* much."

"And now . . . ?"

"A development company wants to build a mini mall on the property. Your father wouldn't agree to paying off the Planning and Zoning Commission, those greedy pigs. He was dictating how I'd live my life."

Thunder rolls in the distance. Rain slashes against the window behind Harry.

"I was sick of the Golden Boy's privilege. He was the big-shot *doctor* and I was a nobody. During the War, he stayed at Fort Hamilton and examined draftees, while poor slobs like me were sent off to combat. I spent two years in the Pacific killing Japs. But when he wouldn't make the payoffs . . . *that* was the final straw."

Another crash of thunder shakes the house.

* * *

There are no more questions.

Rick realizes he'll be slammed with bullets the way Dad was killed and it'll be oblivion, the absence of all he's ever known.

Rick's read that your life flashes before your eyes in the moments before death. But that doesn't happen, not now, because his thoughts streak to wishes and regrets. Yes, there were mistakes, especially when it came to Dad. And he thinks of how strange it is now that Dad's twin brother will end his life. A circle of despair shadows three generations, and it will all come down to the blast of a gun.

He recalls those last words he said to Dad: *Fine, then we'll talk about nothing.*

He could have been a better son. And what pain will this bring to Mom? The agony of a mother's loss. To lose a child—as Harry did.

And Kate. *I could have done more for her. After all, I too was the Golden Boy.*

And there's Jackie. He recalls the evening they met; how the air hummed with possibility. He'd imagined years ahead—a life of caring and commitment.

But as water and ice pour from a lightning-charged sky, he knows there'll be no wedding, no kids; and he'll never again see Jackie's face, feel her body nestled into his, or hear the gentle intake of her breath. At this moment, he realizes she's all he's ever wanted. He's sick with regret.

Harry's voice shatters the realization of these moments. "They say it's best to punish the living and forgive the dead," he says. "But I can't forgive your father. And now I must punish your mother. But, Rick . . . do you forgive your father?"

Rick wonders how life comes down to this—to finding victory over a madman by not answering such an absurd question.

"*Answer* me," Harry growls.

Rick says nothing.

Harry's feasting on his rage. And on loss, sorrow, and envy.

But above all, on hatred, on vengeance.

"I have nothing left to live for," Harry mutters. "I'll rot in prison after killing you. But it doesn't matter. My life's meaningless."

"My life's not meaningless," Rick murmurs.

Am I begging for my life? No, I'm just telling the truth.

"You think your life matters?" Harry rasps. "No one's does. The world will go on without you."

Harry's silhouetted in the storm's gray light as rain and sleet slash against the window behind him. The sky brightens in a flash of white light, then darkens.

Harry's arm extends. The pistol comes closer.

Staring straight ahead, Rick waits for the end.

CHAPTER SIXTY

HARRY'S NOSE WRINKLES.

Air whistles through his nostrils as he gulps more air—it's reflexive—and his head rears back; he's about to sneeze and his eyes close.

Rick hurtles up from the chair, lunges across the desk, slams into Harry and they crash to the floor.

Rick locks his hands onto his uncle's wrist, but Harry rotates it and the pistol slaps against Rick's cheek. He twists his head away from the muzzle, pounces on top of Harry, pins him to the floor, and keeps his hands clutched tightly around Harry's wrist.

Harry begins bucking up and down.

Rick is thrown off him. Still clasping the wrist, Rick flings himself back onto his uncle and tries to wrest the pistol away. But Harry's grip is viselike. The muzzle moves closer to Rick's face. The weapon quivers in the air as they grapple. Rick feels fatigue building in his arms. He's weakening; his arms will turn to spaghetti and the pistol will point at his face.

There's a deafening blast, a kicking recoil, and the gun jumps in their hands. A bullet slams into the wall.

With his ears ringing, Rick rams an elbow into Harry's face. With a fierce twist, he wrenches the pistol away and it's in Rick's hands. Rolling off Harry, he leaps to his feet.

Rick's hand wraps around the pistol's grip; his finger curls around the trigger. The weapon feels like an extension of his arm and he needs only to point and shoot.

Lying on his back, Harry stares at the ceiling. He sobs as his chest heaves and blood oozes from his nostrils, trickles over his lips, drips onto the carpet.

"Don't move. Don't you fucking move. One move and I *will* kill you."

The gun's weight now seems unbearable. So Rick holds the piece with both hands, points it at Harry; the muzzle begins shaking.

Still on his back, Harry grunts, leans sideways, raises himself up on an elbow, stares at Rick. Snot and blood bubble from his nostrils, mix with tears, and it all flows to his mouth; he spits out bloody saliva.

Holding the pistol in his right hand, Rick sidesteps his way toward the desk. He slaps at the telephone with his left hand, knocks the receiver off the cradle. There's a dial tone buzz.

Harry slowly gets to his hands and knees. A thread of crimson drool hangs from his mouth, threads down toward the carpet. "Shoot me," he mutters as he begins rising to his feet.

"Death's too good for you, you son of a bitch."

"You want justice, don't you?"

"Yes."

"Then shoot me."

Rick picks up the receiver. It feels so light, so flimsy. With his left index finger he punches in 911, keeps the pistol in his right hand and pointed at his uncle.

"I'm coming for you," Harry snarls.

"I'll blow you away, you son of a bitch," Rick snarls as a visceral feeling rises from within; it's so powerful every part of him trembles, not because of fear but out of rage so overwhelming that every muscle in his body contracts in coiled readiness. *Shoot him, just blow this bastard away.*

"Do it," Harry shouts. He wobbles for a moment, then begins advancing toward Rick who edges around the desk, puts the receiver to his ear, still pointing the pistol at Harry.

"Nine-one-one. Officer Davenport speaking. What's your emergency?"

"A psychotic man's trying to kill me. I'm in the house at the end of Long Neck Road here in Darien, the house near the water . . . the one owned by Harry Shepherd."

"Yes. We got a call from the New York Police. We've already dispatched officers. Keep calm and stay on the line."

"Tell them to put a move on. I can't hold him off much longer."

Harry staggers, then steadies himself, continues advancing, gets closer.

"Try to stay calm. The police will be there any moment."

"They better get here fast because I'll have to shoot."

The pistol feels heavier so he drops the telephone receiver onto the desk and grasps the gun with both hands.

Harry lumbers toward him.

"Stay back or I'll shoot."

"You don't have the balls to do it."

Rick moves back. "Stay away or I swear to God I'll blast you."

Just pull the trigger. The bastard wants to die, so do it.

Harry trudges forward, falters, steadies himself, keeps coming.

The dispatcher's voice sounds tinny, distant. "Are you there? Can you hear me?"

Harry trundles toward him. One step, then another, slow, wobbling, but he advances.

Just aim for center mass. Shoot him in the chest. Snuff him out like he did Dad.

Harry staggers, regains balance, moves closer. He lunges at Rick who side steps him, and slams the pistol barrel to the side of Harry's head, just above his left ear.

Harry totters, drops to one knee. A gash opens on his scalp. Blood pours down the side of his face. Blood drips from Harry's hair, over his ear down to his jawline and onto his bathrobe. A seeping splotch spreads through the terry cloth.

Harry gets to his feet, turns toward Rick.

Rick's arms are weakening; he can't hold the gun much longer.

Just shoot him, pull the trigger.

Harry closes in and Rick smells the ureic sweat-stench of Harry's bathrobe. And there's the coppery odor of blood pouring from the scalp wound.

Rick launches a kick. It sinks into Harry's belly; his uncle jackknifes and flops facedown onto the floor. Gasping for breath, he lies there, sobbing. Blood sheets from his scalp, forms a spreading puddle that soaks into the carpet. Grunting, Harry begins an alligator crawl toward Rick, a series of clumsy moves—arms and legs, torso slithering—as blood, snot, and saliva leave a trail of bodily fluids on the carpet. He suddenly stops. He's spent, lies on his belly, motionless, mumbling.

Now, Rick sees every second of what happened the night his father died: Dad in the building's vestibule ready to push the button for Catherine Donovan; Harry enters through the outer door, stands behind him and squeezes off a shot, then another, and a third; and Rick's father is slammed forward as the bullets burst through his overcoat and empty him of life.

Murder, done with the same gun Rick now points at the man who killed his father.

This is the time to do it. Kill this son of a bitch.

Yes, do it now. This isn't the time for mercy or understanding or regrets.

Shoot this bastard and put him out of his misery.

CHAPTER SIXTY-ONE

RICK MOVES BEHIND his uncle, holds the weapon at his back.

Harry lies motionless, his face buried in the carpet. His shoulders heave as he sobs.

Rick's hand is steady. There's no shaking, no weakness. Not now, because he has a cause, and it's to end Harry's life. Just a few ounces of pressure will do it: a bullet will slam into Harry's back. Then he'll send another followed by another, exactly what Harry did to his father. He'll die the same way. It'll be a righteous killing, one well deserved.

Harry lies facedown on the carpet, doesn't move.

Lights out, motherfucker.

Rick moves the gun closer; holds it so the muzzle's an inch away from Harry's back at the level of his heart. His finger begins tightening on the trigger.

It's so simple. *Just do it. Pull the fucking trigger.*

Why? Because this son of a bitch stole his father's life, put him in a grave, and stood over that hole in the ground with crocodile tears pouring from his eyes, and after Mom and Katie threw roses onto the coffin, this bastard shoveled soil and rocks and pebbles onto the casket that held his twin brother's mangled body and pretended to mourn his victim in that fucking City of the Dead, as a minister babbled on about God and Jesus and Heaven and ashes and dust and life and loss, while a backhoe stood nearby, ready to dump more soil onto the remains of his dead brother.

Now, he continues to feel only hate and envy for his twin. This son of a bitch did it because of what he claims happened thirty years ago and never mentioned a word about it in all the years since, and his story is nothing but the imaginings of a madman.

Harry's story can't be true. It's the self-justifying fantasy of a jealous man who's lost his mind.

For all Rick knows, this bastard pushed his wife down that stairway and convinced himself his brother was a predator, and he's decided *now*—thirty years later—to punish the living for the so-called sins of the dead. Why?

And now in addition to snuffing out Rick, this madman wants to end his own life. So why not give him what he wants?

Why not give him what he deserves?

Just pull the trigger. Do it. Pull it, and then pull it again. And again.

Rick's arms tremble amid a scalding outpouring of rage. *Yes, do it. You can do it, it should be done, even if it crosses a boundary.*

What boundary? Rick asks himself. What *fucking* boundary?

Fury seethes through Rick's bloodstream, reaches every cell in his body. You can never know your own killing potential until you finally realize how despicable certain people can be.

And here I am, in this moment, where I can take revenge for what Harry did.

The pistol hovers directly over Harry's spinal column.

Rick's hand is steady—no more trembling, no fear—because in this moment, he's beyond conscience or pity or doubt or caring.

His finger tightens on the trigger.

But in a court of law, they'll prove you killed him in cold blood. You'll go to prison for the rest of your life. Fuck it. It doesn't matter.

Harry wants to die.

Just do it. Give him what he wants.

Am I evil? Maybe so. Harry has no corner on malice. On violence. On revenge.

It'll take only an ounce of pressure. A half-ounce. Maybe less.

Death waits for you, Harry. Just as it did for my father.

Death waits for us all.

And for you, Harry, the wait is over.

Rick's finger tightens on the trigger.

Slowly, the trigger begins to depress.

CHAPTER SIXTY-TWO

SIRENS SOUND IN the distance.

Shrieking, keening, carrying on the wind. They come closer, squawk, burp, then wind down, go quiet in front of the house.

There's a lightning flash. A roll of thunder. Rain slashes against the window.

Rick stands in place, frozen, holds the gun to Harry's back. His finger is curled around the trigger, presses it down, but not all the way. Another millimeter, maybe two, and it'll be done. It'll be over.

Do it. Do it now. Before the cops come through the door.

It all seems dreamlike, as though Rick is in a trance.

There's pain in his hand, in his fingers, they're cramping around the pistol grip.

A voice comes through the telephone receiver on the desk. "Can you hear me? The police are outside. They're coming in. If you're still holding the gun, drop it before they enter the premises."

Shouting comes from the foyer, then there's thumping in the living room and in a moment, cops will barge into the office and they'll see Harry lying at Rick's feet with blood everywhere—on the carpet, on Harry's head, his face, his bathrobe—and if Rick's still holding the gun, they'll shoot.

The door to the study bursts open and men pour into the room—guys in tactical helmets and body armor, full riot gear, carrying assault weapons—and the room's thick with cops and guns are pointing at him but his hand is locked around the pistol grip.

"Drop the gun. Drop it. *Now*," shouts a cop.

He's frozen in place, unable to move.

"Drop the goddamned gun. Do it. *Now*."

Rick's hand is numb. The room sways, seems to elongate; the cops look like they're a football field away.

Though he can't feel a thing in his hand, he hears the pistol hit the carpet with a thump.

"On your knees!"

He drops down, feels weak, spent.

"Hands behind your head. Do it. *Now*."

His arms go up with his hands behind his head.

"Clasp your fingers. *Do* it."

His fingers intertwine behind his head.

Radio static, voices, chaos, cops, a swarm of them everywhere. Hands slap his back, his torso, under his arms, the small of his back, his legs, ankles, and there's shouting but he can't make out their words.

"He's clean," says a cop.

Harry is shouting, gets to his feet, stumbles, and lunges at the officers.

"Stay back! Stay back, old man!"

Harry staggers, falls to his knees, tries to get up, but cops pounce on him, pull his arms behind him, snap handcuffs on him. Harry mumbles incoherently while an EMS guy tries staunching the blood pouring from his scalp. He screams and struggles but is held down as a cop helps Rick get to his feet. Another guy picks the pistol up from the carpet.

Rick stumbles toward the couch, sinks onto it, bends forward, and hangs his head between his knees.

Questions come in a cascade of words he can barely decipher. He shakes his head, tries to talk, but his tongue won't obey his commands.

Harry's shouting recedes as he's led from the room into the living room; then he's taken out of the house by the front door and can no longer be heard.

Rick is helped to his feet and is escorted outside to a waiting squad car.

The sky is a turbulent mass of clouds—greenish-black, roiling, ugly. Rain batters down mixed with sleet peppering his face; ice-balls bounce everywhere; puddles are pocked by drops of ice and water; the air is cold and gray. Rainwater drips from the tip of Rick's nose as an officer opens the rear door of the squad car. A hand bends his head down, helps him into the back seat of a patrol car.

Sitting in the vehicle, Rick looks out at Long Island Sound. The water is laced with foam and heaving whitecaps.

Police lights swirl against a darkened sky.

Two cops are in the front seat of the cruiser. A mesh barrier separates the back from the front of the car. A shotgun stands upright on the seat between them.

The road rushes by as sirens shriek and as Harry's house recedes in the distance.

CHAPTER SIXTY-THREE

IT'S A SMALL room, overheated, and smells of steam and sweat.

There's white fluorescent lighting; it's surreal, like being on a flood-lit stage. A Formica-laminated table stands in the middle of the room. Chairs scrape on the floor. There are voices, tumult.

He's sitting in a metal chair. Two detectives sit across from him; another two stand off to the side. More cops wait outside the room.

Rick's heart flutters, his pulse is thready. He feels light-headed, as though he's about to faint. Questions rush by in a flood of words. He draws a deep breath, sucks in as much air as he can, but it doesn't help. He's short of breath, feels like he's suffocating.

"You okay?"

A sound erupts from his mouth, a dry croak.

"You want something to drink?"

He nods.

Give me a goodnight kiss.

His lips are parched; his tongue sticks to the roof of his mouth. He tries to get some saliva going, but no deal, there's none.

An open can of Coca-Cola plops onto the table. He grabs it and with a shaking hand, brings it to his lips. He gulps; it's cold, fizzy, catches in his throat. He coughs, soda froths from his mouth, burns its way out his nostrils, sprays onto the table.

"Hey, guy, take it easy. Drink it slow."

He can't stop coughing; it feels like he's choking and his eyes feel like they'll pop from their sockets. He pushes the can away and when the coughing finally stops, clears his throat. He hears a warbling voice say, "My uncle ... tried to shoot me ... killed my father."

There are questions, but it's a stream of garbled words, floating in the air; and he tries telling them what happened. "There was this gun ... he killed my father with it ... and the other guy in Manhattan ... Harper, and we fought and ... and ... I kicked him and the dispatcher ... she said you were coming ..."

Rick's thoughts slalom through his head, racing like a wind-driven wildfire, and a torrent of gibberish froths forth.

What's happening to me? Am I having a stroke?

"Is that it?"

"Huh?"

"Is that what happened?"

"Yes."

"Can you sign a statement?"

He pressed his lips to hers. It was a filthy, wet kiss.

"Hey, guy, you okay?"

He nods, hears himself say, "... killed my father and that guy Harper ... Robert Harper in Manhattan, back in November."

"Yes, you told us that. We're checking that out."

There are more questions—it's a tsunami of verbiage.

And his hands ... those hands ... I saw them go to her breasts ... and ... he fondled them.

Harry's words: *She tumbled down the stairs and hit bottom.*

He hears the door to the room open.

There are more voices—muffled, indistinct—an unintelligible mixture of words.

Rick hears a voice say, "... we found the other gun ... a Smith & Wesson revolver. It was in his desk. It was probably the one used in the murder on Seventy-Ninth Street."

"... Yes, in Manhattan ..." says a voice that sounds familiar.

"... Ballistics will check it out."

Am I losing my mind?

"Understood ... process him here."

"Shepherd ... Harry Shepherd."

"His uncle."

"The phone call ..."

"Brooklyn."

A hand presses on his shoulder.

"Rick ... ?"

He peers up.

It's Nager. And Callaghan's standing next to him.

Chairs scrape on the floor, voices are everywhere, and it feels like he's on a dizzying merry-go-round.

"C'mon, Rick," Nager says. "We'll take you home."

CHAPTER SIXTY-FOUR

HE'S IN THE back seat of a sedan.

His thoughts are running rampant: Harry, his father, the shooting, the Wilson Pro, how close he came to dying. And how close he came to killing Harry. *The fucker deserves to die.*

Callaghan's driving while Nager's in the front passenger's seat. He catches brief snatches of their conversation.

There are traffic sounds and the rush of wind and rain and a stomach-in-the-throat sensation. They're on the Major Deegan—I-87 now in New York City, somewhere in the Bronx—heading toward Manhattan. How long have they been traveling? It seems like only minutes ago they were in Darien. Has he been sleeping? Like a skipped heartbeat, has he lost a beat of time?

Immense puddles cover parts of the highway; they look like shallow lakes. Cars and trucks wade through them, some go too fast, sending rooster tails of spray into the air, dousing vehicles in the other lanes.

The traffic thickens, then slows to a crawl. Horns honk. Radio static fills the sedan, then Nager's talking to someone at Brooklyn Command but the words are garbled.

Traffic begins moving again. The sleet has abated, but there's now a steady drizzle and the air looks like a gray haze in a pall of exhaust fumes.

". . . pick up the Chevy when you feel up to it," Nager says. "Right now, let's get you home."

He was a hungry man, your father; he was ravenous. For my wife.

Through the whoosh of traffic, the rhythmic slap of the windshield wipers, and the blare of horns, Rick barely hears the detectives as his thoughts spin in succession.

He was an animal, a beast, your father . . . and he was feeding on my wife.

I'll never know the truth. It'll always be a mystery.

What kind of man was Dad?

"Maybe in a day or two, Rick, you'll give the Darien cops another statement," Nager says.

Callaghan adds, "We know you're not in great shape right now."

Nager says, "Lucky we got that fax . . ."

Your father took what was precious from me . . . my wife and my unborn son.

Callaghan asks him something but it's just a ribbon of sound, nothing more.

"There'll be an extradition hearing . . ." he hears Nager say.

Now Rick sees the spittle on Harry's lips, sees those eyes radiating loss, rage, envy, and there's the smell of mold and sweat and rotting food and the stench of death in those walls.

"Why'd he do it?" Nager asks.

"The business," Rick mumbles.

"What about it?"

"Payoffs . . . so they could build a shopping mall," he hears himself say.

Why am I lying?

"But why'd he want *you* dead?"

"He thought I'd take over," Rick mutters even as he tastes another lie. There's no way he'll repeat Harry's sick version of that night. It'll stay buried forever; he won't spread the ugliness of Harry's claims.

Punish the living, forgive the dead.

Hovering between reality and remembrance, he tries to distance himself from that house of decay and death.

His hands . . . they went to her breasts, and he fondled them.

His thoughts stream to his father, then to Harry and all the years of their lives: the Army, war, death, Fort Hamilton, house calls with Dad, the Brooklyn streets, the old Buick he drove back then and now he's a kid going on house calls with his father in those days of innocence, days of wonder, and he thinks of Katie and then Mom and Jackie and a swell of sadness washes over him. It's despair. It's the heartache of knowing the bottomless sorrow of life.

Whatever has been given can be taken away.

The drizzle intensifies. The mist thickens into a fog, a shroud blanketing the world.

Harry's insane world can't *really* be part of his family's story and now part of his own life—it's too ugly—and these things never happen in good families.

The car swerves as Callaghan exits the Major Deegan. They approach the Willis Avenue Bridge. Callaghan stops for a red light at Bruckner Boulevard. Boarded-up buildings, barren lots strewn with garbage and abandoned furniture and broken glass—the air is thick with fog, gloomy, and reeking of misery. It's the south Bronx. Was it just this morning when he drove past this area? It feels like ages ago.

A guy emerges from the mist. Pushing a shopping cart brimming with bottles and cans, he heads toward the sedan. He's unkempt, bearded, ragged, has long hair; he's bedraggled, wears a faded Army fatigue jacket, fingerless gloves; a camouflage hat sits askew on his head and he holds a filthy rag; poor bastard's got that Vietnam vet look; no doubt his soul was stripped bare by the carnage of jungle combat, and he's gonna smear that rag on the windshield, while asking for loose change, but the wipers slap back and forth so he turns away and disappears into the fog.

God, the world's such a fucked-up place.

When the light changes, Callaghan hits the gas and makes a right turn; they streak past Alexander Avenue onto the Willis Avenue Bridge, which spans the Harlem River. Steel girders reel past them in a strobe-like flash and the tires drub over rivets sending vibrations into Rick's spine.

There's a quick turn onto East 128th Street—Manhattan—and then, a right onto Second Avenue and they head downtown passing through a dreamscape of coffee shops, thrift stores, bodegas, and the Good News Manhattan Church. It's Spanish Harlem and there're more fast-food joints, one with a sign reading *Cuchifritoes*.

Now, they're at Ninety-Sixth Street, and the neighborhood suddenly changes. Tenements and bodegas give way to high-rise apartment buildings, trendy boutiques, and pubs filling up with the yuppie lunch crowd.

Moments later, they pull up in front of the building on East Eighty-Fourth Street and it comes to him in a sickening flash: Dad at the top of those stairs, bear-hugging Andrea, fondling and kissing her and she's resisting, she loses her balance as her arms windmill in the air and she's gone.

He feels as though his flesh is shredding.

CHAPTER SIXTY-FIVE

NOW, IN THE apartment, he can't remember seeing the doorman or walking through the lobby or taking the elevator to his floor.

There's only a spotty memory of things since leaving for Darien this morning. It's as though he's in some dream world, a nether land of foggy half-memories. His soaked shoes make a squishing sound as he walks into the kitchen and stands near the refrigerator. Pulling open the door, he sees a half-filled bottle of white wine on the top shelf, snatches it, pops the cork, and with a shaking hand, gulps a mouthful. Swigging another mouthful, he knows he's heading toward oblivion.

Lurching into the living room, he drops down onto the sofa. Spent, he lies on his back, stares at the ceiling. With his head spinning, he closes his eyes, as the sound of street traffic seeps through the windows.

Where's Jackie?

Right, right, right . . . she's at work, won't be back until this evening.

Does he tell her what Harry said? Will that poison her memory of his father?

Of course it will. He'll say nothing. It'll be a lie of omission.

But in the two years they've been together, he's never withheld anything from her.

So, he'll tell her. But not now.

It's impossible to believe what Harry said about his father.

Don't we want heroes in our lives?

Was Dad a hero?

Do we ever know what's really inside another human being? Do we even know ourselves?

I could've killed Harry. If the cops hadn't gotten there at that moment, I'd have blown him away.

Could I do murder?

Was Dad a predator?

Everything fades as Rick's eyelids flutter, and a moment later he falls into merciful darkness.

CHAPTER SIXTY-SIX

It's been weeks since that day at Harry's house.

Rick sits in the first row of the gallery in Courtroom 3A at Brooklyn Criminal Court. The room is high-ceilinged, lit with recessed fluorescent lights. The American flag stands to the right of the judge's bench; New York State's is on the left.

The court clerk sits at a table on the periphery of the courtroom well; he's reading the *New York Post*. The court reporter is perched on her secretary's stool, waiting patiently at her stenographic machine, while sipping a can of Sprite.

A flock of reporters is present. The jury box is empty because none are needed for the sentencing phase of the proceedings against Harry Shepherd.

Nager sits to Rick's right. Callaghan is seated on the other side of Nager. Something's different about them. Rick thinks he saw their hands move toward each other's along the bench and their fingers touched—gently—and it wasn't by accident. They're more than just partners.

But Rick knows it's none of his business.

He recalls a telephone conversation with Nager only two days after the incident at Harry's house.

"Ballistics matched the Wilson Professional to the slugs used in your father's shooting. And Manhattan North confirmed the Smith & Wesson revolver matches up with the bullets in the Harper homicide. Your uncle waived an extradition hearing and he's refused counsel. He's pleading guilty to all three counts."

But Rick is still wondering if Harry's words could possibly be true. *Was Dad a predator?*

*   *   *

The break in the proceedings is over.

The judge enters the courtroom, climbs two steps of the elevated dais, and takes his seat.

This is it: when this witness concludes his testimony, the sentence will be handed down.

Dr. Joel Albert, a forensic psychiatrist, settles into the witness chair. Dressed in a charcoal gray suit, he's a forty-something man with an authoritative-sounding voice. According to Nager, this psychiatrist examined Harry on three occasions at the Brooklyn House of Detention and filed an extensive report detailing his findings.

During his earlier testimony this morning, when asked about Harry's motivation for the murders, Dr. Albert said, "The defendant explained he did it because his brother refused a proposed buyout of their jointly owned business. He also admitted to killing Robert Harper, thinking the man he shot was Rick Shepherd. He said he didn't want his nephew to inherit his brother's share of the business. If that had happened, he'd never have been able to force a buyout on the terms he wanted."

Why did Harry lie about the reason he tried to kill me and then killed Dad?

Ann White, the Assistant DA, a tall woman wearing a tweed suit, moves to the lectern. The stenographer's fingers are poised over her machine.

Ms. White asks, "Doctor, will you please tell the Court your findings concerning the defendant's mental capacity at the times he committed the two murders to which he's confessed?"

"From a strictly medico-legal perspective, Harrison Shepherd knew right from wrong," Dr. Albert explains. "The defendant thought out the method of the shootings and had planned his escape routes. There's no evidence of an irresistible impulse or that he suffered from a state of mind affecting his ability to know his actions were wrong."

Sobbing comes from a woman a few rows behind him. Rick's certain it's Robert Harper's widow or possibly the poor guy's mother.

The judge turns to the witness. "Doctor," he says, "just to be clear, the defendant understood that he acted unlawfully when he committed both crimes?"

"Yes, Your Honor."

"And, Doctor Albert, are you stating with a reasonable degree of medical and psychiatric certainty that from a strictly legal perspective, the defendant was *not* insane at the time he committed the murders?"

"Yes, Your Honor."

*　*　*

Wearing an orange jumpsuit, Harry stands behind the defense table. A waist chain restrains his hands. He's unshaven and his hair, now nearly white, hangs in front of his eyes and over his ears.

Burly corrections officers are nearby. His court-assigned defense counsel stands beside him.

From the first row in the gallery, Rick sits a few feet behind Harry.

As the judge begins talking, Rick feels a squall of rage so incendiary, he could combust. He could leap over the spectator's rail onto Harry's back and lock him in a chokehold, then crank Harry's neck so severely, his spinal column would snap. It would be the revenge he didn't take at Harry's house.

Do it . . . do it . . . end this bastard's life.

Now he has the shakes.

Control . . . control. Let him rot in prison. Don't throw your life away.

Closing his eyes, he clenches his fists, tells himself there are people who give him a reason to live—*Jackie, Mom, and Katie.*

Nager's hand comes to rest gently on his shoulder. Somehow, the guy understands what he's feeling.

The judge—black-robed, white-haired, bespectacled—peers down from the bench and says, "Harrison Shepherd, do you have anything to say before I sentence you?"

Harry shakes his head. "No."

"Harrison Shepherd, you have pleaded guilty to the two criminal offenses of First-Degree Murder, and to one count of Attempted Murder. You have done so with no mental or physical impairment that would interfere with your ability to understand the implications of your acts. By the findings of this Court, you have forfeited the right to live freely among us. Therefore, you are sentenced to a prison term of not less than twenty-five years without the possibility of parole. May God have mercy on your soul."

Rick realizes for Harry, it's a life sentence.

The court officers lead his uncle toward a door at the side of the courtroom.

Rick bends forward, sets his forearms on this thighs, stares down at his shoes.

Nager slips his arm over Rick's shoulders and pats his back.

It's so unfair that his uncle gets to live out his time on earth while Dad is dead.

Will I ever know if Harry's accusations about my father are true?

Was he a predator who did what Harry claimed?

It's the only mystery left.

CHAPTER SIXTY-SEVEN

RICK, JACKIE, AND Mom sit at Mom's dining room table.

"I always thought that, deep down, Harrison resented your father," Mom says, "but it's hard to believe he killed him for *money*. He was a wealthy man. It makes no sense. And your father never said a word about a buyout proposal. And I never heard about some developer wanting to build a mall."

"I'm sure Dad didn't mention it because he didn't think Harry would sell the business against his wishes," Rick says.

Mom sighs. "And what on earth made Harrison think *you'd* inherit the business?" she asks. "He had to know your father's share would go to me when he passed. I should have been the target. I don't understand why he wanted to hurt *you*."

It's Harry's lie, and Rick can live with it because he knows the lie avoids inflicting more pain on Mom.

But why did Harry lie to the psychiatrist and to the Court?

"Mom, do you remember the night Andrea died?"

Her eyes widen. "Of course, but what does that have to do with any of this?"

"Harry never recovered from what happened that night," Rick replies.

"And your father will never recover from what Harry did to *him*." She stifles a sob and cups here face in her hands.

"Mom, tell me what happened the night Andrea died."

"I don't want to rehash it . . . not now." She lets out a trembling breath.

"Maybe if we know more about it, we'll understand Harry better," Rick says, knowing he'll never reveal to Mom what Harry said about his father.

"I don't want to *understand* him. I want to *forget* him. Let him rot in prison . . . forever. And besides, what's done is done."

"Do you remember that night?"

"Of course," she says in a quivering voice.

"When exactly did Andrea die?"

"I don't see why you—"

"Please, Mom. Just tell me the date."

"It was May sixteenth."

"What year was it?"

"Nineteen-fifty-three."

"What exactly happened?" He grasps her hand. Her skin is cold.

"Oh, Rick, I told you years ago." She regards him with a look that's imploring him not to pursue it further, and angry for his having brought it up.

"Please, I know it's unpleasant, Mom, but tell me, again."

She sighs and then reluctantly recounts the story of Andrea's fall down the stairway.

"It was in Brooklyn Heights, right?"

"Yes."

"Do you remember the address?"

"Of course. It was Ninety-Six Pierrepont Street, at a housewarming party. But, Rick, I don't see how this—"

"Where was Dad when she fell?"

"He'd already left to get the car."

"Were the police called?"

She runs her index finger around the rim of her coffee cup. "Yes, and an ambulance came, too. They rushed Andrea to the hospital. But what does this have to do with what Harrison did? And with his wanting to hurt you?"

"Nothing. I guess it's not really important."

I don't know if I'll ever learn what really happened that night.

CHAPTER SIXTY-EIGHT

BROOKLYN'S BOROUGH COMMAND looks medieval, as though it's been standing at the intersection of Wilson and DeKalb Avenues for centuries.

The desk sergeant, a thin guy wearing cop blues, has pale gray eyes and a buzz cut. As Rick approaches, he looks up from the book he's been reading—a paperback edition of *The Godfather*. He shoots an expectant look at Rick. After Rick states his name and the nature of his business, the officer tells him to take the elevator to the third floor.

*   *   *

"Good to see you, Rick," Nager says with a smile as they shake hands.

"Hey, Art. Thanks for agreeing to see me."

"No problem. Liz Callaghan's tied up on a case, so it'll be just you and me. Let's find someplace private where we can talk."

Walking along the corridor, they pass a patrol officer wearing a holstered pistol, and Rick's heart rate spikes. An image of Harry's gun flashes in his mind.

It's a Wilson Combat Professional, the finest pistol money can buy.

Passing the cop, the aroma of a spicy aftershave hits Rick's nostrils, reminding him of the aftershave Dad used when, as a kid, Rick watched him shave in the mornings. It seemed like a magical ritual. How he looked forward to one day being able to shave.

*   *   *

The interrogation room is windowless. A narrow table and three chairs occupy the center of the space. Set amid acoustic ceiling tiles, a buzzing fluorescent light casts a jaundice-yellow hue onto the table. There's no clock on the wall. A sense of timelessness pervades, which must make a suspect feel disoriented while being interrogated.

As Nager closes the door, it makes a sucking sound from the rubberized sealant surrounding the frame. The room is claustrophobic—a suspect's gotta feel the walls closing in, pressuring him to talk, just to get the hell out of the place.

After Rick settles into an uncomfortable metal chair, Nager shakes his head and begins talking. "It makes no sense to me that your uncle would kill his brother and want you dead, too, over a business deal. He must have known your mother would inherit his share of the business, right?"

Rick nods in agreement.

"I know the shrink said that legally, Harry Shepherd's not insane," Nager continues, "but for my money, he's fucking nuts."

So, I took his life for taking Andrea's and our son's lives.

Rick says nothing. There's no way to explain his uncle's story . . . unless he reveals what Harry said.

Was my father an animal? Some kind of pervert?

Nager adds, "Hey, Rick, I'm sorry. This whole topic must be painful for you.

"That's okay."

There's a brief silence.

"So, Rick, what can I do for you?"

"Art, first, I want to thank you and Detective Callaghan for staying in touch the whole time. We really appreciate everything you did."

"It's the least I can do for a family." Nager's eyes look glazed—even wet—as though some powerful emotion just washed over him. At that moment, Rick feels a connection to him, but can't put his finger on what it could be.

After a brief pause, Nager says, "Rick, you said *first* you wanna thank me. You didn't come down here to tell me what you could have said over the phone. What's the *second* thing you want to say?"

"The second thing is that I want to thank you for saving my life."

"Saving your *life*? You got the drop on your uncle and it was game over."

"The truth is, my life *would* be over if you hadn't kept after those people at ATF . . . you know, that form . . ."

"The 4473. The Yellow Form?"

"Yes."

"I don't follow."

"After I got that gun away from Harry, I called 911. The dispatcher told me they'd *already* received a call from Brooklyn and the Darien cops were on their way."

"But you'd already snatched the gun and called the Darien Police . . . and they got there in time. So . . . ?"

"While I was on the line with the dispatcher, Harry kept goading me to shoot him."

"Well, the police got there in time, so it never happened."

"Yes, but I managed to kick him to the floor. I was outta my mind and had the gun pointed at his back. I swear, Art, I was gonna blow him away, even though he was helpless."

"It's a good thing you didn't."

"The truth is, I'd just begun squeezing the trigger when I heard those sirens. That stopped me cold. If the cops got there *ten* seconds later, I'd have shot him in the back . . . at close range."

"Rick, you're right. If you'd shot that bastard in the back, it would have been murder. But I don't know of any man alive who wouldn't have wanted to pull that trigger . . . not after what your uncle did."

Rick realizes Nager understands. Completely.

The silence in the room feels like a welcome interlude.

"Is there anything else you want to say . . . ?"

"Yes, Art. I'd like to ask for a small favor . . ."

"Ask away."

"An incident happened a long time ago . . . it concerns my family."

"A long time ago? When?"

"It happened on May sixteenth, nineteen-fifty-three . . ."

"*Nineteen-fifty-three*? Jesus, that's what . . . almost thirty years ago?"

"Yes. It happened at Ninety-Six Pierrepont Street, here in Brooklyn."

Nager snatches a pen and pad, jots it down. "May sixteenth . . . fifty-three. Ninety-Six Pierrepont? That's Brooklyn Heights, the Eight-Four; that's the Eighty-Fourth Precinct to a civilian. What kind of incident?"

Rick describes Andrea's fall down the stairs. He simply says she tripped, landed on the sidewalk, and died. He gives Nager Andrea's full name and repeats the date.

"Can you get your hands on an Incident Report or any police record of that night, if there *is* one? I'd just like to clear something up. It has no connection to the case."

Like . . . what did Dad do that night?

Nager's lips tighten. "Rick, thirty years is a lifetime as far as records are concerned. I doubt they're still around. Anyone involved in that case would probably be retired by now. And any Incident

Report, if it even exists, would be archived in the Eight-Four's basement, most likely in a carton gathering dust along with dozens of other boxes. If it's even around, it'd be tough to locate."

"Do you know anyone at the Eight-Four who might be willing to look for it?"

"I have a friend there, a guy named Jeff Ketchman. If I can convince him to comb through that basement, there's a chance it might turn up. That is, if the mice and rats haven't eaten through the box. Frankly, it's a helluva long shot."

CHAPTER SIXTY-NINE

WHEN SLEEP ELUDES him—while Jackie sleeps—Rick lies in bed with a transistor radio to his ear.

Ordinarily, he doesn't listen to talk radio, but with the insomnia he's had for the last few months—he's jolted awake after maybe two hours of sleep—the voices in the night keep him company.

The Candy Jones Show is on WMCA. "Tonight, my guest is Dr. Joel Albert," says Candy Jones.

Rick's body stiffens at the mention of the doctor's name.

"He's the psychiatrist who testified at the sentencing phase of Harry Shepherd's trial," Candy Jones continues. "Doctor, you probably know more about what motivated Harrison Shepherd to murder his fraternal twin brother than anyone else. What can you tell us about the Shepherd case?"

"The murder of Dr. James Shepherd provides a clear demonstration of the love-hate relationship that can exist between twins," says the psychiatrist.

"Love and *hate*?" asks Candy Jones.

"Yes, as much as they may love each other, intense competition often exists between twins, whether they're identical *or* fraternal, as they were in the Shepherd case. It can be a very ambivalent relationship."

"But Harrison Shepherd said he killed his brother because of a business deal."

"I don't believe that's true," says Dr. Albert. "I think it's something deeper than that."

Hearing those words, Rick nearly winces. *Did Harry tell the psychiatrist what happened at the top of that stairway?*

"Like what's deeper?" asks Candy Jones.

"Intense rivalry was at the heart of this murderous act. Actually, *all* siblings compete for their parents' affections whether they're twins or not," says Dr. Albert.

I was sick of his privilege, sick and tired of him always being the favorite.

"Tell us more about sibling rivalry," says Candy Jones. "It's something many of us have dealt with as children. And, of course, as parents we see it all the time."

"*Any* family has only a certain amount of resources, emotional and material, to give to kids," Dr. Albert explains. "The bottom line is whether they're twins or not, each child really wants to know, *Am I loved most of all?*

"This is especially true with twins; after all, they live side by side from the very moment of conception. So aside from the love and companionship that can exist between them, there's often intense rivalry. And there can be a good deal of jealousy in any twinship. One thing is certain about what happened to Dr. James Shepherd: his brother Harrison took jealously to a lethal level."

Rick knows the psychiatrist is speaking a basic truth.

I took his life because I was sick of the Golden Boy and his privilege.

He then hears Kate's words repeating in his mind: *Oh, don't kid yourself, Rick. You were his Golden Boy.*

CHAPTER SEVENTY

A FEW DAYS later, Rick and Jackie are heading west along I-84 to spend the weekend with friends in Port Jervis, New York.

Entering the environs of Beacon, the Fishkill Correctional Facility comes into view.

On each side of the highway, the penitentiary sprawls outward to the horizon. The landscape is barren, eerie-looking. It reminds Rick of a Hieronymus Bosch painting: medieval-looking buildings, spread across a vast and treeless expanse, encircled by high walls and watchtowers. Beyond the walls, chain-link fences topped by razor wire are everywhere, and farther from the periphery, strands of looped concertina wire surround the acreage.

Seeing the prison now housing his uncle brings on an onslaught of raw feelings and ugly memories from that horrific day in Darien.

He knows Harry's poisonous words have been successful in shaking him to the core, his beliefs about the kind of man his father actually was.

The proof of their venomous power is that he hasn't been willing to share his uncle's version of Dad's life with the woman, now seated beside him, from whom he's never before kept a secret.

No longer willing to let this lie of omission continue, Rick abruptly turns the wheel, slows down the Malibu, and brings it to a stop on the shoulder of I-84.

"Rick, what's wrong . . . are you okay?"

"There's something I need to tell you."

With traffic streaming by, he tells Jackie everything.

Jackie's eyes are wide as though she's filled with disbelief at what she's hearing.

"I'll never know if my father was a predator."

There's a long moment of silence.

Shaking her head, she says, "Rick, that's horrible, but you know what kind of man your father was. And Harry's a madman. You can't let his insanity eat away at you."

"I get it, honey, but I just wish I knew if Harry's story has even a grain of truth."

CHAPTER SEVENTY-ONE

THIS CELL IS perfect.

It's eight by ten with cinderblock walls. A bunk bed, sink, and toilet are all I need.

Sure beats my time in the Army when I was shipped off to the jungles and mountains of the Pacific. No "three hots and a cot" there.

Just heat, humidity, snakes, bugs . . . and killing, killing, killing.

All the while, the Golden Boy stayed home, in his safe and perfect little world.

I have no trouble shutting out the noise and insanity around me.

At least in here I have all the freedom I need to do what comes next.

And, of course, I'm not insane.

That psychiatrist knew it. He never bought my bullshit that I killed my brother because of a business deal. He could tell I didn't give a damn about money, not anymore. If I'd told the shrink the truth . . . that my brother had to die because of what he did to you and our son . . . he would have had me thrown in the looney bin.

Everyone, including that psychiatrist, believed the good Dr. Shepherd was the finest of men, the last of a dying breed.

Well, the last of that breed is dead, and is now burning in hell because of what he stole from the three of us.

If I'd ended up in a hospital for the insane, I wouldn't be able to do what comes next. They'd have me in restraints or they'd have given me medication, which would have turned me into a dead man walking, a zombie.

At least here, in this cell, I'm the master of my own destiny.

But what's happening?

Andrea, my love, your voice sounds weaker and so far away.

And I can't hear our baby's cries anymore.

Please, tell me, is it time?

What's that you just said?

Oh, yes, I hear you better now.

Of course, I'm ready.

I've been waiting for this moment for so long.

Tell our baby I love him, and you know I've never stopped loving you, not for a moment.

We'll be together, soon.

My life on this ugly earth ended with yours, the night that Golden Boy mauled you with his hands and mouth, and threw you down those stairs.

Okay . . . Now, it's secure around my neck.

And I've looped the bedsheet around that pipe on the ceiling.

Good.

Yes, it's taut.

I'm coming.

The cell darkens.

CHAPTER SEVENTY-TWO

IT'S BEEN TWO weeks since the news broke about Harry Shepherd's suicide.

Rick wasn't surprised. It was clear his uncle wanted to die and it was only a matter of when it would happen. Rick was neither elated nor saddened by hearing about the death. He's trying to get beyond the awful things Harry said about his brother; and knows there'll never come a time when he'll be able to forgive him for having killed Dad. He just hopes the inner fury he feels will lessen.

Sitting at his desk, he thinks back on the day's work. The office was a madhouse and by five in the evening, Rick is thoroughly exhausted. The practice is a hamster wheel spinning at a frenetic pace. And it won't let up. There's been a cold truce with Messner. But it's bound to be broken. And the consequences will be a game changer.

Rick is aware the technicians and physician assistants are complaining about the workload. The patients are bitching, too, because they're forced to wait beyond their appointment times and then are rushed through their exams like they're on a conveyor belt. There's no way the office can keep up with this volume. Any day now, Messner will call for an emergency meeting. The reckoning will come.

There's a soft knock on the door.

Phil Lauria leans in. "I'm still thinking about your suggestion. Not a bad idea."

"Let's talk after the next meeting."

Phil nods. "We'll figure it out. How 'bout lunch tomorrow at the Skyline?"

"Sounds good."

Alone, Rick closes his eyes and thinks about the evening to come. One of Jackie's attorney colleagues and her husband just bought a six-room co-op apartment on West End Avenue. They'll be going to a housewarming party tonight.

An image of his parents at that housewarming party thirty years ago flashes in his mind: the brownstone on Pierrepont Street; a celebratory gathering, mostly doctors; music playing, mixed drinks of the fifties—Seven and Seven, scotch and soda, a few others.

His father loved his Glenfiddich single malt, usually drank a few glasses—straight up—and he'd loosen up, tell a few jokes, make people laugh. Yes, Harry got that one right: Dad could sometimes be the center of attention, the Golden Boy.

And Harry was at the party—squirming with discomfort, wanting to make a hasty exit from the gathering because the others were all professionals. Then, as Mom was making the rounds, saying her good-byes, his father, Harry, and Andrea left the party and stood at the top of the stairway. Is there a chance that Harry's recounting was the truth: that the *real* James Shepherd emerged that night, that he actually did what Harry claimed?

The telephone rings. "Rick, I have a Detective Nager on the line," says Carla, the receptionist.

Rick's chest tightens as he picks up the phone.

"Hey, Art."

"Hello, Rick. I heard about your uncle."

"Yeah, it was no surprise," he says, thinking back to the day he and Jackie drove past the Fishkill Correctional facility.

"To be expected," Nager says, then sighs.

There's a brief pause.

Rick waits, knowing there's a reason for Nager's call.

"Rick, I have some news for you. My friend Jeff Ketchman found that Incident Report. He scrounged around the Eight-Four's basement and came up with it. Maybe the case of wine you sent gave him a bit more motivation to sort through that mess. I just got the fax. I'll read it to you."

CHAPTER SEVENTY-THREE

ON A MILD afternoon in mid-March, Montague Street—the main commercial thoroughfare of Brooklyn Heights—looks exactly like Rick remembers it on any Sunday: it has a neighborhood vibe as people stroll casually along the street, window-shop at boutiques, amble in and out of cafés and coffee shops, push baby carriages or strollers, and buy fresh bagels, bialys, or croissants to take home.

Rick wanted Jackie to accompany him but she's at a last-minute meeting to close the deal on the mega-merger.

Finding a parking space in the Heights is as rare as spying a hundred-dollar bill on a sidewalk. After circling the block three times, Rick sees an available spot on Henry Street; he parallel parks, turns off the ignition, slips a Club steering wheel lock into place, and sets the "NO RADIO" sign on the Malibu's dashboard.

Walking the streets of Brooklyn Heights, a highlight reel of his life loops through his head. It feels like only yesterday when he roamed these streets with the other kids; walked on the promenade overlooking the harbor; or went trick-or-treating on Halloween night. There were sports and games, and life was a fun-filled escapade because he knew so little of the world beyond home and school and friends and baseball.

He's suddenly aware that time can seem to accordion in on itself, taking you from then to now in what seems no more than a few revolutions of the clock's hands. In retrospect, it all seems so linear, so logical and inevitable; but still, how do you go from being a carefree kid to a grown-up with life-and-death responsibilities?

*　　*　　*

He approaches Ninety-Six Pierrepont Street.

Stopping in front of the house, he feels his body tighten as his heart races.

It's a well-kept, four-story brownstone. Standing at the bottom of the stairway, he scans the sandstone-covered steps leading up to the front door.

This is where it happened. And up there, at the entrance, is where, according to Harry, his father assaulted Andrea. It's a steep stairway; the fall would be a brutal one on an unforgiving surface.

This is where it began, this thirty-year-old story leading to five deaths: Andrea, the baby, Robert Harper, Dad, and Harry.

Give me a goodnight kiss.

At this moment, Rick can almost see it happening. Andrea recoils from the hug, loses her balance, tumbles down these stairs, and lands on the sidewalk, right here, where Rick is now standing.

And she dies. Along with the unborn child.

All those years ago.

Nearly breathless, Rick turns and begins walking along Pierrepont Street.

He and Jackie may be the only living souls who know what Harry claims happened that night. Is there anyone who can corroborate Harry's story or provide a different version of that tragedy? Either way, Rick needs to know.

He has time to kill so he'll take one last look at the old house on Cranberry Street before the sale is finalized.

*   *   *

The house is an old Cape Cod structure with a patch of grass in front. It's the house his father left from the night he was murdered.

Standing beneath a massive maple tree, a powerful sense of *déjà vu* overtakes Rick. It feels as familiar as the beat of his heart. A tendril of memory comes to him. It was the day they moved into this house. He stood with his father beneath this same tree, peering at what would become the home where the family would spend years together.

His father pointed upward and said, "Look at that."

Ten feet above them, a squirrel poked its head out of a hole in the tree's massive trunk. Suddenly, the squirrel closed one eye—seemed to wink at them—then made a chirring sound.

They laughed. "The squirrel's welcoming us to our new home," his father said.

Now Rick sees the same hole in the same tree standing in front of the same house.

Of course, all these years later, the squirrel is dead.

And so is his father.

He wonders if other squirrels—generations down the line—still live in this tree.

In that moment, thinking of time gone by and the losses it brings, Rick's eyes well with tears.

CHAPTER SEVENTY-FOUR

THE HOUSE ON Columbia Heights is a six-story, brick-faced building with a Hunter green awning extending to the curb.

Rick looks forward to this meeting but dreads what it may bring. There's no way of knowing what Dr. Sutter will say. That is, if she *did* see anything, and if she does remember it all these years later?

He's come here for the truth. One way or another, he needs to leave with the answer.

Was Dad a predatory beast who did what Harry claims happened that night?

*　　*　　*

Donna Sutter's apartment is on the fifth floor on the harbor side of the building.

Opening the door, she says, "Dr. Shepherd, how good to meet you."

She appears to be in her mid-sixties—about his father's age. With fair skin, kindly blue eyes, chin-length silver hair, and a warm smile, she strikes Rick as a woman with a certain grace.

The living room is furnished in browns, tans, and off-whites. Persian rugs cover much of the blond oak floor. "You have an incredible view," he says as she leads him into the dining room.

The room is dominated by a large picture window providing a panoramic view of New York Harbor from its height of about one hundred feet above the Brooklyn waterfront. Looking west, Rick takes in the vista of the Manhattan skyline across the harbor. It extends from the Brooklyn Bridge to the Statue of Liberty and Governor's Island.

While Dr. Sutter busies herself in the kitchen, Rick gazes out over the harbor. The water appears cobalt blue. The serried towers of Lower Manhattan are backlit by a late winter afternoon red-orange glow. It turns fiery as the sun begins dipping behind the World Trade Center and the downtown skyscrapers.

"I was so sorry to hear about your father," Donna Sutter says as she appears with a pot of freshly brewed coffee, sits at the table, and pours a cup for each of them.

"Thank you," he replies, feeling as he had about Nager's words of condolence—hers are sincere, spoken with genuine feeling. He senses Donna Sutter lives a life of quiet kindness.

"Your phone call brought back so many memories," she says. "Your father and I go back to our medical school days. It seems like only yesterday."

Rick visualizes his father as a younger man: tall, robust-looking, full-cheeked, with blondish hair, vital, and imposing—the way he looks in the framed photo that once stood on the mantelpiece of the house on Cranberry Street. Before the separation. Before the murder.

Donna Sutter's eyes appear to mist over and for a moment Rick thinks she may shed tears. She blinks a few times and sighs. "It's so strange how you live in the moment and yet, what happened years ago stays with you; it never leaves but becomes part of the person you are now.

"Back then, your father and I . . ." She smiles with what Rick thinks may be a hint of regret etched on her face. "Well, what can I say? We had a brief romance. It was intense, the way young people feel things so strongly." She shakes her head. "But then, we went our separate ways. I met my husband and James met your mother. Our lives took different paths."

She pauses and has a faraway look in her eyes.

"Your father was so handsome. You're fortunate to resemble him. You reminded me of him the moment I opened the door. It was almost a flashback."

Does she still have feelings for him?

How will she answer the questions he'll soon ask? Will she—or *can* she—be truthful?

Or objective?

She steeples her fingers. "Like so many young people, we thought we'd change the world. We talked about opening a hospital in Africa, maybe even starting a medical school in one of those poor countries. But life takes over, and those youthful dreams fade."

She reaches out, pats Rick's hand. "Of all the doctors I've known, your father was the only one whose idealism stayed with him, even as an older man." She sighs again. "Everyone who knew him said he practiced medicine with the same enthusiasm and caring at the end of his life as he did when we were young doctors. Was he planning on retiring?"

"No. He'd have continued practicing for as long as he could keep going." Rick's throat thickens as he recalls trying to find work to fill Dad's time.

"Yes, that's the James Shepherd I knew." She falls silent as her lips spread to a thin line and her jaw tightens. "I must admit, Rick, I'm still in the dark about why you're interested in that awful incident. It was so many years ago and I just hate thinking about it."

"As I said on the phone, the woman who fell down the stairs was my aunt. I hope you can tell me a little more about what happened that night."

"I don't know what else I can say other than what I told the police at that time."

He puts his cup down; some coffee slops onto the saucer. He hasn't realized how badly his hands are shaking, and he sets them on his lap to hide them. "The police report named you as a witness," he says. "But it just said my aunt slipped and fell down the stairs. But you saw what happened."

She takes a deep breath. "I'll never forget it. It's so clear in my mind, it might as well have happened yesterday." She sets her palm on her chest and clears her throat; her face turns pale.

"Can you tell me what you saw that night?"

She closes her eyes for a moment, then says, "There were maybe forty people at the party. I was by myself since my husband's flight from Chicago was delayed."

Waiting to hear more, Rick feels his insides begin to tremble.

"It was a lovely housewarming party. It was mostly doctors with their wives and husbands. Your aunt and uncle were there, too. Your father had invited his brother and sister-in-law.

"At about eleven o'clock, I said my goodbyes and headed out the front door. It was a beautiful May night. The air was so fresh, I stopped at the top of the stairs and breathed it in. It's funny how you remember that kind of little detail, isn't it?"

He smiles, then nods. The pores on his cheeks begin to open.

"Anyway, I went down the stairway and walked across the street. You know . . . a few days later, I walked past that house and counted eleven steps from the front door down to the sidewalk."

The skin on her chin begins to tremble.

"How was the lighting that night?"

"Oh, it was good. I distinctly recall there was a streetlight nearby, and since it was springtime, the trees didn't have their full foliage yet, so there was nothing blocking the light. I'd just reached the other side of Pierrepont when I heard something . . . it was a sudden cry. I guess I'd call it a yelp. I'll never forget that sound."

Rick's shirt sticks to his skin like cling wrap. And his scalp grows damp.

She hesitates, then, in a shaky voice continues, "The sound startled me so badly I nearly jumped."

She falls silent, peers down at her coffee cup.

"You heard a sound. And then?"

"I whirled around and saw something I'll never forget: a woman was tumbling down those steps. It seemed like it was happening in slow motion, but of course, it took only a second or two. She landed on the sidewalk. I even remember the sound of her head hitting the steps on the way down. She lay on her back, sprawled on the sidewalk. Her purse and a shoe were on the sidewalk, a few feet away. Even from across the street, I knew she was unconscious."

"Who else was there?"

"Your father was right there, and another man, too, her husband, the poor man."

His muscles tense. The skin on his face feels too tight. "Yes, my Uncle Harry." Rick's mouth goes dry. And a feeling of queasiness slithers through him.

Dad was at the top of the stairway with Harry and Andrea?

In a distant voice he barely recognizes, he says, "My father was there?"

"Yes, he was right there."

He was a hungry man, your father; he was ravenous. For my wife.

His heart feels like it'll beat its way out of his chest.

"He was at the top of the stairs?" he asks.

"I saw her husband there."

"And nobody else was there?"

"Well, yes. Your father was."

Panic threatens to erupt like an electrical storm.

"Exactly *where* was my father?"

"He must have left the party a moment or two after I did. When I turned and saw her fall, I saw him right there . . . standing on the sidewalk."

"He was on the *sidewalk*?"

"Yes, he was maybe ten feet away from where she landed. He must've heard that sound too—because when I turned, I saw him whirl around at the same time I did. And I'm sure we both saw her fall down those stairs."

Rick's heart hammers and he feels light-headed.

"You're sure . . . my father was *already* on the sidewalk when she fell?"

"Yes. He was probably going to get his car because he was alone. Your father was on the sidewalk, not far from where your aunt landed."

His face feels hot. The trembling in his hands intensifies. "What happened then?"

"Your father ran to her. He got down on his knees and bent over her. I rushed back across the street to help him. Your aunt was lying on her back so he put his ear to her chest—listened to her heart—because it was obvious she was seriously injured. It was a critical situation because it was clear she was not only unconscious but was pregnant."

Nodding, Rick watches Donna Sutter slowly shake her head.

"We could hear her struggling for breath," she says. "Just looking at her, I was sure she had a brain injury."

Rick's heart feels like it'll leap into his throat. "And then what . . . ?"

"Your father didn't hesitate; he grabbed her face and pressed his fingers into her cheeks and forced her mouth open. Then, he pinched her nostrils with one hand and began mouth-to-mouth resuscitation. He held her mouth open and breathed for her; he began doing CPR."

He grabbed her face with those huge hands of his; he held her there and pressed her face so her mouth opened. And he put his lips to hers.

Harry's words. Harry's truth.

"Then, he began alternating the mouth-to-mouth breathing along with chest compressions on her sternum; he pumped her chest again and again to keep blood flowing to her brain."

His hands . . . they went to her breasts and he fondled them.

Harry's sick truth. His snow globe reality.

Through the dryness of his mouth, Rick says, "Forgive me for asking again, Donna, but you saw all this clearly?"

It feels like his heart is jumping in his chest.

"Yes. I was standing maybe a foot away. When your father saw me there, he moved over so I could take over doing mouth-to-mouth.

"I got down on my knees and began doing the mouth-to-mouth while he kept up with the chest compressions. We shouted for help and kept up the CPR until an ambulance got there a few minutes later."

"Then what happened?"

"The house emptied out. People were everywhere. The next thing I knew there were sirens and an ambulance and the attendants took over. They began doing CPR; they used an ambu bag to force air into her lungs and then loaded her onto an ambulance. When the police got there maybe a minute or two later, I told them what I saw. They filled out a report, which is how you knew to contact me."

"When the ambulance and police got there, what did my father do?"

"He ran to get his car."

"Where was my uncle?"

"That poor man just stood at the top of that stairway, staring into space. He seemed paralyzed, as though he was in another world."

"Do you think he saw what you and my father did—the mouth-to-mouth and the chest compressions?"

"Who knows? He looked like he was incapacitated."

"What else happened?"

"The ambulance left for the hospital. About a minute later, your father came back with his car. He got out and ran back up the stairs, grabbed your uncle by the arm, and helped him down the stairs. The poor man looked like he was in a trance. Your father, your mother, and your uncle got into the car and went to the hospital."

Rick feels lightness in his chest. It's a sense of relief so intense, it borders on euphoria.

But there's a speck of doubt. "Donna, forgive me, but this happened thirty years ago. We all know memories can get lost or reworked over time. Are you *absolutely* sure that when my aunt fell down those stairs, my *uncle* was the only one up there with her?"

"Oh, yes, I'm positive. I saw *exactly* what happened."

"And my father was *already* on the sidewalk when she fell?"

She smiles in an indulgent way. "I can see you're worried that maybe my memory is faulty."

"Please forgive me, but it was such a long time ago . . ."

"Don't you worry about that. There's not a scintilla of doubt in my mind. Your father was on the sidewalk when your aunt fell down those stairs."

Nodding, he catches his breath.

She sets her hand on top of his. "I can assure you I remember it accurately," she says with a warm smile. "Before I retired, I was a dermatologist. My job involved observing even the smallest details. You know, Rick, dermatology requires very careful observations. Even the tiniest skin lesion can be deadly if it's not picked up early." She pats his hand. "My husband says I'm the most precise person he's ever known."

Her eyes lock onto his.

Rick's pulse slows as a feeling of calm envelops him.

It's the reality of what happened, not some warped revision of it.

"Rick, let me assure you, I saw everything clearly. And I remember it with absolute certainty."

CHAPTER SEVENTY-FIVE

RICK SETTLES BACK in the sofa.

The drive from Brooklyn back to Manhattan seemed to have taken no time at all. Looking back on it, the trip seems to have happened as part of a dream. He wonders why when you're going, it always seems to take longer than when you return. It's one of those little factoids of life he's noticed as far back as he can remember.

Now, in the apartment, he can barely wait for Jackie to get home from the office.

When he hears the key in the door, he rushes to embrace and kiss her.

Her lips spread in a smile and she looks delighted. "How did it go?" she asks.

Sitting on the sofa, he tells her everything Donna Sutter said, leaving nothing out.

"Thank God for her," Jackie exclaims. "Now we know the truth, not just Harry's sick version of what happened."

"And her memory's like a steel trap."

"I think Harry did what many of us do," she says. "He rewrote his memory so it was acceptable to him. It was the only way he could deal with what happened that night. Let's face it, Rick, he was always jealous of your father, so his mind totally distorted what actually happened and created a scenario which fit his lifelong pattern of envy and resentment toward his twin brother. You don't have to be a shrink to figure that out. Harry was a pathetic man whose delusions ate away at him for over thirty years. I've wondered what took him so long to try taking revenge."

"I love the way you think about things."

"And I love the way you *feel* about things."

They laugh and embrace again.

"Memory is such a strange thing," he says. "When you think about it, *this* instant in time is the only one that's not a memory. Our entire lives from this moment back are just memories."

"Yes, without our memories, we'd be empty vessels."

"And Donna Sutter didn't have to rewrite her memory of what happened that night."

"And your father acted exactly like the man we always knew he was."

Embracing again, Rick takes in her scent, and for the first time in months, feels not only warmth, but arousal, and he knows he's starting to feel whole again, as though he's beginning to come back to life.

Their lips meet in a kiss.

Then she whispers, "I love you so much."

"And I love you," he whispers back. "I don't think I've ever told you how much."

"You've told me a thousand times."

Holding each other, they sway back and forth and he's lost in the comfort of the moment.

"There's something else I need to tell you . . ." he whispers.

"There's something *else*?" Her eyes widen.

"Yes, there is."

"What's that?"

"When Harry held that gun on me, I was sure it was the end. And . . . I realized how much I love you . . ." he nearly chokes as tears well in his eyes and his voice breaks . . . "that I'd never see you or be with you again, and I couldn't accept that . . ."

Clinging to each other, it feels as though they could dissolve into one person. Lying together on the sofa, she nestles her body next to his. It's a feeling so comforting, so loving, he could stay this way forever.

Amid their whisperings, Rick is aware of the strangest thing: he wishes time would stop so he could hold onto this moment and not let it become just another memory.

JUNE 1983

CHAPTER SEVENTY-SIX

It's Thursday, seven forty-five in the morning, seven months since Dad's death.

Rick has fifteen minutes before seeing the first patient of the day. The world seems less caked with sadness. He now enjoys being with people, socializing, and feels more alive than at any other time since mid-November of last year. He's sleeping better and has resumed his early morning routine: waking up at six, putting on his sweats, and sprinting the few blocks over to Finley Walk where he jogs along the East River.

It's as if each morning brings a sense of renewal.

There's a knock on the consultation room door.

"Come in."

Jill Kotch opens the door and sticks her head into the room. "This place is so much nicer than the one on Seventy-Ninth Street," she says. "You guys made the right choice."

"I'm glad you came with us, Jill."

"Me too . . ." she says with a smile.

Still at the door, she adds, "I'll see you Saturday."

He nods.

"Another right choice," Jill says. "Jackie's a great girl."

Nodding, he laughs. "Believe me, I know."

"I'm so glad it's an informal wedding and not one of those lavish affairs," she says.

"Yes, it's in Jackie's parents' backyard."

Alone, Rick leans back in his father's chair and gazes across the room. Dad's old textbooks with their yellowed pages and marbled covers stand on two shelves of the bookcase. Rick's books are on another shelf alongside them.

It's a sensible progression. Two generations, aligned. Continuity from father to son.

The Leitz microscope on the credenza draws his gaze. He looks at it quite often, certainly every day. Occasionally, when a nurse draws a patient's blood, before it's sent to the lab, Rick sets a drop on a slide and examines it. How comforting it is to peer through the same lens his father did.

His father's college and medical school diplomas with their gold seals and black Gothic fonts hang on the wall behind the desk. His own diplomas are mounted next to them.

Beside them hangs a framed Certificate of Appreciation dated in 1945 and signed by President Harry S. Truman. Made out to James L. Shepherd, MD, it says, "In grateful recognition of services patriotically rendered his country in the administration of the Selective Service System for the period of three years." The gold presidential seal is embossed in the lower right corner.

Only last night, Jackie remarked, "Setting up an office with Dave and Phil was the best thing you could ever do. Your father would have been so proud."

"But we don't make house calls," Rick said with a laugh.

"No one does anymore. But you're not running a medical factory. Speaking of a factory, did you speak with the lawyer handling Harry's property?"

"Yes. He's the executor of the will and the deal's done. There'll be a mini mall on the site. They'll be breaking ground in a few months. And Harry's will specifies that the money from the sale of the property and the house goes to ChildFund International."

"What's that?"

"It's a foundation that helps abused kids."

"That sums up Harry's life . . . he was an abused kid."

"A damaged soul," he says. "If what he said about my grandfather is true, Harry's entire life was poisoned, just like his fish."

Rick will keep in mind an important lesson from his ordeal with Harry: the preciousness of life.

And of family.

Beyond the tragedy of his father's death, Rick knows his life is a good one.

Yes, he feels a pang of remorse when he recalls those last words he spoke to his father only a day before he died. He now realizes they were little more than an expression of youthful impatience.

Rick also knows he was mistaken to have felt he'd been living the wrong life.

He's made his choices and is living his own life.

The life Harry wanted to end.

The life Nager and Callaghan saved.

The life he has now and will have into the future with Jackie.

This life.

It's a good life.

He knows the people who love him—and whom he loves—are at the core of it all. They provide purpose and a sense of belonging.

And while there's no going back, Rick knows he's burdened by the weight of regret, knows that if he could redo any one moment of his life, there's nothing he would change but a single thing: if only he could have one more chance to tell his father how much he loved him.

AUTHOR'S NOTE

Since *Downfall* is fiction, I took liberties with geography, locales, with certain police procedures, and with some aspects of life in New York City during the early 1980s. I've altered certain facts and timelines in the service of storytelling. Those changes have no consequences in so far as a work of fiction is concerned.

Readers familiar with Manhattan's Upper East Side may recognize some familiar landmarks from the 1980s. They may also note that I've changed, tweaked, or obliterated certain physical features that were present during that time. Any mistakes in the recounting or description of these places are strictly my own.

Along with well-known places, there are fictitious restaurants, and other details that are the products of imagination. The same thing was done with certain parts of Brooklyn though I remained true to the geography of Brooklyn Heights.

Those who know southwestern Connecticut from the 1980s may be aware of changes in geographical descriptions and other details of little consequence when telling a story.

Other than these minor alterations, I hope *Downfall*, though fiction, remains faithful to the truth of what it means to be a human being struggling with an extreme event (as Cormack McCarthy put it, the fiction of mortal events) while dealing with love and work, with family conflicts, the power of the past, the inevitability of regrets, the beguiling mysteries of memory, and the struggles that bedevil each of us in our lives.

ACKNOWLEDGMENTS

As I've said before, though every novel I've written feels like I'm on a solitary journey, it really is not. The truth is I never write alone. While it took time to realize this, my writing has benefited from the collective wisdom imparted to me by people who've been important in my life.

Among them are relatives, friends, teachers, and authors who've been instrumental in my life and who've influenced the person I've become.

I am grateful to Pat and Bob Gussin and the entire staff of Oceanview Publishing for believing in me.

I owe a special debt of gratitude to three teachers who influenced me deeply during my years of training to become a psychiatrist. They are Drs. Bill Console, Dick Simons, and Warren Tanenbaum. They imparted to me a degree of insight into human behavior I cherish and which has been central to my life as a reasonably sentient human being and writer. Over the years, Dick and Warren have become treasured friends in whom I find the deepest understanding of what it means to be human.

Certain authors are prized friends and have been important to my growth as a writer. I've shared lunches, dinners, telephone conversations, and emails with them and have read most of their novels.

Foremost among them are Don Winslow and his wife, Jean; David Morrell; Simon Toyne; Jon Land; and Lisa Gardner. I can never thank them enough for having shared so many insights about the writing life, its challenges, disappointments, and the role it plays in all our lives.

A small coterie of people has helped ease my way through the choppy waters of the publishing world. Foremost among them are Sharon Goldinger, Kristen Weber, Skye Wentworth, Victoria Colatta, Andrea Reider, and Penina Lopez. It's always been great to have these people on my team.

Relatives and friends have been vitally important over the years They include Claire and Dr. David Copen, Laura and Dr. Roger Rahtz, Bert and Joyce Serwitz, Alan Steinberg and Mindi Stark-Steinberg, Phil (Dog Man) Kaufman and Helen Kaufman, Dr. Jeff (the engineer) Ketchman and Niki (the sculptor) Ketchman, Chief John Lynch of the Wilton PD, Dr. Warren Tanenbaum and Nina Tanenbaum, Phil Lauria and Elaine Tai-Lauria, Lou LeJaq, Dr. Peter LeJaq, Dr. Barry Nathanson and Susan Nathanson, Bruce Glaser, Harriet Senie, Scott Williams, Terry Williams, Harvey (Harv-Hog) Morgan and Valentina Belyanko Morgan, Ann White and Steve White, Dr. Joel Albert, Ann Chernow and Martin West, Judith Marks White, and many others with whom I've spent so many good times over the years.

I owe a debt of gratitude to librarians Elaine Tai-Lauria, Cindy Bloom Lahey, and Elizabeth Joseph who have provided me with opportunities for author talks and luncheon gatherings at various venues.

Certain bookstores have been important in my writing life. They include Books on the Common in Ridgefield, Connecticut, the Elm Street Bookstore in New Canaan, Connecticut, R.J. Julia Bookstore in Madison, Connecticut, the Bank Square Book Store in Mystic,

Connecticut, Yale University Bookstore in New Haven, Connecticut, and the Fairfield University Bookstore in Fairfield, Connecticut.

Connecticut libraries have supported me by hosting author talks and discussion groups as well as luncheons and special events. They include the Wilton Library, the New Canaan Library, the Bethel Library, the Ridgefield Library, the Stamford Library, the Westport Library, the Bridgeport Library, and the Yale University Library.

My heartfelt gratitude goes out to all the readers who have been loyal fans and given over their precious time to read my books. Time is the greatest gift and I appreciate the generosity of readers in devoting some of it to my writings. Without readers, a book is no more than an untold tale stored on a shelf. I've said this before but it bears repeating. Many readers have virtually begged for a continuation of the Mad Dog trilogy with Roddy Dolan and Danny Burns, but I must leave Roddy to his relatively peaceful life without my muckracking intrusions. We must all move on, including Roddy.

And, of course, there are more stories to tell.

My deepest thanks to Sidney, Billy, Maggie, Hannah, Hank, Jenny, and Jake.

My wife, Linda, has been a source of creative inspiration, selfless input, and boundless encouragement. She's a first-rate grammarian and editor, conceptually and in many other ways. I must repeat two basic truths: Linda has rescued every novel I've ever written. Above all, she's given me the love that has made my life worthwhile.

BOOK CLUB
DISCUSSION QUESTIONS

1. William Faulkner said, "The past is never dead. It's not even past." Do you believe this to be true? How does this pertain to certain characters in *Downfall*?

2. Is *Downfall* a fitting title for this novel? If so, why?

3. What role does memory play in *Downfall*, and how does memory affect our lives?

4. Are sibling relationships often characterized by rivalry? As the story unfolded, how would you characterize the relationships in *Downfall*? Between Rick's father and uncle? Rick and his sister?

5. Discuss Rick's father's inability to adapt to changes in the medical profession.

6. Is Rick Shepherd adapting realistically to the changes in medicine, or is he modeling his professional life too closely to that of his idealized father?

7. How frequently are children "forced" or "pushed" into following the career of a parent?

8. Rick came very close to exacting revenge for his father's death. Are there times when revenge is not only understandable but acceptable?

9. Is suicide a reasonable choice when dealing with certain life challenges?

10. Is there any one question you would like to ask the author?